## THE ONLY GOD LIVING IN GREEN TOWN, ILLINOIS, THAT DOUGLAS SPAULDING KNEW OF.

The facts about John Huff, aged twelve, are simple and soon stated.

He could pathfind more trails than any Choctaw or Cherokee since time began.

Could leap from the sky like a chimpanzee from a vine.

Could live underwater two minutes and slide fifty yards downstream.

Could hit baseballs into apple trees, knocking down harvests.

Could jump six-foot orchard walls.

Ran laughing. Sat easy. Was not a bully. Was kind. Knew the words to all the cowboy songs and would teach you if you asked.

Knew the names of all the wild flowers and when the moon would rise or set and when the tides came in or out.

He was, in fact, the only god living in the whole of Green Town, Illinois, during the twentieth century that Douglas Spaulding knew of.

# DANDELION WINE

## Ray Bradbury

**BANTAM BOOKS**
Toronto • New York • London • Sydney

All of the characters in this book are fictitious,
and any resemblance to persons, living or dead,
is purely coincidental.

## RL 5, IL age 12 and up

DANDELION WINE

*A Bantam Book / published by arrangement with
Doubleday & Company, Inc.*

### PRINTING HISTORY

*Doubleday edition published September 1957
3 printings through October 1957*

*Excerpt appeared in Best-in-Books May 1958
4 printings through September 1958*

*Knopf edition published April 1975
Bantam edition / May 1959*

*Bantam Pathfinder edition / February 1964
25 printings through July 1975*

*Revised Bantam edition / January 1976
11 printings through August 1982*

*Small portions of this book appeared as follows: "Season of
Sitting" in* CHARM, *Copyright 1951 by Street and Smith Publica-
tions, Inc.; "A Story About Love" in* MCCALL'S *Magazine;
"The Swan" in* COSMOPOLITAN; *"The Magic Kitchen" in* EVER-
WOMAN'S FAMILY CIRCLE.

ISBN 0-553-20519-6

*Published simultaneously in the United States and Canada*

*Bantam Books are published by Bantam Books, Inc. Its trade-
mark, consisting of the words "Bantam Books" and the por-
trayal of a rooster, is Registered in U.S. Patent and Trademark
Office and in other countries. Marca Registrada. Bantam
Books, Inc., 666 Fifth Avenue, New York, New York 10103.*

PRINTED IN THE UNITED STATES OF AMERICA

H    20 19 18 17 16 15 14 13

*For Walter I. Bradbury
neither uncle nor cousin
but most decidedly
editor and friend.*

## JUST THIS SIDE OF BYZANTIUM
### An Introduction

This book, like most of my books and stories, was a surprise. I began to learn the nature of such surprises, thank God, when I was fairly young as a writer. Before that, like every beginner, I thought you could beat, pummel, and thrash an idea into existence. Under such treatment, of course, any decent idea folds up its paws, turns on its back, fixes its eyes on eternity, and dies.

It was with great relief, then, that in my early twenties I floundered into a word-association process in which I simply got out of bed each morning, walked to my desk, and put down any word or series of words that happened along in my head.

I would then take arms against the word, or for it, and bring on an assortment of characters to weigh the word and show me its meaning in my own life. An hour or two hours later, to my amazement, a new story would be finished and done. The surprise was total and lovely. I soon found that I would have to work this way for the rest of my life.

First I rummaged my mind for words that could describe my personal nightmares, fears of night and time from my childhood, and shaped stories from these.

Then I took a long look at the green apple trees and the old house I was born in and the house next door where lived my grandparents, and all the lawns of the summers I grew up in, and I began to try words for all that.

What you have here in this book then is a gathering of dandelions from all those years. The wine metaphor which appears again and again in these pages is wonderfully apt. I was gathering images all of my life, storing them away, and forgetting them. Somehow I had to send myself back, with words as catalysts, to open the memories out and see what they had to offer.

So from the age of twenty-four to thirty-six hardly a day passed when I didn't stroll myself across a recollection of my grandparents' northern Illinois grass, hoping to come across some old half-burnt firecracker, a rusted toy, or a fragment of letter written to myself in some young year hoping to contact the older person I became to remind him of his past, his life, his people, his joys, and his drenching sorrows.

It became a game that I took to with immense gusto: to see how much I could remember about dandelions themselves, or picking wild grapes with my father and brother, rediscovering the mosquito-breeding ground rain barrel by the side bay window, or searching out the smell of the gold-fuzzed bees that hung around our back porch grape arbor. Bees do have a smell, you know, and if they don't they should, for their feet are dusted with spices from a million flowers.

And then I wanted to call back what the ravine was like, especially on those nights when walking home late across town, after seeing Lon Chaney's delicious fright *The Phantom of the Opera*, my brother Skip would run ahead and hide under the ravine-creek bridge like the Lonely One and leap out and grab me, shrieking, so I ran, fell, and ran again, gibbering all the way home. That was great stuff.

Along the way I came upon and collided, through word-association, with old and true friendships. I borrowed my friend John Huff from my childhood in Arizona and shipped him East to Green Town so that I could say goodbye to him properly.

Along the way, I sat me down to breakfasts, lunches, and dinners with the long dead and much loved. For I was a boy who did indeed love his parents and grandparents and his brother, even when that brother "ditched" him.

Along the way, I found myself in the basement working the wine-press for my father, or on the front porch Independence night helping my Uncle Bion load and fire his homemade brass cannon.

Thus I fell into surprise. No one told me to surprise myself, I might add. I came on the old and best ways of writing through ignorance and experiment and was startled when truths leaped out of bushes like quail before gunshot. I blundered into creativity as blindly as any child learning to walk and see. I learned to let my senses and my Past tell me all that was somehow true.

So, I turned myself into a boy running to bring a dipper of clear rainwater out of that barrel by the side of the house. And, of course, the more water you dip out the more flows in. The flow has never ceased. Once I learned to keep going back and back again to those times, I had plenty of memories and sense impressions to play with, not work with, no, play with. *Dandelion Wine* is nothing if it is not the boy-hid-in-the-man playing in the fields of the Lord on the green grass of other Augusts in the midst of starting to grow up, grow old, and sense darkness waiting under the trees to seed the blood.

I was amused and somewhat astonished at a critic a few years back who wrote an article analyzing *Dandelion Wine* plus the more realistic works of Sinclair Lewis, wondering how I could have been born and raised in Waukegan, which I renamed Green Town for my novel, and not noticed how ugly the harbor was and how depressing the coal docks and railyards down below the town.

But, of course, I had noticed them and, genetic enchanter that I was, was fascinated by their beauty. Trains and boxcars and the smell of coal and fire are not ugly to children. Ugliness is a concept that we happen on later and become self-conscious about. Counting boxcars is a prime activity of boys. Their elders fret and fume and jeer at the train that holds them up, but boys happily count and cry the names of the cars as they pass from far places.

And again, that supposedly ugly railyard was where carnivals and circuses arrived with elephants who washed the brick pavements with mighty steaming acid waters at five in the dark morning.

As for the coal from the docks, I went down in my basement every autumn to await the arrival of the truck and its metal chute, which clanged down and released a ton of beauteous meteors that fell out of far space into my cellar and threatened to bury me beneath dark treasures.

In other words, if your boy is a poet, horse manure can only mean flowers to him; which is, of course, what horse manure has always been about.

Perhaps a new poem of mine will explain more than this introduction about the germination of all the summers of my life into one book.

Here's the start of the poem:

> *Byzantium, I come not from,*
> *But from another time and place*
> *Whose race was simple, tried and true;*
> *As boy*
> *I dropped me forth in Illinois.*
> *A name with neither love nor grace*
> *Was Waukegan, there I came from*
> *And not, good friends, Byzantium.*

The poem continues, describing my lifelong relationship to my birthplace:

> *And yet in looking back I see*
> *From topmost part of farthest tree*
> *A land as bright, beloved and blue*
> *As any Yeats found to be true.*

Waukegan, visited by me often since, is neither homelier nor more beautiful than any other small midwestern town. Much of it is green. The trees *do* touch in the middle of streets. The street in front of my old home is still paved with red bricks. In what way then was the town special? Why, I was born there. It was my life. I had to write of it as I saw fit:

> So we grew up with mythic dead
> To spoon upon midwestern bread
> And spread old gods' bright marmalade
> To slake in peanut-butter shade,
> Pretending there beneath our sky
> That it was Aphrodite's thigh . . .
> While by the porch-rail calm and bold
> His words pure wisdom, stare pure gold
> My grandfather, a myth indeed,
> Did all of Plato supersede
> While Grandmama in rockingchair
> Sewed up the raveled sleeve of care
> Crocheted cool snowflakes rare and bright
> To winter us on summer night.
> And uncles, gathered with their smokes
> Emitted wisdoms masked as jokes,
> And aunts as wise as Delphic maids
> Dispensed prophetic lemonades
> To boys knelt there as acolytes
> To Grecian porch on summer nights;
> Then went to bed, there to repent
> The evils of the innocent;
> The gnat-sins sizzling in their ears
> Said, through the nights and through the years
> Not Illinois nor Waukegan
> But blither sky and blither sun.
> Though mediocre all our Fates
> And Mayor not as bright as Yeats
> Yet still we knew ourselves. The sum?
> Byzantium.
> Byzantium.

Waukegan/Green Town/Byzantium.
Green Town *did* exist, then?
Yes, and again, yes.
Was there a real boy named John Huff?
There was. And that was truly his name. But he

didn't go away from me, I went away from him. But, happy ending, he is still alive, forty-two years later, and remembers our love.

Was there a Lonely One?

There was. And that was *his* name. And he moved around at night in my home town when I was six years old and he frightened everyone and was never captured.

Most importantly, did the big house itself, with Grandpa and Grandma and the boarders and uncles and aunts in it exist? I have already answered that.

Is the ravine real and deep and dark at night? It was, it is. I took my daughters there a few years back, fearful that the ravine might have gone shallow with time. I am relieved and happy to report that the ravine is deeper, darker, and more mysterious than ever. I would not, even now, go home through there after seeing *The Phantom of the Opera.*

So there you have it. Waukegan was Green Town was Byzantium, with all the happiness that that means, with all the sadness that these names imply. The people there were gods and midgets and knew themselves mortal and so the midgets walked tall so as not to embarrass the gods and the gods crouched so as to make the small ones feel at home. And, after all, isn't that what life is all about, the ability to go around back and come up inside other people's heads to look out at the damned fool miracle and say: oh, so that's how you see it!? Well, now, I must remember that.

Here is my celebration, then, of death as well as life, dark as well as light, old as well as young, smart and dumb combined, sheer joy as well as complete terror written by a boy who once hung upside down in trees, dressed in his bat costume with candy fangs in his mouth, who finally fell out of the trees when he was twelve and went and found a toy-dial type-writer and wrote his first "novel."

A final memory.

Fire balloons.

You rarely see them these days, though in some

countries, I hear, they are still made and filled with warm breath from a small straw fire hung beneath.

But in 1925 Illinois, we still had them, and one of the last memories I have of my grandfather is the last hour of a Fourth of July night forty-eight years ago when Grandpa and I walked out on the lawn and lit a small fire and filled the pear-shaped red-white-and-blue-striped paper balloon with hot air, and held the flickering bright-angel presence in our hands a final moment in front of a porch lined with uncles and aunts and cousins and mothers and fathers, and then, very softly, let the thing that was life and light and mystery go out of our fingers up on the summer air and away over the beginning-to-sleep houses, among the stars, as fragile, as wondrous, as vulnerable, as lovely as life itself.

I see my grandfather there looking up at that strange drifting light, thinking his own still thoughts. I see me, my eyes filled with tears, because it was all over, the night was done, I knew there would never be another night like this.

No one said anything. We all just looked up at the sky and we breathed out and in and we all thought the same things, but nobody said. Someone finally had to say, though, didn't they? And that one is me.

The wine still waits in the cellars below.

My beloved family still sits on the porch in the dark.

The fire balloon still drifts and burns in the night sky of an as yet unburied summer.

Why and how?

Because I say it is so.

Ray Bradbury
*Summer, 1974*

I T was a quiet morning, the town covered over with darkness and at ease in bed. Summer gathered in the weather, the wind had the proper touch, the breathing of the world was long and warm and slow. You had only to rise, lean from your window, and know that this indeed was the first real time of freedom and living, this was the first morning of summer.

Douglas Spaulding, twelve, freshly wakened, let summer idle him on its early-morning stream. Lying in this third-story cupola bedroom, he felt the tall power it gave him, riding high in the June wind, the grandest tower in town. At night, when the trees washed together, he flashed his gaze like a beacon from this lighthouse in all directions over swarming seas of elm and oak and maple. Now . . .

"Boy," whispered Douglas.

A whole summer ahead to cross off the calendar, day by day. Like the goddess Siva in the travel books, he saw his hands jump everywhere, pluck sour apples, peaches, and midnight plums. He would be clothed in trees and bushes and rivers. He would freeze, gladly, in the hoarfrosted icehouse door. He would bake, happily, with ten thousand chickens, in Grandma's kitchen.

But now—a familiar task awaited him.

One night each week he was allowed to leave his father, his mother, and his younger brother Tom asleep in their small house next door and run here, up the dark spiral stairs to his grandparents' cupola, and in this sorcerer's tower sleep with thunders and

1

visions, to wake before the crystal jingle of milk bottles and perform his ritual magic.

He stood at the open window in the dark, took a deep breath and exhaled.

The street lights, like candles on a black cake, went out. He exhaled again and again and the stars began to vanish.

Douglas smiled. He pointed a finger.

There, and there. Now over here, and here . . .

Yellow squares were cut in the dim morning earth as house lights winked slowly on. A sprinkle of windows came suddenly alight miles off in dawn country.

"Everyone yawn. Everyone up."

The great house stirred below.

"Grandpa, get your teeth from the water glass!" He waited a decent interval. "Grandma and Greatgrandma, fry hot cakes!"

The warm scent of fried batter rose in the drafty halls to stir the boarders, the aunts, the uncles, the visiting cousins, in their rooms.

"Street where all the Old People live, wake up! Miss Helen Loomis, Colonel Freeleigh, Miss Bentley! Cough, get up, take pills, move around! Mr. Jonas, hitch up your horse, get your junk wagon out and around!"

The bleak mansions across the town ravine opened baleful dragon eyes. Soon, in the morning avenues below, two old women would glide their electric Green Machine, waving at all the dogs. "Mr. Tridden, run to the carbarn!" Soon, scattering hot blue sparks above it, the town trolley would sail the rivering brick streets.

"Ready John Huff, Charlie Woodman?" whispered Douglas to the Street of Children. "Ready!" to baseballs sponged deep in wet lawns, to rope swings hung empty in trees.

"Mom, Dad, Tom, wake up."

Clock alarms tinkled faintly. The courthouse clock boomed. Birds leaped from trees like a net thrown by his hand, singing. Douglas, conducting an orchestra, pointed to the eastern sky.

The sun began to rise.

He folded his arms and smiled a magician's smile. Yes, sir, he thought, everyone jumps, everyone runs when I yell. It'll be a fine season.

He gave the town a last snap of his fingers.

Doors slammed open; people stepped out.

Summer 1928 began.

CROSSING the lawn that morning, Douglas Spaulding broke a spider web with his face. A single invisible line on the air touched his brow and snapped without a sound.

So, with the subtlest of incidents, he knew that this day was going to be different. It would be different also, because, as his father explained, driving Douglas and his ten-year-old brother Tom out of town toward the country, there were some days compounded completely of odor, nothing but the world blowing in one nostril and out the other. And some days, he went on, were days of hearing every trump and trill of the universe. Some days were good for tasting and some for touching. And some days were good for all the senses at once. This day now, he nodded, smelled as if a great and nameless orchard had grown up overnight beyond the hills to fill the entire visible land with its warm freshness. The air felt like rain, but there were no clouds. Momentarily, a stranger might laugh off in the woods, but there was silence. . . .

Douglas watched the traveling land. He smelled no orchards and sensed no rain, for without apple trees or clouds he knew neither could exist. And as for that stranger laughing deep in the woods . . . ?

Yet the fact remained—Douglas shivered—this, without reason, was a special day.

The car stopped at the very center of the quiet forest.

"All right, boys, behave."

They had been jostling elbows.

"Yes, sir."

They climbed out, carrying the blue tin pails away from the lonely dirt road into the smell of fallen rain.

"Look for bees," said Father. "Bees hang around grapes like boys around kitchens, Doug?"

Douglas looked up suddenly.

"You're off a million miles," said Father. "Look alive. Walk with us."

"Yes, sir."

And they walked through the forest, Father very tall, Douglas moving in his shadow, and Tom, very small, trotting in his brother's shade. They came to a little rise and looked ahead. Here, here, did they see? Father pointed. Here was where the big summer-quiet winds lived and passed in the green depths, like ghost whales, unseen.

Douglas looked quickly, saw nothing, and felt put upon by his father who, like Grandpa, lived on riddles. But . . . But, still . . . Douglas paused and listened.

Yes, something's going to happen, he thought, I know it!

"Here's maidenhair fern," Dad walked, the tin pail belling in his fist. "Feel this?" He scuffed the earth. "A million years of good rich leafmold laid down. Think of the autumns that got by to make this."

"Boy, I walk like an Indian," said Tom. "Not a sound."

Douglas felt but did not feel the deep loam, listening, watchful. We're surrounded! he thought. It'll happen! What? He stopped. Come out, wherever you are, whatever you are! he cried silently.

Tom and Dad strolled on the hushed earth ahead.

"Finest lace there is," said Dad quietly.

And he was gesturing up through the trees above to show them how it was woven across the sky or how the sky was woven into the trees, he wasn't sure which. But there it was, he smiled, and the weaving went on, green and blue, if you watched and saw the

5

forest shift its humming loom. Dad stood comfortably saying this and that, the words easy in his mouth. He made it easier by laughing at his own declarations just so often. He liked to listen to the silence, he said, if silence could be listened to, for, he went on, in that silence you could hear wildflower pollen sifting down the bee-fried air, by God, the bee-fried air! Listen! the waterfall of birdsong beyond those trees!

Now, thought Douglas, here it comes! Running! I don't see it! Running! Almost on me!

"Fox grapes!" said Father. "We're in luck, look here!"

Don't! Douglas gasped.

But Tom and Dad bent down to shove their hands deep in rattling bush. The spell was shattered. The terrible prowler, the magnificent runner, the leaper, the shaker of souls, vanished.

Douglas, lost and empty, fell to his knees. He saw his fingers sink through green shadow and come forth stained with such color that it seemed he had somehow cut the forest and delved his hand in the open wound.

"Lunch time, boys!"

With buckets half burdened with fox grapes and wild strawberries, followed by bees which were, no more, no less, said Father, the world humming under its breath, they sat on a green-mossed log, chewing sandwiches and trying to listen to the forest the same way Father did. Douglas felt Dad watching him, quietly amused. Dad started to say something that had crossed his mind, but instead tried another bite of sandwich and mused over it.

"Sandwich outdoors isn't a sandwich anymore. Tastes different than indoors, notice? Got more spice. Tastes like mint and pinesap. Does wonders for the appetite."

Douglas's tongue hesitated on the texture of bread and deviled ham. No . . . no . . . it was just a sandwich.

6

Tom chewed and nodded. "Know just what you mean, Dad!"

It almost happened, thought Douglas. Whatever it was it was Big, my gosh, it was Big! Something scared it off. Where is it now? Back of that bush! No, behind me! No here . . . almost *here* . . . He kneaded his stomach secretly.

If I wait, it'll come back. It won't hurt; somehow I know it's not here to hurt me. What then? What? What?

"You know how many baseball games we played this year, last year, year before?" said Tom, apropos of nothing.

Douglas watched Tom's quickly moving lips.

"Wrote it down! One thousand five hundred sixty-eight games! How many times I brushed my teeth in ten years? Six thousand! Washed my hands: fifteen thousand. Slept: four thousand some-odd times, not counting naps. Ate: six hundred peaches, eight hundred apples. Pears: two hundred. I'm not hot for pears. Name a thing, I got the statistics! Runs to the billion millions, things I done, add 'em up, in ten years."

Now, thought Douglas, it's coming close again. Why? Tom talking? But why Tom? Tom chatting along, mouth crammed with sandwich, Dad there, alert as a mountain cat on the log, and Tom letting the words rise like quick soda bubbles in his mouth:

"Books I read: four hundred. Matinees I seen: forty Buck Joneses, thirty Jack Hoxies, forty-five Tom Mixes, thirty-nine Hoot Gibsons, one hundred and ninety-two single and separate Felix-the-Cat cartoons, ten Douglas Fairbankses, eight repeats on Lon Chaney in *The Phantom of the Opera,* four Milton Sillses, and one Adolph Menjou thing about love where I spent ninety hours in the theater toilet waiting for the mush to be over so I could see *The Cat and the Canary* or *The Bat,* where everybody held onto everybody else and screamed for two hours without letting go. During that time I figure four hundred lollipops, three hundred Tootsie Rolls, seven hundred ice-cream cones . . .

Tom rolled quietly along his way for another five minutes and then Dad said, "How many berries you picked so far, Tom?"

"Two hundred fifty-six on the nose!" said Tom instantly.

Dad laughed and lunch was over and they moved again into the shadows to find fox grapes and the tiny wild strawberries, bent down, all three of them, hands coming and going, the pails getting heavy, and Douglas holding his breath, thinking, Yes, yes, it's near again! Breathing on my neck, almost! Don't look! Work. Just pick, fill up the pail. If you look you'll scare it off. Don't lose it this time! But how, do you bring it around here where you can see it, stare it right in the eye? How? How?

"Got a snowflake in a matchbox," said Tom, smiling at the wine-glove on his hand.

Shut up! Douglas wanted to yell. But no, the yell would scare the echoes, and run the Thing away!

And, wait . . . the more Tom talked, the closer the great Thing came, it wasn't scared of Tom, Tom drew it with his breath, Tom was part of it!

"Last February," said Tom, and chuckled. "Held a matchbox up in a snowstorm, let one old snowflake fall in, shut it up, ran inside the house, stashed it in the icebox!"

Close, very close. Douglas stared at Tom's flickering lips. He wanted to jump around, for he felt a vast tidal wave lift up behind the forest. In an instant it would smash down, crush them forever . . .

"Yes, sir," mused Tom, picking grapes, "I'm the only guy in all Illinois who's got a snowflake in summer. Precious as diamonds, by gosh. Tomorrow I'll open it. Doug, you can look, too. . . ."

Any other day Douglas might have snorted, struck out, denied it all. But now, with the great Thing rushing near, falling down in the clear air above him, he could only nod, eyes shut.

Tom, puzzled, stopped picking berries and turned to stare over at his brother.

Douglas, hunched over, was an ideal target. Tom leaped, yelling, landed. They fell, thrashed, and rolled.

No! Douglas squeezed his mind shut. No! But suddenly . . . Yes, it's all right! Yes! The tangle, the contact of bodies, the falling tumble had not scared off the tidal sea that crashed now, flooding and washing them along the shore of grass deep through the forest. Knuckles struck his mouth. He tasted rusty warm blood, grabbed Tom hard, held him tight, and so in silence they lay, hearts churning, nostrils hissing. And at last, slowly, afraid he would find nothing, Douglas opened one eye.

And everything, absolutely everything, was there.

The world, like a great iris of an even more gigantic eye, which has also just opened and stretched out to encompass everything, stared back at him.

And he knew what it was that had leaped upon him to stay and would not run away now.

*I'm alive,* he thought.

His fingers trembled, bright with blood, like the bits of a strange flag now found and before unseen, and him wondering what country and what allegiance he owed to it. Holding Tom, but not knowing him there, he touched his free hand to that blood as if it could be peeled away, held up, turned over. Then he let go of Tom and lay on his back with his hand up in the sky and he was a head from which his eyes peered like sentinels through the portcullis of a strange castle out along a bridge, his arm, to those fingers where the bright pennant of blood quivered in the light.

"You all right, Doug?" asked Tom.

His voice was at the bottom of a green moss well somewhere underwater, secret, removed.

The grass whispered under his body. He put his arm down, feeling the sheath of fuzz on it, and, far away, below, his toes creaking in his shoes. The wind sighed over his shelled ears. The world slipped bright over the glassy round of his eyeballs like images

9

sparked in a crystal sphere. Flowers were suns and
fiery spots of sky strewn through the woodland. Birds
flickered like skipped stones across the vast inverted
pond of heaven. His breath raked over his teeth, going
in ice, coming out fire. Insects shocked the air with
electric clearness. Ten thousand individual hairs
grew a millionth of an inch on his head. He heard the
twin hearts beating in each ear, the third heart
beating in his throat, the two hearts throbbing his
wrists, the real heart pounding his chest. The million
pores on his body opened.

I'm *really* alive! he thought. I never knew it
before, or if I did I don't remember!

He yelled it loud but silent, a dozen times! Think
of it, think of it! Twelve years old and only now! Now
discovering this rare timepiece, this clock gold-
bright and guaranteed to run threescore and ten, left
under a tree and found while wrestling.

"Doug, you okay?"

Douglas yelled, grabbed Tom, and rolled.

"Doug, you're crazy!"

"Crazy!"

They spilled downhill, the sun in their mouths,
in their eyes like shattered lemon glass, gasping like
trout thrown out on a bank, laughing till they cried.

"Doug, you're not mad?"

"No, no, no, no, no!"

Douglas, eyes shut, saw spotted leopards pad in
the dark.

"Tom!" Then quieter. "Tom . . . does everyone
in the world . . . know he's alive?"

"Sure. Heck, yes!"

The leopards trotted soundlessly off through
darker lands where eyeballs could not turn to follow.

"I hope they do," whispered Douglas. "Oh, I sure
hope they know."

Douglas opened his eyes. Dad was standing
high above him there in the green-leaved sky, laughing, hands on hips. Their eyes met. Douglas
quickened. Dad knows, he thought. It was all
planned. He brought us here on purpose, so this could

happen to me! He's in on it, he knows it all. And now he knows that I know.

A hand came down and seized him through the air. Swayed on his feet with Tom and Dad, still bruised and rumpled, puzzled and awed, Douglas held his strange-boned elbows tenderly and licked the fine cut lip with satisfaction. Then he looked at Dad and Tom.

"I'll carry all the pails," he said. "This once, let me haul everything."

They handed over the pails with quizzical smiles.

He stood swaying slightly, the forest collected, full-weighted and heavy with syrup, clenched hard in his down-slung hands. I want to feel all there is to feel, he thought. Let me feel tired, now, let me feel tired. I mustn't forget, I'm alive, I know I'm alive, I mustn't forget it tonight or tomorrow or the day after that.

The bees followed and the smell of fox grapes and yellow summer followed as he walked heavy-laden and half drunk, his fingers wonderously cal-loused, arms numb, feet stumbling so his father caught his shoulder.

"No," mumbled Douglas, "I'm all right. I'm fine. . . ."

It took half an hour for the sense of the grass, the roots, the stones, the bark of the mossy log, to fade from where they had patterned his arms and legs and back. While he pondered this, let it slip, slide, dissolve away, his brother and his quiet father followed behind, allowing him to pathfind the forest alone out toward that incredible highway which would take them back to the town. . . .

THE town, later in the day.

And yet another harvest.

Grandfather stood on the wide front porch like a captain surveying the vast unmotioned calms of a season dead ahead. He questioned the wind and the untouchable sky and the lawn on which stood Douglas and Tom to question only him.

"Grandpa, are they ready? Now?"

Grandfather pinched his chin. "Five hundred, a thousand, two thousand easy. Yes, yes, a good supply. Pick 'em easy, pick 'em all. A dime for every sack delivered to the press!"

"Hey!"

The boys bent, smiling. They picked the golden flowers. The flowers that flooded the world, dripped off lawns onto brick streets, tapped softly at crystal cellar windows and agitated themselves so that on all sides lay the dazzle and glitter of molten sun.

"Every year," said Grandfather. "They run amuck; I let them. Pride of lions in the yard. Stare, and they burn a hole in your retina. A common flower, a weed that no one sees, yes. But for us, a noble thing, the dandelion."

So, plucked carefully, in sacks, the dandelions were carried below. The cellar dark glowed with their arrival. The wine press stood open, cold. A rush of flowers warmed it. The press, replaced, its screw rotated, twirled by Grandfather, squeezed gently on the crop.

"There . . . so . . ."

The golden tide, the essence of this fine fair

month ran, then gushed from the spout below, to be crocked, skimmed of ferment, and bottled in clean ketchup shakers, then ranked in sparkling rows in cellar gloom.

Dandelion wine.

The words were summer on the tongue. The wine was summer caught and stoppered. And now that Douglas knew, he really knew he was alive, and moved turning through the world to touch and see it all, it was only right and proper that some of his new knowledge, some of this special vintage day would be sealed away for opening on a January day with snow falling fast and the sun unseen for weeks or months and perhaps some of the miracle by then forgotten and in need of renewal. Since this was going to be a summer of unguessed wonders, he wanted it all salvaged and labeled so that any time he wished, he might tiptoe down in this dank twilight and reach up his fingertips.

And there, row upon row, with the soft gleam of flowers opened at morning, with the light of this June sun glowing through a faint skin of dust, would stand the dandelion wine. Peer through it at the wintry day—the snow melted to grass, the trees were reinhabited with bird, leaf, and blossoms like a continent of butterflies breathing on the wind. And peering through, color sky from iron to blue.

Hold summer in your hand, pour summer in a glass, a tiny glass of course, the smallest tingling sip for children; change the season in your veins by raising glass to lip and tilting summer in.

"Ready, now, the rain barrel!"

Nothing else in the world would do but the pure waters which had been summoned from the lakes far away and the sweet fields of grassy dew on early morning, lifted to the open sky, carried in laundered clusters nine hundred miles, brushed with wind, electrified with high voltage, and condensed upon cool air. This water, falling, raining, gathered yet more of the heavens in its crystals. Taking something of the east wind and the west wind and the north wind and the south, the water made rain and the rain, within this hour of rituals, would be well on its way to wine.

Douglas ran with the dipper. He plunged it deep in the rain barrel. "Here we go!"

The water was silk in the cup; clear, faintly blue silk. It softened the lip and the throat and the heart, if drunk. This water must be carried in dipper and bucket to the cellar, there to be leavened in freshets, in mountain streams, upon the dandelion harvest.

Even Grandma, when snow was whirling fast, dizzying the world, blinding windows, stealing breath from gasping mouths, even Grandma, one day in February, would vanish to the cellar.

Above, in the vast house, there would be coughings, sneezings, wheezings, and groans, childish fevers, throats raw as butcher's meat, noses like bottled cherries, the stealthy microbe everywhere.

Then, rising from the cellar like a June goddess, Grandma would come, something hidden but obvious under her knitted shawl. This, carried to every miserable room upstairs-and-down would be dispensed with aroma and clarity into neat glasses, to be swigged neatly. The medicines of another time, the balm of sun and idle August afternoons, the faintly heard sounds of ice wagons passing on brick avenues, the rush of silver skyrockets and the fountaining of lawn mowers moving through ant countries, all these, all these in a glass.

Yes, even Grandma, drawn to the cellar of winter for a June adventure, might stand alone and quietly, in secret conclave with her own soul and spirit, as did Grandfather and Father and Uncle Bert, or some of the boarders, communing with a last touch of a calendar long departed, with the picnics and the warm rains and the smell of fields of wheat and new popcorn and bending hay. Even Grandma, repeating and repeating the fine and golden words, even as they were said now in this moment when the flowers were dropped into the press, as they would be repeated every winter for all the white winters in time. Say-

14

ing them over and over on the lips, like a smile, like a sudden patch of sunlight in the dark.

Dandelion wine. Dandelion wine. Dandelion wine.

Y ou did not hear them coming. You hardly heard them go. The grass bent down, sprang up again. They passed like cloud shadows downhill . . . the boys of summer, running.

Douglas, left behind, was lost. Panting, he stopped by the rim of the ravine, at the edge of the softly blowing abyss. Here, ears pricked like a deer, he snuffed a danger that was old a billion years ago. Here the town, divided, fell away in halves. Here civilization ceased. Here was only growing earth and a million deaths and rebirths every hour.

And here the paths, made or yet unmade, that told of the need of boys traveling, always traveling, to be men.

Douglas turned. This path led in a great dusty snake to the ice house where winter lived on the yellow days. This path raced for the blast-furnace sands of the lake shore in July. This to trees where boys might grow like sour and still-green crab apples, hid among leaves. This to peach orchard, grape arbor, watermelons lying like tortoise-shell cats slumbered by sun. That path, abandoned, but wildly swiveling, to school! This, straight as an arrow, to Saturday cowboy matinees. And this, by the creek waters, to wilderness beyond town. . . .

Douglas squinted.

Who could say where town or wilderness began? Who could say which owned what and what owned which? There was always and forever that indefinable place where the two struggled and one of them won for a season to possess a certain avenue, a dell, a glen, a tree, a bush. The thin lapping of the great continental sea of grass and flower, starting far out in lonely farm country, moved inward with the thrust of seasons. Each night the wilderness, the meadows, the far country flowed down-creek through ravine and welled up in town with a smell of grass and water, and the town was disinhabited and dead and gone back to earth. And each morning a little more of the ravine edged up into town, threatening to swamp garages like leaking rowboats, devour ancient cars which had been left to the flaking mercies of rain and therefore rust.

"Hey! Hey!" John Huff and Charlie Woodman ran through the mystery of ravine and town and time. "Hey!"

Douglas moved slowly down the path. The ravine was indeed the place where you came to look at the two things of life, the ways of man and the ways of the natural world. The town was, after all, only a large ship filled with constantly moving survivors, bailing out the grass, chipping away the rust. Now and again a lifeboat, a shanty, kin to the mother ship, lost out to the quiet storm of seasons, sank down in silent waves of termite and ant into swallowing ravine to feel the flicker of grasshoppers rattling like dry paper in hot weeds, become soundproofed with spider dust and finally, in avalanche of shingle and tar, collapse like kindling shrines into a bonfire, which thunderstorms ignited with blue lightning, while flash-photographing the triumph of the wilderness.

It was this then, the mystery of man seizing from the land and the land seizing back, year after year, that drew Douglas, knowing the towns never really won, they merely existed in calm peril, fully accoutered with lawn mower, bug spray and hedge shears, swimming steadily as long as civilization said to swim, but each house ready to sink in green tides, buried forever, when the last man ceased and his trowels and mowers shattered to cereal flakes of rust.

The town. The wilderness. The houses. The ravine. Douglas blinked back and forth. But how to

relate the two, make sense of the interchange when
. . .

His eyes moved down to the ground.

The first rite of summer, the dandelion picking,
the starting of the wine, was over. Now the second
rite waited for him to make the motions, but he
stood very still.

"Doug . . . come on . . . Doug . . . !" The running
boys faded.

"I'm alive," said Douglas. "But what's the use?
They're more alive than me. How come? How come?"

And standing alone, he knew the answer, staring
down at his motionless feet . . .

L ATE that night, going home from the show with his mother and father and his brother Tom, Douglas saw the tennis shoes in the bright store window. He glanced quickly away, but his ankles were seized, his feet suspended, then rushed. The earth spun; the shop awnings slammed their canvas wings overhead with the thrust of his body running. His mother and father and brother walked quietly on both sides of him. Douglas walked backward, watching the tennis shoes in the midnight window left behind.

"It was a nice movie," said Mother.

Douglas murmured, "It was . . ."

It was June and long past time for buying the special shoes that were quiet as a summer rain falling on the walks. June and the earth full of raw power and everything everywhere in motion. The grass was still pouring in from the country, surrounding the sidewalks, stranding the houses. Any moment the town would capsize, go down and leave not a stir in the clover and weeds. And here Douglas stood, trapped on the dead cement and the red-brick streets, hardly able to move.

"Dad!" He blurted it out. "Back there in that window, those Cream-Sponge Para Litefoot Shoes . . ."

His father didn't even turn. "Suppose you tell me why you need a new pair of sneakers. Can you do that?"

"Well . . ."

It was because they felt the way it feels every

19

summer when you take off your shoes for the first time and run in the grass. They felt like it feels sticking your feet out of the hot covers in wintertime to let the cold wind from the open window blow on them suddenly and you let them stay out a long time until you pull them back in under the covers again to feel them, like packed snow. The tennis shoes felt like it always feels the first time every year wading in the slow waters of the creek and seeing your feet below, half an inch further downstream, with refraction, than the real part of you above water.

"Dad," said Douglas, "it's hard to explain."

Somehow the people who made tennis shoes knew what boys needed and wanted. They put marshmallows and coiled springs in the soles and they wove the rest out of grasses bleached and fired in the wilderness. Somewhere deep in the soft loam of the shoes the thin hard sinews of the buck deer were hidden. The people that made the shoes must have watched a lot of winds blow the trees and a lot of rivers going down to the lakes. Whatever it was, it was in the shoes, and it was summer.

Douglas tried to get all this in words.

"Yes," said Father, "but what's wrong with last year's sneakers? Why can't you dig *them* out of the closet?"

Well, he felt sorry for boys who lived in California where they wore tennis shoes all year and never knew what it was to get winter off your feet, peel off the iron leather shoes all full of snow and rain and run barefoot for a day and then lace on the first new tennis shoes of the season, which was better than barefoot. The magic was always in the new pair of shoes. The magic night might die by the first of September, but now in late June there was still plenty of magic, and shoes like these could jump you over trees and rivers and houses. And if you wanted, they could jump you over fences and sidewalks and dogs.

"Don't you see?" said Douglas. "I just *can't* use last year's pair."

For last year's pair were dead inside. They had

20

been fine when he started them out, last year. But by the end of summer, every year, you always found out, you always knew, you couldn't really jump over rivers and trees and houses in them, and they were dead. But this was a new year, and he felt that this time, with this new pair of shoes, he could do anything, anything at all.

They walked up on the steps to their house. "Save your money," said Dad. "In five or six weeks—"

"Summer'll be over!"

Lights out, with Tom asleep, Douglas lay watching his feet, far away down there at the end of the bed in the moonlight, free of the heavy iron shoes, the big chunks of winter fallen away from them.

"Reasons. I've got to think of reasons for the shoes."

Well, as anyone knew, the hills around town were wild with friends putting cows to riot, playing barometer to the atmospheric changes, taking sun, peeling like calendars each day to take more sun. To catch those friends, you must run much faster than foxes or squirrels. As for the town, it steamed with enemies grown irritable with heat, so remembering every winter argument and insult. *Find friends, ditch enemies!* That was the Cream-Sponge Para Litefoot motto. *Does the world run too fast? Want to catch up? Want to be alert, stay alert? Litefoot, then! Litefoot!*

He held his coin bank up and heard the faint small tinkling, the airy weight of money there.

Whatever you want, he thought, you got to make your own way. During the night now, let's find that path through the forest. . . .

Downtown, the store lights went out, one by one. A wind blew in the window. It was like a river going downstream and his feet wanting to go with it.

In his dreams he heard a rabbit running running running in the deep warm grass.

Old Mr. Sanderson moved through his shoe store as the proprietor of a pet shop must move through his shop where are kenneled animals from everywhere in the world, touching each one briefly along the way. Mr. Sanderson brushed his hands over the shoes in the window, and some of them were like cats to him and some were like dogs; he touched each pair with concern, adjusting laces, fixing tongues. Then he stood in the exact center of the carpet and looked around, nodding.

There was a sound of growing thunder.

One moment, the door to Sanderson's Shoe Emporium was empty. The next, Douglas Spaulding stood clumsily there, staring down at his leather shoes as if these heavy things could not be pulled up out of the cement. The thunder had stopped when his shoes stopped. Now, with painful slowness, daring to look only at the money in his cupped hand, Douglas moved out of the bright sunlight of Saturday noon. He made careful stacks of nickels, dimes, and quarters on the counter, like someone playing chess and worried if the next move carried him out into sun or deep into shadow.

"Don't say a word!" said Mr. Sanderson.

Douglas froze.

"First, I know just what you want to buy," said Mr. Sanderson. "Second, I see you every afternoon at my window; you think I don't see? You're wrong. Third, to give it its full name, you want the Royal Crown Cream-Sponge Para Litefoot Tennis Shoes: 'LIKE MENTHOL ON YOUR FEET!' Fourth, you want credit."

"No!" cried Douglas, breathing hard, as if he'd run all night in his dreams. "I got something better than credit to offer!" he gasped. "Before I tell, Mr. Sanderson, you got to do me one small favor. Can you remember when was the last time you yourself wore a pair of Litefoot sneakers, sir?"

Mr. Sanderson's face darkened. "Oh, ten, twenty, say, thirty years ago. Why . . . ?"

"Mr. Sanderson, don't you think you owe it to your customers, sir, to at least try the tennis shoes you sell, for just one minute, so you know how they feel? People forget if they don't keep testing things. United Cigar Store man smokes cigars, don't he? Candy-store man samples his own stuff, I should think. So . . ."

"You may have noticed," said the old man, "I'm wearing shoes."

"But not sneakers, sir! How you going to sell sneakers unless you can rave about them and how you going to rave about them unless you know them?"

Mr. Sanderson backed off a little distance from the boy's fever, one hand to his chin. "Well . . ."

"Mr. Sanderson," said Douglas, "you sell me something and I'll sell you something just as valuable."

"Is it absolutely necessary to the sale that I put on a pair of the sneakers, boy?" said the old man.

"I sure wish you could, sir!"

The old man sighed. A minute later, seated panting quietly, he laced the tennis shoes to his long narrow feet. They looked detached and alien down there next to the dark cuffs of his business suit. Mr. Sanderson stood up.

"How do they *feel?*" asked the boy.

"How do they feel, he asks; they feel fine." He started to sit down.

"Please!" Douglas held out his hand. "Mr. Sanderson, now could you kind of rock back and forth a little, sponge around, bounce kind of, while I tell you the rest? It's this: I give you my money, you give me the shoes, I owe you a dollar. But, Mr. Sanderson, *but*—soon as I get those shoes on, you know what *happens?*"

"What?"

"Bang! I deliver your packages, pick up packages, bring you coffee, burn your trash, run to the post office, telegraph office, library! You'll see twelve of me in and out, in and out, every minute. Feel those shoes, Mr. Sanderson, *feel* how fast they'd take me? All those springs inside? Feel all the running inside? Feel how they kind of grab hold and can't let you alone and don't like you just *standing* there?

Feel how quick I'd be doing the things you'd rather not bother with? You stay in the nice cool store while I'm jumping all around town! But it's not me really, it's the shoes. They're going like mad down alleys, cutting corners, and back! There they go!"

Mr. Sanderson stood amazed with the rush of words. When the words got going the flow carried him; he began to sink deep in the shoes, to flex his toes, limber his arches, test his ankles. He rocked softly, secretly, back and forth in a small breeze from the open door. The tennis shoes silently hushed themselves deep in the carpet, sank as in a jungle grass, in loam and resilient clay. He gave one solemn bounce of his heels in the yeasty dough, in the yielding and welcoming earth. Emotions hurried over his face as if many colored lights had been switched on and off. His mouth hung slightly open. Slowly he gentled and rocked himself to a halt, and the boy's voice faded and they stood there looking at each other in a tremendous and natural silence.

A few people drifted by on the sidewalk outside, in the hot sun.

Still the man and boy stood there, the boy glowing, the man with revelation in his face.

"Boy," said the old man at last, "in five years, how would you like a job selling shoes in this emporium?"

"Gosh, thanks, Mr. Sanderson, but I don't know what I'm going to be yet."

"Anything you want to be, son," said the old man, "you'll be. No one will ever stop you."

The old man walked lightly across the store to the wall of ten thousand boxes, came back with some shoes for the boy, and wrote up a list on some paper while the boy was lacing the shoes on his feet and then standing there, waiting.

The old man held out his list. "A dozen things you got to do for me this afternoon. Finish them, we're even Stephen, and you're fired."

"Thanks, Mr. Sanderson!" Douglas bounded away.

"Stop!" cried the old man.

Douglas pulled up and turned.

Mr. Sanderson leaned forward. "How do they *feel?*"

The boy looked down at his feet deep in the rivers, in the fields of wheat, in the wind that already was rushing him out of the town. He looked up at the old man, his eyes burning, his mouth moving, but no sound came out.

"Antelopes?" said the old man, looking from the boy's face to his shoes. "Gazelles?"

The boy thought about it, hesitated, and nodded a quick nod. Almost immediately he vanished. He just spun about with a whisper and went off. The door stood empty. The sound of the tennis shoes faded in the jungle heat.

Mr. Sanderson stood in the sun-blazed door, listening. From a long time ago, when he dreamed as a boy, he remembered the sound. Beautiful creatures leaping under the sky, gone through brush, under trees, away, and only the soft echo their running left behind.

"Antelopes," said Mr. Sanderson. "Gazelles."

He bent to pick up the boy's abandoned winter shoes, heavy with forgotten rains and long-melted snows. Moving out of the blazing sun, walking softly, lightly, slowly, he headed back toward civilization. . . .

H E brought out a yellow nickel tablet. He brought out a yellow Ticonderoga pencil. He opened the tablet. He licked the pencil.

"Tom," he said, "you and your statistics gave me an idea. I'm going to do the same, keep track of things. For instance: you realize that every summer we do things over and over we did the whole darn summer before?"

"Like what, Doug?"

"Like making dandelion wine, like buying these new tennis shoes, like shooting off the first firecracker of the year, like making lemonade, like getting slivers in our feet, like picking wild fox grapes. Every year the same things, same way, no change, no difference. That's one half of summer, Tom."

"What's the other half?"

"Things we do for the first time ever."

"Like eating olives?"

"Bigger than that. Like finding out maybe that Grandpa or Dad don't know everything in the world."

"They know every darn thing there is to know, and don't you forget it!"

"Tom, don't argue, I already got it written down under Discoveries and Revelations. They don't know everything. But it's no crime. That I discovered, too."

"What other new crazy stuff you got in there?"

"I'm alive."

"Heck, that's old!"

"*Thinking* about it, *noticing* it, is new. You do things and don't watch. Then all of a sudden you look and see what you're doing and it's the first time,

26

really. I'm going to divide the summer up in two parts. First part of this tablet is titled: RITES AND CEREMONIES. The first root beer pop of the year. The first time running barefoot in the grass of the year. First time almost drowning in the lake of the year. First watermelon. First mosquito. First harvest of dandelions. Those are the things we do over and over and over and never think. Now here in back, like I said, is DISCOVERIES AND REVELATIONS or maybe ILLUMINATIONS, that's a swell word, or INTUITIONS, okay? In other words you do an old familiar thing, like bottling dandelion wine, and you put that under RITES AND CEREMONIES. And then you think about it, and what you think, crazy or not, you put under DISCOVERIES AND REVELATIONS. Here's what I got on the wine: *Every time you bottle it, you got a whole chunk of 1928 put away, safe.* How you like that, Tom?"

"I got lost a mile back somewhere."

"Let me show you another. Up front under CEREMONIES I got: *First argument and licking of Summer 1928 by Dad, morning of June 24th.* In back under REVELATIONS I got: *The reason why grownups and kids fight is because they belong to separate races. Look at them, different from us. Look at us, different from them. Separate races, and 'never the twain shall meet.'* Put that in your pipe and smoke it, Tom!"

"Doug, you hit it, you hit it! That's right! That's exactly why we don't get along with Mom or Dad. Trouble, trouble, from sunrise to supper! Boy, you're a genius!"

"Any time this next three months you see something done over and over, tell me. Think about it, and tell me *that.* Come Labor Day, we'll add up the summer and see what we got!"

"I got a statistic for you right now. Grab your pencil, Doug. There are five billion trees in the world. I looked it up. Under every tree is a shadow, right? So, then, what makes night? I'll tell you: shadows crawling out from under five billion trees! Think of it! Shadows running around in the air, muddying the waters you might say. If only we could figure a way to keep those darn five billion shadows under those trees, we could stay up half the night, Doug, because there'd be no night! There you are; something old, something new."

"That's old and new, all right." Douglas licked the yellow Ticonderoga pencil, whose name he dearly loved. "Say it again."

*"Shadows are under five billion trees . . ."*

YES, summer was rituals, each with its natural time and place. The ritual of lemonade or ice-tea making, the ritual of wine, shoes, or no shoes, and at last, swiftly following the others, with quiet dignity, the ritual of the front-porch swing.

On the third day of summer in the late afternoon Grandfather reappeared from the front door to gaze serenely at the two empty eye rings in the ceiling of the porch. Moving to the geranium-pot-lined rail like Ahab surveying the mild mild day and mild-looking sky, he wet his finger to test the wind, and shucked his coat to see how shirt sleeves felt in the westering hours. He acknowledged the salutes of other captains on yet other flowered porches, out themselves to discern the gentle ground swell of weather, oblivious to their wives chirping or snapping like fuzzball hand dogs hidden behind black porch screens.

"All right, Douglas, let's set it up."

In the garage they found, dusted, and carried forth the howdah, as it were, for the quiet summer-night festivals, the swing chair which Grandpa chained to the porch-ceiling eyelets.

Douglas, being lighter, was first to sit in the swing. Then, after a moment, Grandfather gingerly settled his pontifical weight beside the boy. Thus they sat, smiling at each other, nodding, as they swung silently back and forth, back and forth.

Ten minutes later Grandma appeared with water buckets and brooms to wash down and sweep off the porch. Other chairs, rockers and straight-backs, were summoned from the house.

"Always like to start sitting early in the season," said Grandpa, "before the mosquitoes thicken."

About seven o'clock you could hear the chairs scraping back from the tables, someone experimenting with a yellow-toothed piano, if you stood outside the dining-room window and listened. Matches being struck, the first dishes bubbling in the suds and tinkling on the wall racks, somewhere, faintly, a phonograph playing. And then as the evening changed the hour, at house after house on the twilight streets, under the immense oaks and elms, on shady porches, people would begin to appear, like those figures who tell good or bad weather in rain-or-shine clocks.

Uncle Bert, perhaps, Grandfather, then Father, and some of the cousins; the men all coming out first into the syrupy evening, blowing smoke, leaving the women's voices behind in the cooling-warm kitchen to set their universe aright. Then the first male voices under the porch brim, the feet up, the boys fringed on the worn steps or wooden rails where sometime during the evening something, a boy or a geranium pot, would fall off.

At last, like ghosts hovering momentarily behind the door screen, Grandma, Great-grandma, and Mother would appear, and the men would shift, move, and offer seats. The women carried varieties of fans with them, folded newspapers, bamboo whisks, or perfumed kerchiefs, to start the air moving about their faces as they talked.

What they talked of all evening long, no one remembered next day. It wasn't important to anyone what the adults talked about; it was only important that the sounds came and went over the delicate ferns that bordered the porch on three sides; it was only important that the darkness filled the town like black water being poured over the houses, and that the cigars glowed and that the conversations went on, and on. The female gossip moved out, disturbing the first mosquitoes so they danced in frenzies on the air. The male voices invaded the old house timbers; if you closed your eyes and put your head down against the floor boards you could hear the men's voices rumbling like a distant, political earthquake, constant, unceasing, rising or falling a pitch.

Douglas sprawled back on the dry porch planks, completely contented and reassured by these voices, which would speak on through eternity, flow in a stream of murmurings over his body, over his closed eyelids, into his drowsy ears, for all time. The rocking chairs sounded like crickets, the crickets sounded like rocking chairs, and the moss-covered rain barrel by the dining-room window produced another generation of mosquitoes to provide a topic of conversation through endless summers ahead.

Sitting on the summer-night porch was so good, so easy and so reassuring that it could never be done away with. These were rituals that were right and lasting; the lighting of pipes, the pale hands that moved knitting needles in the dimness, the eating of foil-wrapped, chilled Eskimo Pies, the coming and going of all the people. For at some time or other during the evening, everyone visited here; the neighbors down the way, the people across the street; Miss Fern and Miss Roberta humming by in their electric runabout, giving Tom or Douglas a ride around the block and then coming up to sit down and fan away the fever in their cheeks; or Mr. Jonas, the junkman, having left his horse and wagon hidden in the alley, and ripe to bursting with words, would come up the steps looking as fresh as if his talk had never been said before, and somehow it never had. And last of all, the children, who had been off squinting their way through a last hide-and-seek or kick-the-can, panting, glowing, would sickle quietly back like boomerangs along the soundless lawn, to sink beneath the talking talking talking of the porch voices which would weigh and gentle them down. . . .

Oh, the luxury of lying in the fern night and the grass night and the night of susurrant, slumbrous voices weaving the dark together. The grownups had forgotten he was there, so still, so quiet Douglas lay, noting the plans they were making for his and their own futures. And the voices chanted, drifted, in moonlit clouds of cigarette smoke while the moths, like late appleblossoms come alive, tapped faintly about the far street lights, and the voices moved on into the coming years. . . .

IN front of the United Cigar Store this evening the men were gathered to burn dirigibles, sink battle ships, blow up dynamite works and, all in all, savor the very bacteria in their porcelain mouths that would some day stop them cold. Clouds of annihilation loomed and blew away in their cigar smoke about a nervous figure who could be seen dimly listening to the sound of shovels and spades and the intonations of "ashes to ashes, dust to dust." This figure was that of Leo Auffmann, the town jeweler, who, widening his large liquid-dark eyes, at last threw up his childlike hands and cried out in dismay.

"Stop! In God's name, get out of that graveyard!"

"Leo, how right you are," said Grandfather Spaulding, passing on his nightly stroll with his grandsons Douglas and Tom. "But, Leo, only you can shut these doom-talkers up. Invent something that will make the future brighter, well rounded, infinitely joyous. You've invented bicycles, fixed the penny-arcade contraptions, been our town movie projectionist, haven't you?"

"Sure," said Douglas. "Invent us a happiness machine!"

The men laughed.

"Don't," said Leo Auffmann. "How have we used machines so far, to make people cry? Yes! Every time man and the machine look like they will get on all right—boom! Someone adds a cog, airplanes drop bombs on us, cars run us off cliffs. So is the boy wrong to ask? No! No . . ."

His voice faded as Leo Auffmann moved to the curb to touch his bicycle as if it were an animal.

"What can I lose?" he murmured. "A little skin off my fingers, a few pounds of metal, some sleep? I'll do it, so help me!"

"Leo," said Grandfather, "we didn't mean——"

But Leo Auffmann was gone, pedaling off through the warm summer evening, his voice drifting back. ". . . I'll do it. . . ."

"You know," said Tom, in awe, "I bet he *will*."

WATCHING him cycle the brick streets of evening, you could see that Leo Auffmann was a man who coasted along, enjoying the way the thistles ticked in the hot grass when the wind blew like a furnace, or the way the electric power lines sizzled on the rain-wet poles. He was a man who did not suffer but pleasured in sleepless nights of brooding on the great clock of the universe running down or winding itself up, who could tell? But many nights, listening, he decided first one way and then the other . . .

The shocks of life, he thought, biking along, what were they? Getting born, growing up, growing old, dying. Not much to do about the first. But—the other three?

The wheels of his Happiness Machine spun whirling golden light spokes along the ceiling of his head. A machine, now, to help boys change from peach fuzz to briar bramble, girls from toadstool to nectarine. And in the years when your shadow leaned clear across the land as you lay abed nights with your heartbeat mounting to the billions, his invention must let a man drowse easy in the falling leaves like the boys in autumn who, comfortably strewn in the dry stacks, are content to be a part of the death of the world. . . .

"Papa!"

His six children, Saul, Marshall, Joseph, Rebecca, Ruth, Naomi, all ages from five to fifteen, came rushing across the lawn to take his bike, each touching him at once.

"We waited. We got ice cream!"

Moving toward the porch, he could feel his wife's smile there in the dark.

Five minutes passed in comfortable eating silence, then, holding a spoonful of moon-colored ice cream up as if it were the whole secret of the universe to be tasted carefully he said, "Lena? What would you think if I tried to invent a Happiness Machine?"

"Something's wrong?" she asked quickly.

GRANDFATHER walked Douglas and Tom home. Halfway there, Charlie Woodman and John Huff and some other boys rushed by like a swarm of meteors, their gravity so huge they pulled Douglas away from Grandfather and Tom and swept him off toward the ravine.

"Don't get lost, son!"

"I won't . . . I won't . . ."

The boys plunged into darkness.

Tom and Grandfather walked the rest of the way in silence, except when they turned in at home and Tom said, "Boy, a Happiness Machine—hot diggety!"

"Don't hold your breath," said Grandpa.

The courthouse clock struck eight.

The courthouse clock struck nine and it was getting late and it was really night on this small street in a small town in a big state on a large continent on a planet earth hurtling down the pit of space toward nowhere or somewhere and Tom feeling every mile of the long drop. He sat by the front-door screen looking out at that rushing blackness that looked very innocent, as if it was holding still. Only when you closed your eyes and lay down could you feel the world spinning under your bed and hollowing your ears with a black sea that came in and broke on cliffs that weren't there.

There was a smell of rain. Mother was ironing and sprinkling water from a corked ketchup bottle over the crackling dry clothes behind Tom.

One store was still open about a block away—Mrs. Singer's.

Finally, just before it was time for Mrs. Singer to close her store, Mother relented and told Tom, "Run get a pint of ice cream and be sure she packs it tight."

He asked if he could get a scoop of chocolate on top, because he didn't like vanilla, and Mother agreed. He clutched the money and ran barefooted over the warm evening cement sidewalk, under the apple and oak trees, toward the store. The town was so quiet and far off you could hear only the crickets sounding in the spaces beyond the hot indigo trees that hold back the stars.

His bare feet slapped the pavement. He crossed the street and found Mrs. Singer moving ponderously about her store, singing Yiddish melodies.

"Pint ice cream?" she said. "Chocolate on top? Yes!"

He watched her fumble the metal top off the ice-cream freezer and manipulate the scoop, packing the cardboard pint chock-full with "chocolate on top, yes!" He gave the money, received the chill, icy pack, and rubbing it across his brow and cheek, laughing, thumped barefootedly homeward. Behind him the lights of the lonely little store blinked out and there was only a street light shimmering on the corner, and the whole city seemed to be going to sleep.

Opening the screen door, he found Mom still ironing. She looked hot and irritated but she smiled just the same.

"When will Dad be home from lodge meeting?" he asked.

"About eleven or eleven-thirty," Mother replied. She took the ice cream to the kitchen, divided it. Giving him his special portion of chocolate, she dished out some for herself and the rest was put away, "for Douglas and your father when they come."

They sat enjoying the ice cream, wrapped at the core of the deep quiet summer night. His mother and himself and the night all around their small house on the small street. He licked each spoonful of

38

ice cream thoroughly before digging for another, and Mom put her ironing board away and the hot iron in its open case cooling, and she sat in the armchair by the phonograph, eating her dessert and saying, "My land, it was a hot day today. Earth soaks up all the heat and lets it out at night. It'll be soggy sleeping."

They both sat listening to the night, pressed down by every window and door and complete silence because the radio needed a new battery, and they had played all the Knickerbocker Quartet records and Al Jolson and Two Black Crows records to exhaustion; so Tom just sat on the hardwood floor and looked out into the dark dark dark, pressing his nose against the screen until the flesh of its tip was molded into small dark squares.

"I wonder where Doug is? It's almost nine-thirty."

"He'll be here," Tom said, knowing very well that Douglas would be.

He followed Mom out to wash the dishes. Each sound, each rattle of spoon or dish was amplified in the baked evening. Silently they went to the living room, removed the couch cushions and, together, yanked it open and extended it down into the double bed it secretly was. Mother made the bed, punching pillows neatly to flump them up for their heads. Then, as he was unbuttoning his shirt, she said, "Wait awhile, Tom."

"Why?"

"Because I say so."

"You look funny, Mom."

Mom sat down a moment, then stood up, went to the door and called. He listened to her calling and calling, "Douglas, Douglas, oh Doug! Douglasssssss!" over and over. Her calling floated out into the summer warm dark and never came back. The echoes paid no attention.

Douglas. Douglas. Douglas.

*Douglas!*

And as he sat on the floor, a coldness that was not ice cream and not winter, and not part of summer's heat, went through Tom. He noticed Mom's eyes sliding, blinking; the way she stood undecided and was nervous. All of these things.

She opened the screen door. Stepping out into the night, she walked down the steps and down the front sidewalk under the lilac bush. He listened to her moving feet.

She called again.

Silence.

She called twice more. Tom sat in the room. Any moment now, Douglas would answer from down the long long narrow street, "All right, Mom! All right, Mother! Hey!"

But he didn't answer. And for two minutes Tom sat looking at the made-up bed, the silent radio, the silent phonograph, at the chandelier with the crystal bobbins gleaming quietly, at the rug with the scarlet and purple curlicues on it. He stubbed his toe on the bed purposely to see if it hurt. It did.

Whining, the screen door opened and Mother said, "Come on, Tom. We'll take a walk."

"Where to?"

"Just down the block. Come on."

He took her hand. Together they walked down St. James Street. Underfoot the concrete was still warm, and the crickets were sounding louder against the darkening dark. They reached a corner, turned, and walked toward the West Ravine.

Off somewhere a car floated by, flashing its lights in the distance. There was such a complete lack of life, light, and activity. Here and there, back off from where they were walking, faint squares of light glowed where people were still up. But most of the houses, darkened, were sleeping already, and there were a few lightless places where the occupants of a dwelling sat talking low night talk on their front porches. You heard a porch swing squeaking as you walked by.

"I wish your father was home," said Mother. Her large hand squeezed around his small one. "Just wait'll I get that boy. The Lonely One's around again. Killing people. No one's safe any more. You never know when the Lonely One'll turn up or where. So help me, when Doug gets home I'll spank him within an inch of his life."

Now they had walked another block and were standing by the holy black silhouette of the German Baptist Church at the corner of Chapel Street and Glen Rock. In back of the church, a hundred yards away, the ravine began. He could smell it. It had a dark-sewer, rotten-foliage, thick-green odor. It was a wide ravine that cut and twisted across town—a jungle by day, a place to let alone at night, Mother often declared.

He should have felt encouraged by the nearness of the German Baptist Church but he was not, because the building was not illumined, was cold and useless as a pile of ruins on the ravine edge.

He was only ten years old. He knew little of death, fear, or dread. Death was the waxen effigy in the coffin when he was six and Great-grandfather passed away, looking like a great fallen vulture in his casket, silent, withdrawn, no more to tell him how to be a good boy, no more to comment succinctly on politics. Death was his little sister one morning when he awoke at the age of seven, looked into her crib, and saw her staring up at him with a blind, blue, fixed and frozen stare until the men came with a small wicker basket to take her away. Death was when he stood by her high chair four weeks later and suddenly realized she'd never be in it again, laughing and crying and making him jealous of her because she was born. That was death. And Death was the Lonely One, unseen, walking and standing behind trees, waiting in the country to come in, once or twice a year, to this town, to these streets, to these many places where there was little light, to kill one, two, three women in the past three years. That was Death. . . .

But this was more than Death. This summer

night deep down under the stars was all things you would ever feel or see or hear in your life, drowning you all at once.

Leaving the sidewalk, they walked along a trodden, pebbled, weed-fringed path while the crickets rose in a loud full drumming chorus. He followed obediently behind brave, fine, tall Mother—defender of the universe. Together, then, they approached, reached, and paused at the very end of civilization.

The Ravine.

Here and now, down in that pit of jungled blackness were suddenly all the things he would never know or understand; all the things without names lived in the huddled tree shadow, in the odor of decay.

He realized he and his mother were alone.

Her hand *trembled*.

He felt the tremble. . . . Why? But she was bigger, stronger, more intelligent than himself, wasn't she? Did she, too, feel that intangible menace, that groping out of darkness, that crouching malignancy down below? Was there, then, no strength in growing up? No solace in being an adult? No sanctuary in life? No fleshly citadel strong enough to withstand the scrabbling assault of midnights? Doubts flushed him. Ice cream lived again in his throat, stomach, spine and limbs; he was instantly cold as a wind out of December gone.

He realized that all men were like this; that each person was to himself one alone. One oneness, a unit in a society, but always afraid. Like here, standing. If he should scream, if he should holler for help, would it matter?

Blackness could come swiftly, swallowing; in one titanically freezing moment all would be concluded. Long before dawn, long before police with flashlights might probe the dark, disturbed pathway, long before men with trembling brains could rustle down the pebbles to his help. Even if they were within five hundred yards of him now, and help *certainly* was, in

42

three seconds a dark tide could rise to take all ten years from him and——

The essential impact of life's loneliness crushed his beginning-to-tremble body. Mother was alone, too. She could not look to the sanctity of marriage, the protection of her family's love, she could not look to the United States Constitution or the City Police, she could not look anywhere, in this very instant, save into her heart, and there she would find nothing but uncontrollable repugnance and a will to fear. In this instant it was an individual problem seeking an individual solution. He must accept being alone and work on from there.

He swallowed hard, clung to her. *Oh, Lord, don't let her die, please,* he thought. *Don't do anything to us. Father will be coming home from lodge meeting in an hour and if the house is empty——*

Mother advanced down the path into the primeval jungle. His voice trembled. "Mom, Doug's all right. Doug's all right. He's all right. Doug's all right!"

Mother's voice was strained, high. "He always comes through here. I tell him not to, but those darned kids, they come through here anyway. Some night he'll come through and never come out again——"

*Never come out again.* That could mean anything, Tramps. Criminals. Darkness. Accident. Most of all—death!

Alone in the universe.

There were a million small towns like this all over the world. Each as dark, as lonely, each as removed, as full of shuddering and wonder. The reedy playing of minor-key violins was the small towns' music, with no lights, but many shadows. Oh, the vast swelling loneliness of them. The secret damp ravines of them. Life was a horror lived in them at night, when at all sides sanity, marriage, children, happiness, were threatened by an ogre called Death.

Mother raised her voice into the dark. "Doug! Douglas!"

Suddenly both of them realized something was wrong.

The crickets had stopped chirping.

Silence was complete.

Never in his life a silence like this one. One so utterly complete. Why should the crickets cease? Why? What reason? They'd never stopped ever before. Not ever.

Unless. Unless——

Something was going to happen.

It was as if the whole ravine was tensing, bunching together its black fibers, drawing in power from sleeping countrysides all about, for miles and miles. From dew-sodden forest and dells and rolling hills where dogs tilted heads to moons, from all around the great silence was sucked into one center, and they were the core of it. In ten seconds now, something would happen, something would happen. The crickets kept their truce, the stars were so low he could almost brush the tinsel. There were swarms of them, hot and sharp.

Growing, growing, the silence. Growing, growing, the tenseness. Oh, it was so dark, so far away from everything. Oh, God!

And then, way way off across the ravine:

"Okay, Mom! Coming, Mother!"

And again: "Hi, Mom! Coming, Mom!"

And then the quick scuttering of tennis shoes padding down through the pit of the ravine as three kids came dashing, giggling. His brother Douglas, Chuck Woodman, and John Huff. Running, giggling . . .

The stars sucked up like the stung antennae of ten million snails.

The crickets sang!

The darkness pulled back, startled, shocked, angry. Pulled back, losing its appetite at being so rudely interrupted as it prepared to feed. As the dark retreated like a wave on the shore, three children piled out of it, laughing.

"Hi, Mom! Hi, Tom! Hey!"

It smelled like Douglas, all right. Sweat and grass and the odor of trees and branches and the creek about him.

"Young man, you're going to get a licking," declared Mother. She put away her fear instantly. Tom knew she would never tell anyone of it, ever. It would be in her heart, though, for all time, as it was in his heart for all time.

They walked home to bed in the late summer night. He was glad Douglas was alive. Very glad. For a moment there he had thought——

Far off in the dim moonlit country, over a viaduct and down a valley, a train rushed along whistling like a lost metal thing, nameless and running. Tom went to bed shivering, beside his brother, listening to that train whistle, and thinking of a cousin who lived way out in the country where that train ran now; a cousin who died of pneumonia late at night years and years ago——

He smelled the sweat of Doug beside him. It was magic. Tom stopped trembling.

"Only two things I know for sure, Doug," he whispered.

"What?"

"Nighttime's awful dark—is one."

"What's the other?"

"The ravine at night don't belong in Mr. Auffmann's Happiness Machine, if he ever builds it."

Douglas considered this awhile. "You can say that again."

They stopped talking. Listening, suddenly they heard footsteps coming down the street, under the trees, outside the house now, on the sidewalk. From her bed Mother called quietly,

"That's your father."

It was.

L ATE at night, on the front porch, Leo Auffmann
wrote a list he could not see in the dark, ex-
claiming, "Ah!" or, "That's another!" when he hit
upon a fine component. Then the front-door screen
made a moth sound, tapping.

"Lena?" he whispered.

She sat down next to him on the swing, in her
nightgown, not slim the way girls get when they are
not loved at seventeen, not fat the way women get
when they are not loved at fifty, but absolutely right,
a roundness, a firmness, the way women are at any
age, he thought, when there is no question.

She was miraculous. Her body, like his, was always thinking for her, but in a different way, shaping
the children, or moving ahead of him into any room to
change the atmosphere there to fit any particular
mood he was in. There seemed no long periods of
thought for her; thinking and doing moved from her
head to her hand and back in a natural and gentle
circuiting he could not and cared not to blueprint.

"That machine," she said at last, ". . . we don't
need it."

"No," he said, "but sometimes you got to build
for others. I been figuring, what to put in. Motion
pictures? Radios? Stereoscopic viewers? All those in
one place so any man can run his hand over it and
smile and say, 'Yes, sir, that's happiness.' "

Yes, he thought, to make a contraption that in
spite of wet feet, sinus trouble, rumpled beds, and
those three-in-the-morning hours when monsters ate
your soul, would manufacture happiness, like that

magic salt mill that, thrown in the ocean, made salt forever and turned the sea to brine. Who wouldn't sweat his soul out through his pores to invent a machine like that? he asked the world, he asked the town, he asked his wife!

In the porch swing beside him, Lena's uneasy silence was an opinion.

Silent now, too, head back, he listened to the elm leaves above hissing in the wind.

Don't forget, he told himself, that sound, too, must be in the machine.

A minute later the porch swing, the porch, stood empty in the dark.

G RANDFATHER smiled in his sleep.
Feeling the smile and wondering why it was
there, he awoke. He lay quietly listening, and
the smile was explained.

For he heard a sound which was far more important than birds or the rustle of new leaves. Once each year he woke this way and lay waiting for the sound which meant that summer had officially begun. And it began on a morning such as this when a boarder, a nephew, a cousin, a son or a grandson came out on the lawn below and moved in consecutively smaller quadrangles north and east and south and west with a clatter of rotating metal through the sweet summer grass. Clover blossoms, the few unharvested dandelion fires, ants, sticks, pebbles, remnants of last year's July Fourth squibs and punks, but predominantly clear green, a fount leaped up from the chattering mower. A cool soft fount; Grandfather imagined it tickling his legs, spraying his warm face, filling his nostrils with the timeless scent of a new season begun, with the promise that, yes, we'll *all* live another twelve months.

God bless the lawn mower, he thought. Who was the fool who made January first New Year's Day? No, they should set a man to watch the grasses across a million Illinois, Ohio, and Iowa lawns, and on that morning when it was long enough for cutting, instead of rachets and horns and yelling, there should be a great swelling symphony of lawn mowers reaping fresh grass upon the prairie lands. Instead of confetti and serpentine, people should throw grass spray at each other on the one day each year that really represents the Beginning!

He snorted at his own lengthy discussion of the affair, went to the window and leaned out into the mellow sunshine, and sure enough, there was a boarder, a young newspaperman named Forrester, just finishing a row.

"Morning, Mr. Spaulding!"

"Give 'em hell, Bill!" cried Grandpa heartily, and was soon downstairs eating Grandma's breakfast, with the bay window open so the rattling buzz of the lawn mower lolled about his eating.

"It gives you confidence," Grandpa said. "That lawn mower. *Listen* to it!"

"Won't be using the lawn mower much longer." Grandma set down a stack of wheat cakes. "They got a new kind of grass Bill Forrester's putting in this morning, never needs cutting. Don't know what they call it, but it just grows so long and no longer."

Grandpa stared at the woman. "You're finding a poor way to joke with me."

"Go look for yourself. Land's sake," said Grandma, "it was Bill Forrester's idea. The new grass is waiting in little flats by the side of the house. You just dig small holes here and there and put the new grass in spots. By the end of the year the new grass kills off the old, and you sell your lawn mower."

Grandpa was up from his chair, through the hall, and out the front door in ten seconds.

Bill Forrester left his machine and came over, smiling, squinting in the sun. "That's right," he said. "Bought the grass yesterday. Thought, while I'm on vacation I'd just plant it for you."

"Why wasn't I consulted about this? It's *my* lawn!" cried Grandfather.

"Thought you'd appreciate it, Mr. Spaulding."

"Well, I don't think I do appreciate it. Let's see this confounded grass of yours."

They stood by the little square pads of new grass. Grandpa toed at it with one end of his shoe suspiciously. "Looks like plain old grass to me. You sure some horse trader didn't catch you early in the morning when you weren't fully awake?"

"I've seen the stuff growing in California. Only so high and no higher. If it survives our climate it'll save us getting out here next year, once a week, to keep the darned stuff trimmed."

"That's the trouble with your generation," said Grandpa. "Bill, I'm ashamed of you, you a newspaperman. All the things in life that were put here to savor, you eliminate. Save time, save work, you say." He nudged the grass trays disrespectfully. "Bill, when you're my age, you'll find out it's the little savors and little things that count more than big ones. A walk on a spring morning is better than an eighty-mile ride in a hopped-up car, you know why? Because it's full of flavors, full of a lot of things growing. You've time to seek and find. I know—you're after the broad effect now, and I suppose that's fit and proper. But for a young man working on a newspaper, you got to look for grapes as well as watermelons. You greatly admire skeletons and I like fingerprints; well and good. Right now such things are bothersome to you, and I wonder if it isn't because you've never learned to use them. If you had your way you'd pass a law to abolish all the little jobs, the little things. But then you'd leave yourselves nothing to do between the big jobs and you'd have a devil of a time thinking up things to do so you wouldn't go crazy. Instead of that, why not let nature show you a few things? Cutting grass and pulling weeds can be a way of life, son."

Bill Forrester was smiling quietly at him.

"I know," said Grandpa, "I talk too much."

"There's no one I'd rather hear."

"Lecture continued, then. Lilacs on a bush are better than orchids. And dandelions and devil grass are better! Why? Because they bend you over and turn you away from all the people and the town for a little while and sweat you and get you down where you remember you got a nose again. And when you're all to yourself that way, you're really yourself for a little while; you get to thinking things through, alone.

Gardening is the handiest excuse for being a philosopher. Nobody guesses, nobody accuses, nobody knows, but there you are, Plato in the peonies, Socrates force-growing his own hemlock. A man toting a sack of blood manure across his lawn is kin to Atlas letting the world spin easy on his shoulder. As Samuel Spaulding, Esquire, once said, 'Dig in the earth, delve in the soul.' Spin those mower blades, Bill, and walk in the spray of the Fountain of Youth. End of lecture. Besides, a mess of dandelion greens is good eating once in a while."

"How many years since you had dandelion greens for supper, sir?"

"We won't go into that!"

Bill kicked one of the grass flats slightly and nodded. "About this grass now. I didn't finish telling. It grows so close it's guaranteed to kill off clover and dandelions——"

"Great God in heaven! That means no dandelion wine next year! That means no bees crossing our lot! You're out of your mind, son! Look here, how much did all this cost you?"

"A dollar a flat. I bought ten flats as a surprise."

Grandpa reached into his pocket, took out the old deep-mouthed purse, unclasped the silver clasp, and removed from it three five-dollar bills. "Bill, you've just made a great profit of five dollars on this transaction. I want you to deliver this load of unromantic grass into the ravine, the garbage dump—anywhere—but I ask you in a civil and humble voice not to plant it in my yard. Your motives are above reproach, but my motives, I feel, because I'm approaching my tenderest years, must be considered first."

"Yes, sir." Bill pocketed the bills reluctantly.

"Bill, you just plant this new grass some other year. The day after I die, Bill, you're free to tear up the whole damn lawn. Think you can wait another five years or so for an old orator to kick off?"

"I know darn well I can wait," Bill said.

"There's a thing about the lawn mower I can't

even tell you, but to me it's the most beautiful sound in the world, the freshest sound of the season, the sound of summer, and I'd miss it fearfully if it wasn't there, and I'd miss the smell of cut grass."

Bill bent to pick up a flat. "Here I go to the ravine."

"You're a good, understanding young man, and will make a brilliant and sensitive reporter," said Grandfather, helping him. "This I predict!"

The morning passed, noon came on, Grandpa retired after lunch, read a little Whittier, and slept well on through the day. When he awoke at three the sun was streaming through the windows, bright and fresh. He lay in bed and was startled to hear the old, the familiar, the memorable sound.

"Why," he said, "someone's using the lawn mower! But the lawn was just cut this morning!"

He listened again. And yes, there it was, the endless droning chatter up and down, up and down.

He leaned out the window and gaped. "Why, it's Bill. Bill Forrester, you there! Has the sun got you? You're cutting the lawn *again!*"

Bill looked up, smiled a white smile, and waved. "I know! I think I missed a few spots!"

And while Grandpa lay in bed for the next five minutes, smiling and at ease, Bill Forrester cut the lawn north, then west, then south, and finally, in a great green spraying fountain, toward the east.

ON Sunday morning Leo Auffmann moved slowly through his garage, expecting some wood, a curl of wire, a hammer or wrench to leap up crying, "Start here!" But nothing leaped, nothing cried for a beginning.

Should a Happiness Machine, he wondered, be something you can carry in your pocket?

Or, he went on, should it be something that carries you in *its* pocket?

"One thing I absolutely *know*," he said aloud. "It should be *bright!*"

He set a can of orange paint in the center of the workbench, picked up a dictionary, and wandered into the house.

"Lena?" He glanced at the dictionary. "Are you 'pleased, contented, joyful, delighted'? Do you feel 'Lucky, fortunate'? Are things 'clever and fitting,' 'successful and suitable' for you?"

Lena stopped slicing vegetables and closed her eyes. "Read me the list again, please," she said.

He shut the book.

"What have I done, you got to stop and think an hour before you can tell me? All I ask is a simple yes or no! You're *not* contented, delighted, joyful?"

"Cows are contented, babies and old people in second childhood are delighted, God help them," she said. "As for 'joyful,' Leo? Look how I laugh scrubbing out the sink. . . ."

He peered closely at her and his face relaxed. "Lena, it's true. A man doesn't appreciate. Next month, maybe, we'll get away."

"*I'm* not complaining!" she cried. "*I'm* not the one comes in with a list saying, 'Stick out your tongue.' Leo, do you ask what makes your heart beat all night? No! Next will you ask, What's marriage? Who knows, Leo? Don't ask. A man who thinks like that, how it runs, how things work, falls off the trapeze in the circus, chokes wondering how the muscles work in the throat. Eat, sleep, breathe, Leo, and stop staring at me like I'm something new in the house!"

Lena Auffmann froze. She sniffed the air.

"Oh, my God, look what you done!"

She yanked the oven door open. A great cloud of smoke poured through the kitchen.

"Happiness!" she wailed. "And for the first time in six months we have a fight! Happiness, and for the first time in twenty years it's not bread, it's charcoal for supper!"

When the smoke cleared, Leo Auffmann was gone.

The fearful clangor, the collision of man and inspiration, the flinging about of metal, lumber, hammer, nails, T square, screwdriver, continued for many days. On occasion, defeated, Leo Auffmann loitered out through the streets, nervous, apprehensive, jerking his head at the slightest sound of distant laughter, listened to children's jokes, watching what made them smile. At night he sat on neighbors' crowded porches, listening to the old folks weigh and balance life, and at each explosion of merriment Leo Auffmann quickened like a general who has seen the forces of darkness routed and whose strategy has been reaffirmed. On his way home he felt triumphant until he was in his garage with the dead tools and the inanimate lumber. Then his bright face fell away in a pale funk, and to cover his sense of failure he banged and crashed the parts of his machine about as if they really did make sense. At last it began to shape itself and at the end of the ten days and nights, trembling with fatigue, self-dedicated, half starved, fumbling and looking as if he had been riven by lightning, Leo Auffmann wandered into his house.

The children, who had been screaming horribly at each other, fell silent, as if the Red Death had entered at the chiming of the clock.

"The Happiness Machine," husked Leo Auffmann, "is ready."

"Leo Auffmann," said his wife, "has lost fifteen pounds. He hasn't talked to his children in two weeks, they are nervous, they fight, listen! His wife is nervous, she's gained ten pounds, she'll need new clothes, look! Sure—the machine is ready. But happy? Who can say? Leo, leave off with the clock you're building. You'll never find a cuckoo big enough to go in it! Man was not made to tamper with such things. It's not against God, no, but it sure looks like it's against Leo Auffmann. Another week of this and we'll bury him in his machine!"

But Leo Auffmann was too busy noticing that the room was falling swiftly up.

How interesting, he thought, lying on the floor.

Darkness closed in a great wink on him as someone screamed something about that Happiness Machine, three times.

The first thing he noticed the next morning was dozens of birds fluttering around in the air stirring up ripples like colored stones thrown into an incredibly clear stream, gonging the tin roof of the garage softly.

A pack of multibred dogs pawfooted one by one into the yard to peer and whine gently through the garage door; four boys, two girls, and some men hesitated in the driveway and then edged along under the cherry trees.

Leo Auffmann, listening, knew what it was that had reached out and called them all into the yard.

The sound of the Happiness Machine.

It was the sort of sound that might be heard coming from a giant's kitchen on a summer day. There were all kinds of hummings, low and high, steady and then changing. Incredible foods were being baked there by a host of whirring golden bees as big as teacups. The giantess herself, humming contentedly under her breath, might glide to the door, as vast as all summer, her face a huge peach-colored moon gazing calmly out upon smiling dogs, corn-haired boys and flour-haired old men.

"Wait," said Leo Auffmann out loud. "I didn't turn the machine on this morning! Saul!"

Saul, standing in the yard below, looked up.

"Saul, did you turn it on?"

"You told me to warm it up half an hour ago!"

"All right, Saul, I forgot. I'm not awake." He fell back in bed.

His wife, bringing his breakfast up, paused by the window, looking down at the garage.

"Tell me," she said quietly. "If that machine is like you say, has it got an answer to making babies in it somewhere? Can that machine make seventy-year-old people twenty? Also, how does death look when you hide in there with all that happiness?"

"Hide!"

"If you died from overwork, what should I do today, climb in that big box down there and be happy? Also tell me, Leo, how is our life? You know how our house is. Seven in the morning, breakfast, the kids; all of you gone by eight-thirty and it's just me and washing and me and cooking and socks to be darned, weeds to be dug, or I run to the store or polish silver. Who's complaining? I'm just reminding you how the house is put together, Leo, what's in it! So now answer: How do you get all those things I said in one machine?"

"That's not how it's built!"

"I'm sorry. I got no time to look, then."

And she kissed his cheek and went from the room and he lay smelling the wind that blew from the hidden machine below, rich with the odor of those roasted chestnuts that sold in the autumn streets of a Paris he had never known. . . .

A cat moved, unseen among the hypnotized dogs

and boys to purr against the garage door, in the sound of snow-waves crumbling down a faraway and rhythmically breathing shore.

Tomorrow, thought Leo Auffmann, we'll try the machine, all of us, together.

Late that night he awoke and knew something had wakened him. Far away in another room he heard someone crying.

"Saul?" he whispered, getting out of bed.

In his room Saul wept, his head buried in his pillow. "No . . . no . . ." he sobbed. "Over . . . over . . ."

"Saul, you had a nightmare? Tell me about it, son."

But the boy only wept.

And sitting there on the boy's bed, Leo Auffmann suddenly thought to look out the window. Below, the garage doors stood open.

He felt the hairs rise along the back of his neck.

When Saul slept again, uneasily, whimpering, his father went downstairs and out to the garage where, not breathing, he put his hand out.

In the cool night the Happiness Machine's metal was too hot to touch.

So, he thought, Saul was here tonight.

Why? Was Saul unhappy, in need of the machine? No, happy, but wanting to hold onto happiness always. Could you blame a boy wise enough to know his position who tried to keep it that way? No! And yet . . .

Above, quite suddenly, something white was exhaled from Saul's window. Leo Auffmann's heart thundered. Then he realized the window curtain had blown out into the open night. But it had seemed as intimate and shimmering a thing as a boy's soul escaping his room. And Leo Auffmann had flung up his hands as if to thwart it, push it back into the sleeping house.

Cold, shivering, he moved back into the house and up to Saul's room where he seized the blowing curtain in and locked the window tight so the pale thing could not escape again. Then he sat on the bed and put his hand on Saul's back.

"*A Tale of Two Cities?* Mine. *The Old Curiosity Shop?* Ha, that's Leo Auffmann's all right! *Great Expectations?* That *used* to be mine. But let *Great Expectations* be his, now!"

"What's this?" asked Leo Auffmann, entering.

"This," said his wife, "is sorting out the community property! When a father scares his son at night it's time to chop everything in half! Out of the way, Mr. Bleak House, Old Curiosity Shop. In all these books, no mad scientist lives like Leo Auffmann, none!"

"You're leaving, and you haven't even tried the machine!" he protested. "Try it on, you'll unpack, you'll stay!"

"*Tom Swift and His Electric Annihilator*—whose is that?" she asked. "Must I *guess?*"

Snorting, she gave *Tom Swift* to Leo Auffmann.

Very late in the day all the books, dishes, clothes, linens had been stacked one here, one there, four here, four there, ten here, ten there. Lena Auffmann, dizzy with counting, had to sit down. "All right," she gasped. "Before I go, Leo, prove you don't give nightmares to innocent sons!"

Silently Leo Auffmann led his wife into the twilight. She stood before the eight-foot-tall, orange-colored box.

"That's *happiness?*" she said. "Which button do I press to be overjoyed, grateful, contented, and much-obliged?"

The children had gathered now.

"Mama," said Saul, "don't!"

"I got to know what I'm yelling about, Saul." She got in the machine, sat down, and looked out at her husband, shaking her head. "It's not me needs this, it's you, a nervous wreck, shouting."

"Please," he said, "you'll see!"

He shut the door.

"Press the button!" he shouted in at his unseen wife.

There was a click. The machine shivered quietly, like a huge dog dreaming in its sleep.

"Papa!" said Saul, worried.

"Listen!" said Leo Auffmann.

At first there was nothing but the tremor of the machine's own secretly moving cogs and wheels.

"Is Mama all right?" asked Naomi.

"All right, she's fine! There, now . . . there!"

And inside the machine Lena Auffmann could be heard saying, "Oh!" and then again, "Ah!" in a startled voice. "Look at that!" said his hidden wife. "Paris!" and later, "London! There goes Rome! The Pyramids! The Sphinx!"

"The Sphinx, you hear, children?" Leo Auffmann whispered and laughed.

"Perfume!" cried Lena Auffmann, surprised.

Somewhere a phonograph played "The Blue Danube" faintly.

"Music! I'm dancing!"

"Only *thinks* she's dancing," the father confided to the world.

"Amazing!" said the unseen woman.

Leo Auffmann blushed. "What an understanding wife."

And then inside the Happiness Machine, Lena Auffmann began to weep.

The inventor's smile faded.

"She's crying," said Naomi.

"She can't be!"

"She is," said Saul.

"She simply can't be crying!" Leo Auffmann, blinking, pressed his ear to the machine. "But . . . yes . . . like a baby . . ."

He could only open the door.

"Wait." There his wife sat, tears rolling down her cheeks. "Let me finish." She cried some more.

Leo Auffmann turned off the machine, stunned.

"Oh, it's the saddest thing in the world!" she wailed. "I feel awful, terrible." She climbed out through the door. "First, there was Paris . . ."

"What's wrong with Paris?"

"I never even *thought* of being in Paris in my life. But now you got me thinking: Paris! So suddenly I want to be in Paris and I know I'm not!"

"It's almost as good, this machine."

"No. Sitting in there, I knew. I thought, it's not real!"

"Stop crying, Mama."

She looked at him with great dark wet eyes. "You had me dancing. We haven't danced in twenty years."

"I'll take you dancing tomorrow night!"

"No, no! It's not important, it *shouldn't* be important. But your machine says it's important! So I believe! It'll be all right, Leo, after I cry some more."

"What else?"

"What else? The machine says, 'You're young.' I'm not. It lies, that Sadness Machine!"

"Sad in what way?"

His wife was quieter now. "Leo, the mistake you made is you forgot some hour, some day, we all got to climb out of that thing and go back to dirty dishes and the beds not made. While you're in that thing, sure, a sunset lasts forever almost, the air smells good, the temperature is fine. All the things you want to last, last. But outside, the children wait on lunch, the clothes need buttons. And then let's be frank, Leo, how long can you *look* at a sunset? Who *wants* a sunset to last? Who wants perfect temperature? Who wants air smelling good always? So after awhile, who would notice? Better, for a minute or two, a sunset. After that, let's have something else. People are like that, Leo. How could you forget?"

"Did I?"

"Sunsets we always liked because they only happen once and go away."

"But Lena, that's sad."

"No, if the sunset stayed and we got bored, that

would be a real sadness. So two things you did you should never have. You made quick things go slow and stay around. You brought things faraway to our backyard where they don't belong, where they just tell you, 'No, you'll never travel, Lena Auffmann, Paris you'll never see! Rome you'll *never* visit.' But I *always* knew that, so why tell me? Better to forget and make do, Leo, make do, eh?"

Leo Auffmann leaned against the machine for support. He snatched his burned hand away, surprised.

"So now what, Lena?" he said.

"It's not for me to say. I know only so long as this thing is here I'll want to come out, or Saul will want to come out like he did last night, and against our judgment sit in it and look at all those places so far away and every time we will cry and be no fit family for you."

"I don't understand," he said, "how I could be so wrong. Just let me check to see what you say is true." He sat down inside the machine. "You won't go away?"

His wife nodded. "We'll wait, Leo."

He shut the door. In the warm darkness he hesitated, pressed the button, and was just relaxing back in color and music, when he heard someone screaming.

"Fire, Papa! The machine's on fire!"

Someone hammered the door. He leaped up, bumped his head, and fell as the door gave way and the boys dragged him out. Behind him he heard a muffled explosion. The entire family was running now. Leo Auffmann turned and gasped, "Saul, call the fire department!"

Lena Auffmann caught Saul as he ran. "Saul," she said. "Wait."

There was a gush of flame, another muffled explosion. When the machine was burning very well indeed, Lena Auffmann nodded.

"All right, Saul," she said. "Run call the fire department."

Everybody who was anybody came to the fire. There was Grandpa Spaulding and Douglas and Tom and most of the boarders and some of the old men from across the ravine and all the children from six blocks around. And Leo Auffmann's children stood out front, proud of how fine the flames looked jumping from the garage roof.

Grandfather Spaulding studied the smoke ball in the sky and said, quietly, "Leo, was that it? Your Happiness Machine?"

"Some year," said Leo Auffmann, "I'll figure it and tell you."

Lena Auffmann, standing in the dark now, watched as the fireman ran in and out of the yard; the garage, roaring, settled upon itself.

"Leo," she said, "it won't take a year to figure. Look around. Think. Keep quiet a little bit. Then come tell me. I'll be in the house, putting books back on shelves, and clothes back in closets, fixing supper, supper's late, look how dark. Come, children, help Mama."

When the firemen and the neighbors were gone, Leo Auffmann was left with Grandfather Spaulding and Douglas and Tom, brooding over the smoldering ruin. He stirred his foot in the wet ashes and slowly said what he had to say.

"The first thing you learn in life is you're a fool. The last thing you learn in life is you're the same fool. In one hour, I've done a lot of thinking. I thought, Leo Auffmann is blind! . . . You want to see the *real* Happiness Machine? The one they patented a couple thousand years ago, it still runs, not good all the time, no! but it runs. It's been here all along."

"But the fire——" said Douglas.

"Sure, the fire, the garage! But like Lena said, it don't take a year to figure; what burned in the garage don't count!"

They followed him up the front-porch steps.

"Here," whispered Leo Auffmann, "the front window. Quiet, and you'll see it."

Hesitantly, Grandfather, Douglas, and Tom peered through the large windowpane.

And there, in small warm pools of lamplight, you could see what Leo Auffmann wanted you to see. There sat Saul and Marshall, playing chess at the coffee table. In the dining room Rebecca was laying out the silver. Naomi was cutting paper-doll dresses. Ruth was painting water colors. Joseph was running his electric train. Through the kitchen door, Lena Auffmann was sliding a pot roast from the steaming oven. Every hand, every head, every mouth made a big or little motion. You could hear their faraway voices under glass. You could hear someone singing in a high sweet voice. You could smell bread baking, too, and you knew it was real bread that would soon be covered with real butter. Everything was there and it was working.

Grandfather, Douglas, and Tom turned to look at Leo Auffmann, who gazed serenely through the window, the pink light on his cheeks.

"Sure," he murmured. "There it is." And he watched with now-gentle sorrow and now-quick delight, and at last quiet acceptance as all the bits and pieces of this house mixed, stirred, settled, poised, and ran steadily again. "The Happiness Machine," he said. "The Happiness Machine."

A moment later he was gone.

Inside, Grandfather, Douglas, and Tom saw him tinkering, make a minor adjustment here, eliminate friction there, busy among all those warm, wonderful, infinitely delicate, forever mysterious, and ever-moving parts.

Then smiling, they went down the steps into the fresh summer night.

TWICE a year they brought the big flapping rugs out into the yard and laid them where they looked out of place and uninhabited, on the lawn. Then Grandma and Mother came from the house with what looked to be the back rungs of those beautiful looped wire chairs downtown in the soda-fountain place. These great wire wands were handed around so they stood, Douglas, Tom, Grandma, Great-grandma, and Mother poised like a collection of witches and familiars over the dusty patterns of old Armenia. Then at a signal from Great-grandma, a blink of the eyes or a gumming of the lips, the flails were raised, the harping wires banged down again and again upon the rugs.

"Take that! And that!" said Great-grandma. "Get the flies, boys, kill the cooties!"

"Oh, you!" said Grandma to her mother.

They all laughed. The dust storm puffed up about them. Their laughing became choked.

Showers of lint, tides of sand, golden flakes of pipe tobacco fluttered, shivered on the exploded and re-exploded air. Pausing, the boys saw the tread of their shoes and the older people's shoes pressed a billion times in the warp and woof of this rug, now to be smoothed clean as the tide of their beating swept again and again along the oriental shore.

"There's where your husband spilled that coffee!" Grandma gave the rug a blow.

"Here's where you dropped the cream!" Great-grandma whacked up a great twister of dust.

"Look at the scuff marks. Boys, boys!"

"Double-Grandma, here's the ink from your pen!"

"Pshaw! Mine was purple ink. That's common blue!"

Bang!

"Look at the path worn from the hall door here to the kitchen door. Food. That's what brings the lions to the water hole. Let's shift it, put it back the other way around."

"Better yet, lock the men out of the house."

"Make them leave their shoes outside the door."

Bang, bang!

They hung the rugs on the wash line now, to finish the job. Tom looked at the intricate scrolls and loops, the flowers, the mysterious figures, the shuttling patterns.

"Tom, don't stand there. Strike, boy!"

"It's fun, seeing things," said Tom.

Douglas glanced up suspiciously. "What do you see?"

"The whole darn town, people, houses, here's our house!" Bang! "Our street!" Bang! "That black part there's the ravine!" Bang! "There's school!" Bang! "This funny cartoon here's you, Doug!" Bang! "Here's Great-grandma, Grandma, Mom." Bang! "How many years this rug been down?"

"Fifteen."

"Fifteen years of people stomping across it; I see every shoe print," gasped Tom.

"Land, boy, you got a tongue," said Great-grandma.

"I see all the things happened in that house in all those years right here!" Bang! "All the past, sure, but I can see the future, too. Just squinch up my eyes and peek around at the patterns, there, to see where we'll be walking, running around, tomorrow."

Douglas stopped swinging the beater. "What else you see in the rug?"

"Threads mostly," said Great-grandma. "Not much left but the underskin. See how the manufacturer wove the thing."

"Right!" said Tom mysteriously. "Threads one way, threads another. I see it all. Dire fiends. Deadly sinners. There's bad weather, there's good. Picnics. Banquets. Strawberry festivals." He tapped the beater from place to place portentously.

"That's some boardinghouse you got me running," said Grandma, glowing with exertion.

"It's all there, fuzzylike. Hold your head on one side, Doug, get one eye almost shut. It's better at night, of course, inside, the rug on the floor, lamplight and all. Then you get shadows all shapes, light and dark, and watch the threads running off, feel the nap, run your hand around on the fur. Smells just like a desert, I bet. All hot and sandy, like inside a mummy case, maybe. Look, that red spot, that's the Happiness Machine burning up!"

"Catsup from somebody's sandwich, no doubt," said Mom.

"No, Happiness Machine," said Douglas, and was sad to see it burning there. He had been counting on Leo Auffmann to keep things in order, keep everybody smiling, keep the small gyroscope he often felt inside himself tilting toward the sun every time the earth tilted toward outer space and darkness. But no, there was Auffmann's folly, ashes and cinders. Bang! Bang! Douglas struck.

"Look, there's the green electric runabout! Miss Fern! Miss Roberta!" said Tom. "Honk, Honk!" Bang!

They all laughed.

"There's your life-strings, Doug, running along in knots. Too many sour apples. Pickles at bedtime!"

"Which one, where?" cried Douglas, peering.

"This one, one year from now, this one, two years from now, and this one, three, four, five years from now!"

Bang! The wire beater hissed like a snake in the blind sky.

"And one to grow on!" said Tom.

He hit the rug so hard all the dust of five thousand centuries jumped from the shocked texture, paused on the air a terrible moment, and even as

Douglas stood, eyes squinted to see the warp, the woof, the shivering pattern, the Armenian avalanche of dust roared soundless upon, over, down and around, burying him forever before their eyes. . . .

How it began with the children, old Mrs. Bentley never knew. She often saw them, like moths and monkeys, at the grocer's among the cabbages and hung bananas, and she smiled at them and they smiled back. Mrs. Bentley watched them making footprints in winter snow, filling their lungs with autumn smoke, shaking down blizzards of spring appleblossoms, but felt no fear of them. As for herself, her house was in extreme good order, everything set to its station, the floors briskly swept, the foods neatly tinned, the hatpins thrust through cushions, and the drawers of her bedroom bureaus crisply filled with the paraphernalia of years.

Mrs. Bentley was a saver. She saved tickets, old theatre programs, bits of lace, scarves, rail transfers; all the tags and tokens of existence.

"I've a stack of records," she often said. "Here's Caruso. That was in 1916, in New York; I was sixty and John was still alive. Here's June Moon, 1924, I think, right after John died."

That was the huge regret of her life, in a way. The one thing she had most enjoyed touching and listening to and looking at she hadn't saved. John was far out in the meadow country, dated and boxed and hidden under grasses, and nothing remained of him but his high silk hat and his cane and his good suit in the closet. So much of the rest of him had been devoured by moths.

But what she could keep she had kept. Her pink-flowered dresses crushed among moth balls in vast black trunks, and cut-glass dishes from her childhood—she had brought them all when she moved to this town five years ago. Her husband had owned rental property in a number of towns, and, like a yellow ivory chess piece, she had moved and sold one after another, until now she was here in a strange town, left with only the trunks and furniture, dark and ugly, crouched about her like the creatures of a primordial zoo.

The thing about the children happened in the middle of summer. Mrs. Bentley, coming out to water the ivy upon her front porch, saw two cool-colored sprawling girls and a small boy lying on her lawn, enjoying the immense prickling of the grass.

At the very moment Mrs. Bentley was smiling down upon them with her yellow mask face, around a corner like an elfin band came an ice-cream wagon. It jingled out icy melodies, as crisp and rimmed as crystal wineglasses tapped by an expert, summoning all. The children sat up, turning their heads, like sunflowers after the sun.

Mrs. Bentley called, "Would you like some? Here!" The ice-cream wagon stopped and she exchanged money for pieces of the original Ice Age. The children thanked her with snow in their mouths, their eyes darting from her buttoned-up shoes to her white hair.

"Don't you want a bite?" said the boy.

"No, child. I'm old enough and cold enough; the hottest day won't thaw me," laughed Mrs. Bentley.

They carried the miniature glaciers up and sat, three in a row, on the shady porch glider.

"I'm Alice, she's Jane, and that's Tom Spaulding."

"How nice. And I'm Mrs. Bentley. They called me Helen."

They stared at her.

"Don't you believe they called me Helen?" said the old lady.

"I didn't know old ladies had first names," said Tom, blinking.

Mrs. Bentley laughed dryly.

"You never hear them used, he means," said Jane.

"My dear, when you are as old as I, they won't call you Jane, either. Old age is dreadfully formal. It's always 'Mrs.' Young people don't like to call you 'Helen.' It seems much too flip."

"How old *are* you?" asked Alice.

"I remember the pterodactyl." Mrs. Bentley smiled.

"No, but how old?"

"Seventy-two."

They gave their cold sweets an extra long suck, deliberating.

"That's *old*," said Tom.

"I don't feel any different now than when I was your age," said the old lady.

"*Our* age?"

"Yes. Once I was a pretty little girl just like you, Jane, and you, Alice."

They did not speak.

"What's the matter?"

"Nothing." Jane got up.

"Oh, you don't have to go so soon, I hope. You haven't finished eating. . . . Is something the matter?"

"My mother says it isn't nice to fib," said Jane.

"Of course it isn't. It's very bad," agreed Mrs. Bentley.

"And not to *listen* to fibs."

"Who was fibbing to you, Jane?"

Jane looked at her and then glanced nervously away. "You were."

"I?" Mrs. Bentley laughed and put her withered claw to her small bosom. "About what?"

"About your age. About being a little girl."

Mrs. Bentley stiffened. "But I *was*, many years ago, a little girl just like you."

"Come on, Alice, Tom."

"Just a moment," said Mrs. Bentley. "Don't you believe me?"

"I don't know," said Jane. "No."

"But how ridiculous! It's perfectly obvious. Everyone was young once!"

"Not you," whispered Jane, eyes down, almost to herself. Her empty ice stick had fallen in a vanilla puddle on the porch floor.

"But of course I was eight, nine, ten years old, like all of you."

The two girls gave a short, quickly-sealed-up laugh.

Mrs. Bentley's eyes glittered. "Well, I can't waste a morning arguing with ten-year-olds. Needless to say, I was ten myself once and just as silly."

The two girls laughed. Tom looked uneasy.

"You're joking with us," giggled Jane. "You weren't really ten ever, were you, Mrs. Bentley?"

"You run on home!" the woman cried suddenly, for she could not stand their eyes. "I won't have you laughing."

"And your name's not really Helen?"

"Of course it's Helen!"

"Good-by," said the two girls, giggling away across the lawn under the seas of shade, Tom followed them slowly. "Thanks for the ice cream!"

"Once I played *hopscotch!*" Mrs. Bentley cried after them, but they were gone.

Mrs. Bentley spent the rest of the day slamming teakettles about, loudly preparing a meager lunch, and from time to time going to the front door, hoping to catch those insolent fiends on their laughing excursions through the late day. But if they had appeared, what could she say to them, why should she worry about them?

"The idea!" said Mrs. Bentley to her dainty, rose-clustered teacup. "No one ever doubted I was a girl before. What a silly, horrible thing to do. I don't mind being old—not really—but I *do* resent having my childhood taken away from me."

She could see the children racing off under the cavernous trees with her youth in their frosty fingers, invisible as air.

After supper, for no reason at all, with a senseless certainty of motion, she watched her own hands, like a pair of ghostly gloves at a seance, gather together certain items in a perfumed kerchief. Then she went to her front porch and stood there stiffly for half an hour.

As suddenly as night birds the children flew by, and Mrs. Bentley's voice brought them to a fluttering rest.

"Yes, *Mrs.* Bentley?"

"Come up on this porch!" she commanded them, and the girls climbed the steps, Tom trailing after.

"Yes, Mrs. Bentley?" They thumped the "Mrs." like a bass piano chord, extra heavily, as if that were her first name.

"I've some treasures to show you." She opened the perfumed kerchief and peered into it as if she herself might be surprised. She drew forth a hair comb, very small and delicate, its rim twinkling with rhinestones.

"I wore this when I was nine," she said.

Jane turned it in her hand and said, "How nice."

"Let's see!" cried Alice.

"And here is a tiny ring I wore when I was eight," said Mrs. Bentley. "It doesn't fit my finger now. You look through it and see the Tower of Pisa ready to fall."

"Let's see it lean!" The girls passed it back and forth between them until Jane fitted it to her hand. "Why, it's just *my* size!" she exclaimed.

"And the comb fits *my* head!" gasped Alice.

Mrs. Bentley produced some jackstones. "Here," she said. "I once played with these."

She threw them. They made a constellation on the porch.

"And here!" In triumph she flashed her trump card, a postal picture of herself when she was seven years old, in a dress like a yellow butterfly, with her golden curls and blown blue-glass eyes and angelic pouting lips.

"Who's this little girl?" asked Jane.

"It's *me!*"

The two girls held onto it.

"But it doesn't look like you," said Jane simply. "Anybody could get a picture like this, somewhere."

They looked at her for a long moment.

"Any more pictures, Mrs. Bentley?" asked Alice. "Of you, later? You got a picture of you at fifteen, and one at twenty, and one at forty and fifty?"

The girls chortled.

"I don't have to show you anything!" said Mrs. Bentley.

"Then we don't have to believe you," replied Jane.

"But this picture proves I was young!"

"That's some other little girl, like us. You borrowed it."

"I was married!"

"Where's *Mr.* Bentley?"

"He's been gone a long time. If he were here, he'd tell you how young and pretty I was when I was twenty-two."

"But he's not here and he can't tell, so what does that prove?"

"I have a marriage certificate."

"You could have borrowed that, too. Only way I'll believe you were ever young"—Jane shut her eyes to emphasize how sure she was of herself—"is if you have someone say they saw you when you were ten."

"Thousands of people saw me but they're dead, you little fool—or ill, in other towns. I don't know a soul here, just moved here a few years ago, so no one saw me young."

"Well, there you *are!*" Jane blinked at her companions. "Nobody *saw* her!"

"Listen!" Mrs. Bentley seized the girl's wrist. "You must take these things on faith. Someday you'll be as old as I. People will say the same. 'Oh, no,' they'll say, 'those vultures were never hummingbirds, those owls were never orioles, those parrots were never bluebirds!' One day you'll be like me!"

"No, we won't!" said the girls. "Will we?" they asked one another.

"Wait and see!" said Mrs. Bentley.

And to herself she thought, Oh, God, children are children, old women are old women, and nothing in between. They can't imagine a change they can't see.

"Your mother," she said to Jane. "Haven't you noticed, over the years, the change?"

"No," said Jane. "She's always the same."

And that was true. You lived with people every day and they never altered a degree. It was only when people had been off on a long trip, for years, that they shocked you. And she felt like a woman who has been on a roaring black train for seventy-two years, landing at last upon the rail platform and everyone crying: "Helen Bentley, is that *you?*"

"I guess we better go home," said Jane. "Thanks for the ring. It just fits me."

"Thanks for the comb. It's fine."

"Thanks for the picture of the little girl."

"Come back—you can't have those!" Mrs. Bentley shouted as they raced down the steps. "They're *mine!*"

"Don't!" said Tom, following the girls. "Give them back!"

"No, she stole them! They belonged to some other little girl. She stole them. Thanks!" cried Alice.

So no matter how she called after them, the girls were gone, like moths through darkness.

"I'm sorry," said Tom, on the lawn, looking up at Mrs. Bentley. He went away.

They took my ring and my comb and my picture, thought Mrs. Bentley, trembling there on the steps. Oh, I'm empty, empty; it's part of my life.

She lay awake for many hours into the night, among her trunks and trinkets. She glanced over at the neat stacks of materials and toys and opera plumes and said, aloud, "Does it really belong to me?"

Or was it the elaborate trick of an old lady convincing herself that she had a past? After all, once a time was over, it was done. You were always in the present. She may have been a girl once, but was not now. Her childhood was gone and nothing could fetch it back.

A night wind blew in the room. The white curtain fluttered against a dark cane, which had leaned against the wall near the other bric-a-brac for many years. The cane trembled and fell out into a patch of moonlight, with a soft thud. Its gold ferrule glittered. It was her husband's opera cane. It seemed as if he were pointing it at her, as he often had, using his soft, sad, reasonable voice when they, upon rare occasions, disagreed.

"Those children are right," he would have said. "They stole nothing from you, my dear. These things don't belong to you *here*, you *now*. They belonged to her, that other you, so long ago."

Oh, thought Mrs. Bentley. And then, as though an ancient phonograph record had been set hissing under a steel needle, she remembered a conversation she had once had with Mr. Bentley—Mr. Bentley, so prim, a pink carnation in his whisk-broomed lapel, saying, "My dear, you never will understand time, will you? You're always trying to be the things you were, instead of the person you are tonight. Why do you save those ticket stubs and theater programs? They'll only hurt you later. Throw them away, my dear."

But Mrs. Bentley had stubbornly kept them.

"It won't work," Mr. Bentley continued, sipping his tea. "No matter how hard you try to be what you once were, you can only be what you are here and now. Time hypnotizes. When you're nine, you think you've always been nine years old and will always be. When you're thirty, it seems you've always been balanced there on that bright rim of middle life. And then when you turn seventy, you are always and forever seventy. You're in the present, you're trapped in a young now or an old now, but there is no other now to be seen."

It had been one of the few, but gentle, disputes of their quiet marriage. He had never approved of her bric-a-brackery. "Be what you are, bury what you are not," he had said. "Ticket stubs are trickery. Saving things is a magic trick, with mirrors."

If he were alive tonight, what would he say?

"You're saving cocoons." That's what he'd say. "Corsets, in a way, you can never fit again. So why save them? You can't really prove you were ever young. Pictures? No, they lie. You're not the picture."

"Affidavits?"

"No, my dear, you're not the dates, or the ink, or the paper. You're not these trunks of junk and dust. You're only you, here, now—the present you."

Mrs. Bentley nodded at the memory, breathing easier.

"Yes, I see. I see."

The gold-ferruled cane lay silently on the moon-lit rug.

"In the morning," she said to it, "I will do something final about this, and settle down to being only me, and nobody else from any other year. Yes, that's what I'll do."

She slept. . . .

The morning was bright and green, and there at her door, bumping softly on the screen, were the two girls. "Got any more to give us, Mrs. Bentley? More of the little girl's things?"

She led them down the hall to the library.

"Take this." She gave Jane the dress in which she had played the mandarin's daughter at fifteen. "And this, and this." A kaleidoscope, a magnifying glass. "Pick anything you want," said Mrs. Bentley. "Books, skates, dolls, everything—they're yours."

"Ours?"

"Only yours. And will you help me with a little work in the next hour? I'm building a big fire in my back yard. I'm emptying the trunks, throwing out this trash for the trashman. It doesn't belong to me. Nothing ever belongs to anybody."

"We'll help," they said.

Mrs. Bentley led the procession to the back yard, arms full, a box of matches in her hand.

So the rest of the summer you could see the two little girls and Tom like wrens on a wire, on Mrs. Bentley's front porch, waiting. And when the silvery chimes of the icicle man were heard, the front door opened, Mrs. Bentley floated out with her hand deep down the gullet of her silver-mouthed purse, and for half an hour you could see them there on the porch, the children and the old lady putting coldness into warmness, eating chocolate icicles, laughing. At last they were good friends.

"How old are you, Mrs. Bentley?"

"Seventy-two."

"How old were you fifty years ago?"

"Seventy-two."

"You weren't ever young, were you, and never wore ribbons or dresses like these?"

"No."

"Have you got a first name?"

"My name is Mrs. Bentley."

"And you've always lived in this one house?"

"Always."

"And never were pretty?"

"Never."

"Never in a million trillion years?" The two girls would bend toward the old lady, and wait in the pressed silence of four o'clock on a summer afternoon.

"Never," said Mrs. Bentley, "in a million trillion years."

Y ou got the nickel tablet ready, Doug?"

"Sure." Doug licked his pencil good.

"What you got in there so far?"

"All the ceremonies."

"July Fourth and all that, dandelion-wine making and junk like bringing out the porch swing, huh?"

"Says here, I ate the first Eskimo Pie of the summer season June first, 1928."

"That wasn't summer, that was still spring."

"It was a 'first' anyway, so I put it down. Bought those new tennis shoes June twenty-fifth. Went barefoot in the grass June twenty-sixth. Busy, busy, busy, heck! Well, what you got to report this time, Tom? A new first, a fancy ceremony of some sort to do with vacation like a creek-crab catching or water-strider-spider grabbing?"

"Nobody ever grabbed a water-strider-spider in his life. You ever *know* anybody grabbed a water-strider-spider? Go ahead, think!"

"I'm thinking."

"Well?"

"You're right. Nobody ever did. Nobody ever will, I guess. They're just too fast."

"It's not that they're fast. They just don't exist," said Tom. He thought about it and nodded. "That's right, they just never did exist at all. Well, what I got to report is this."

He leaned over and whispered in his brother's ear.

Douglas wrote it.

They both looked at it.

"I'll be darned!" said Douglas. "I never thought of that. That's brilliant! It's true. Old people never *were* children!"

"And it's kind of sad," said Tom, sitting still. "There's nothing we can do to help them."

S EEMS like the town is full of machines," said Douglas, running. "Mr. Auffmann and his Happiness Machine, Miss Fern and Miss Roberta and their Green Machine. Now, Charlie, what you handing me?"

"A Time Machine!" panted Charlie Woodman, pacing him. "Mother's, scout's, Injun's honor!"

"Travels in the past and future?" John Huff asked, easily circling them.

"Only in the past, but you can't have everything. Here we are."

Charlie Woodman pulled up at a hedge.

Douglas peered in at the old house. "Heck, that's Colonel Freeleigh's place. Can't be no Time Machine in there. He's no inventor, and if he was, we'd known about an important thing like a Time Machine years ago."

Charlie and John tiptoed up the front-porch steps. Douglas snorted and shook his head, staying at the bottom of the steps.

"Okay, Douglas," said Charlie. "Be a knucklehead. Sure, Colonel Freeleigh didn't *invent* this Time Machine. But he's got a proprietary interest in it, and it's been here all the time. We were too darned dumb to notice! So long, Douglas Spaulding, to you!"

Charlie took John's elbow as though he was escorting a lady, opened the front-porch screen and went in. The screen door did not slam.

Douglas had caught the screen and was following silently.

Charlie walked across the enclosed porch, knocked, and opened the inside door. They all peered down a long dark hall toward a room that was lit like an undersea grotto, soft green, dim, and watery.

"Colonel Freeleigh?"

Silence.

"He don't hear so good," whispered Charlie. "But he told me to just come on in and yell. *Colonel!*"

The only answer was the dust sifting down and around the spiral stair well from above. Then there was a faint stir in that undersea chamber at the far end of the hall.

They moved carefully along and peered into a room which contained but two pieces of furniture— an old man and a chair. They resembled each other, both so thin you could see just how they had been put together, ball and socket, sinew and joint. The rest of the room was raw floor boards, naked walls and ceiling, and vast quantities of silent air.

"He looks dead," whispered Douglas.

"No, he's just thinking up new places to travel to," said Charlie, very proud and quiet. "Colonel?"

One of the pieces of brown furniture moved and it was the colonel, blinking around, focusing, and smiling a wild and toothless smile. "Charlie!"

"Colonel, Doug and John here came to——"

"Welcome, boys; sit down, sit down!"

The boys sat, uneasily, on the floor.

"But where's the——" said Douglas. Charlie jabbed his ribs quickly.

"Where's the what?" asked Colonel Freeleigh.

"Where's the point in *us* talking, he means." Charlie grimaced at Douglas, then smiled at the old man. "We got nothing to say. Colonel, *you* say something."

"Beware, Charlie, old men only lie in wait for people to ask them to talk. Then they rattle on like a rusty elevator wheezing up a shaft."

"Ching Ling Soo," suggested Charlie casually.

"Eh?" said the colonel.

"Boston," Charlie prompted, "1910."

"Boston, 1910 . . ." The colonel frowned. "Why, Ching Ling Soo, of course!"

"Yes, sir, Colonel."

"Let me see, now . . ." The colonel's voice murmured, it drifted away on serene lake waters. "Let me see . . ."

The boys waited.

Colonel Freeleigh closed his eyes.

"October first, 1910, a calm cool fine autumn night, the Boston Variety Theatre, yes, there it *is*. Full house, all waiting. Orchestra, fanfare, curtain! Ching Ling Soo, the great Oriental Magician! There he is, on stage! And there I am, front row center! 'The Bullet Trick!' he cries. 'Volunteers!' The man next to me goes up. 'Examine the rifle!' says Ching. 'Mark the bullet!' says he. 'Now, fire this marked bullet from this rifle, using my face for a target, and,' says Ching, 'at the far end of the stage I will catch the bullet in my *teeth!*' "

Colonel Freeleigh took a deep breath and paused.

Douglas was staring at him, half puzzled, half in awe. John Huff and Charlie were completely lost. Now the old man went on, his head and body frozen, only his lips moving.

" 'Ready, aim, fire!' cries Ching Ling Soo. Bang! The rifle cracks. Bang! Ching Ling Soo shrieks, he staggers, he falls, his face all red. Pandemonium. Audience on its feet. Something wrong with the rifle. 'Dead,' someone says. And they're right. Dead. Horrible, horrible . . . I'll always remember . . . his face a mask of red, the curtain coming down fast and the women weeping . . . 1910 . . . Boston . . . Variety Theatre . . . poor man . . . poor man . . ."

Colonel Freeleigh slowly opened his eyes.

"Boy, Colonel," said Charlie, "that was fine. Now how about Pawnee Bill?"

"Pawnee Bill . . . ?"

"And the time you was on the prairie way back in '75."

"Pawnee Bill . . ." The colonel moved into darkness. "Eighteen seventy-five . . . yes, me and Pawnee Bill on a little rise in the middle of the prairie, waiting. 'Shh!' says Pawnee Bill. 'Listen.' The prairie like a big stage all set for the storm to come. Thunder. Soft. Thunder again. Not so soft. And across that prairie as far as the eye could see this big ominous yellow-dark cloud full of black lightning, somehow sunk to earth, fifty miles wide, fifty miles long, a mile high, and no more than an inch off the ground. 'Lord!' I cried, 'Lord!'—from up on my hill—'Lord!' The earth pounded like a mad heart, boys, a heart gone to panic. My bones shook fit to break. The earth shook: rat-a-tat rat-a-tat, boom! Rumble. That's a rare word: rumble. Oh, how that mighty storm rumbled along down, up, and over the rises, and all you could see was the cloud and nothing inside. 'That's them!' cried Pawnee Bill. And the cloud was dust! Not vapors or rain, no, but prairie dust flung up from the tinder-dry grass like fine corn meal, like pollen all blazed with sunlight now, for the sun had come out. I shouted again! Why? Because in all that hell-fire filtering dust now a veil moved aside and I saw them, I swear it! The grand army of the ancient prairie: the bison, the buffalo!"

The colonel let the silence build, then broke it again.

"Heads like giant Negroes' fists, bodies like locomotives! Twenty, fifty, two hundred thousand iron missiles shot out of the west, gone off the track and flailing cinders, their eyes like blazing coals, rumbling toward oblivion!

"I saw that the dust rose up and for a little while showed me that sea of humps, of dolloping manes, black shaggy waves rising, falling . . . 'Shoot!' says Pawnee Bill. 'Shoot!' And I cock and aim. 'Shoot!' he says. And I stand there feeling like God's right hand, looking at the great vision of strength and violence going by, going by, midnight at noon, like a glinty funeral train all black and long and sad and forever and you don't fire at a funeral train, now do you, boys? *do* you? All I wanted then was for the dust to sink again and cover the black shapes of doom which pummeled and jostled on in great burdensome commotions. And, boys, the dust came down. The cloud hid the million feet that were drumming up the thunder and dusting out the storm. I heard Pawnee Bill curse and hit my arm. But I was glad I hadn't touched that cloud or the power within that cloud with so much as a pellet of lead. I just wanted to stand watching time bundle by in great trundlings all hid by the storm the bison made and carried with them toward eternity.

"An hour, three hours, six, it took for the storm to pass on away over the horizon toward less kind men than me. Pawnee Bill was gone, I stood alone, stone deaf. I walked all numb through a town a hundred miles south and heard not the voices of men and was satisfied not to hear. For a little while I wanted to remember the thunder. I hear it still, on summer afternoons like this when the rain shapes over the lake; a fearsome, wondrous sound . . . one I wish you might have heard. . . ."

The dim light filtered through Colonel Freeleigh's nose which was large and like white porcelain which cupped a very thin and tepid orange tea indeed.

"Is he asleep?" asked Douglas at last.

"No," said Charlie. "Just recharging his batteries."

Colonel Freeleigh breathed swiftly, softly, as if he'd run a long way. At last he opened his eyes.

"Yes, *sir!*" said Charlie, in admiration.

"Hello, Charlie." The colonel smiled at the boys puzzledly.

"That's Doug and that's John," said Charlie.

"How-de-do, boys."

The boys said hello.

"But——" said Douglas. "Where is the——?"

"My gosh, you're dumb!" Charlie jabbed Douglas in the arm. He turned to the colonel. "You were saying, sir?"

"*Was* I?" murmured the old man.

"The Civil War," suggested John Huff quietly. "Does he remember that?"

"Do I remember?" said the colonel. "Oh, I do, I do!" His voice trembled as he shut up his eyes again. "Everything! Except . . . which side I fought on . . ."

"The *color* of your uniform——" Charlie began.

"Colors begin to run on you," whispered the colonel. "It's gotten hazy. I see soldiers with me, but a long time ago I stopped seeing color in their coats or caps. I was born in Illinois, raised in Virginia, married in New York, built a house in Tennessee and now, very late, here I am, good Lord, back in Green Town. So you see why the colors run and blend. . . ."

"But you remember which side of hills you fought on?" Charlie did not raise his voice. "Did the sun rise on your left or right? Did you march toward Canada or Mexico?"

"Seems some mornings the sun rose on my good right hand, some mornings over my left shoulder. We marched all directions. It's most seventy years since. You forget suns and mornings that long past."

"You remember winning, don't you? A battle won, somewhere?"

"No," said the old man, deep under. "I don't remember anyone winning anywhere any time. War's never a winning thing, Charlie. You just lose all the time, and the one who loses last asks for terms. All I remember is a lot of losing and sadness and nothing good but the end of it. The end of it, Charles, that was a winning all to itself, having nothing to do with guns. But I don't suppose that's the kind of victory you boys mean for me to talk on."

"Antietam," said John Huff. "Ask about Antietam."

"I was there."

The boys' eyes grew bright. "Bull Run, ask him Bull Run . . ."

"I was there." Softly.

"What about Shiloh?"

"There's never been a year in my life I haven't thought, what a lovely name and what a shame to see it only on battle records."

"Shiloh, then. Fort Sumter?"

"I saw the first puffs of powder smoke." A dreaming voice. "So many things come back, oh, so many things. I remember songs. 'All's quiet along the Potomac tonight, where the soldiers lie peacefully dreaming; their tents in the rays of the clear autumn moon, or the light of the watchfire, are gleaming.' Remember, remember . . . 'All quiet along the Potomac tonight; no sound save the rush of the river; while soft falls the dew on the face of the dead—the picket's off duty forever!' . . . After the surrender, Mr. Lincoln, on the White House balcony asked the band to play, 'Look away, look away, look away, Dixie land . . .' And then there was the Boston lady who one night wrote a song will last a thousand years: 'Mine eyes have seen the glory of the coming of the Lord; He is trampling out the vintage where the grapes of wrath are stored.' Late nights I feel my mouth move singing back in another time. 'Ye Cavaliers of Dixie! Who guard the Southern shores . . .' 'When the boys come home in triumph, brother, with the laurels they shall gain . . .' So many songs, sung on both sides, blowing north, blowing south on the night winds. 'We are coming, Father Abraham, three hundred thousand more . . .' 'Tenting tonight, tenting tonight, tenting on the old camp ground.' 'Hurrah, hurrah, we bring the Jubilee, hurrah, hurrah, the flag that makes us free . . .'"

The old man's voice faded.

The boys sat for a long while without moving. Then Charlie turned and looked at Douglas and said, "Well, is he or isn't he?"

Douglas breathed twice and said, "He sure *is*."

The colonel opened his eyes.

"I sure am *what*?" he asked.

"A Time Machine," murmured Douglas. "A Time Machine."

The colonel looked at the boys for a full five seconds. Now it was his voice that was full of awe.

"Is that what you boys call me?"

"Yes, sir, Colonel."

"Yes, sir."

The colonel sat slowly back in his chair and looked at the boys and looked at his hands and then looked at the blank wall beyond them steadily.

Charlie arose. "Well, I guess we better go. So long and thanks, Colonel."

"What? Oh, so long, boys."

Douglas and John and Charlie went on tiptoe out the door.

Colonel Freeleigh, though they crossed his line of vision, did not see them go.

In the street, the boys were startled when someone shouted from a first-floor window above, "Hey!"

They looked up.

"Yes, sir, Colonel?"

The colonel leaned out, waving one arm.

"I thought about what you said, boys!"

"Yes, sir?"

"And—you're right! Why didn't I *think* of it before! A Time Machine, by God, a Time Machine!"

"Yes, sir."

"So long, boys. Come aboard any time!"

At the end of the street they turned again and the colonel was still waving. They waved back, feeling warm and good, then went on.

"Chug-a-chug," said John. "I can travel twelve years into the past. Wham-chug-ding!"

"Yeah," said Charlie, looking back at that quiet house, "but you can't go a hundred years."

"No," mused John, "I can't go a hundred years. That's really traveling. That's really some machine."

They walked for a full minute in silence, looking at their feet. They came to a fence.

"Last one over this fence," said Douglas, "is a girl."

All the way home they called Douglas "Dora."

L ONG after midnight Tom woke to find Douglas scribbling rapidly in the nickel tablet, by flashlight.

"Doug, what's up?"

"Up? Everything's up! I'm counting my blessings, Tom! Look here; the Happiness Machine didn't work out, did it? But, who cares! I got the whole year lined up, anyway. Need to run anywhere on the main streets, I got the Green Town Trolley to look around and spy on the world from. Need to run anywhere *off* the main streets, I knock on Miss Fern and Miss Roberta's door and they charge up the batteries on their electric runabout and we go sailing down the sidewalks. Need to run down alleys and over fences, to see that part of Green Town you only see around back and behind and creep up on, and I got my brand-new sneakers. Sneakers, runabout, trolley! I'm set! But even better, Tom, even better, listen! If I want to go where no one else can go because they're not smart enough to even think of it, if I want to charge back to 1890 and then transfer to 1875 and transfer again crosstown to 1860 I just hop on the old Colonel Freeleigh Express! I'm writing it down here this way: 'Maybe old people were never children, like we claim with Mrs. Bentley, but, big or little, some of them were standing around at Appomattox the summer of 1865.' They got Indian vision and can sight back further than you and me will ever sight ahead."

"That sounds swell, Doug; what does it mean?"

Douglas went on writing. "It means you and me

ain't got half the chance to be far-travelers they have.
If we're lucky we'll hit forty, forty-five, fifty. That's
just a jog around the block to them. It's when you hit
ninety, ninety-five, a hundred, that you're far-traveling like heck."

The flashlight went out.

They lay there in the moonlight.

"Tom," whispered Douglas. "I got to travel all
those ways. See what I can see. But most of all I got
to visit Colonel Freeleigh once, twice, three times a
week. He's better than all the other machines. He
talks, you listen. And the more he talks the more he
gets you to peering around and noticing things. He
tells you you're riding on a very special train, by
gosh, and sure enough, it's true. He's been down the
track, and knows. And now here we come, you and
me, along the same track, but further on, and so much
looking and snuffing and handling things to do, you
need old Colonel Freeleigh to shove and say look
alive so you remember every second! Every darn
thing there is to remember! So when kids come
around when you're real old, you can do for them
what the colonel once did for you. That's the way it
is, Tom, I got to spend a lot of time visiting him and
listening so I can go far-traveling with him as often
as he can."

Tom was silent a moment. Then he looked over
at Douglas there in the dark.

"Far-traveling. You make that up?"

"Maybe yes and maybe no."

"Far-traveling," whispered Tom.

"Only one thing I'm sure of," said Douglas, closing his eyes. "It sure sounds lonely."

**B**ANG!
A door slammed. In an attic dust jumped off bureaus and bookcases. Two old women collapsed against the attic door, each scrabbling to lock it tight, tight. A thousand pigeons seemed to have leaped off the roof right over their heads. They bent as if burdened, ducked under the drum of beating wings. Then they stopped, their mouths surprised. What they heard was only the pure sound of panic, their hearts in their chests. . . . Above the uproar, they tried to make themselves heard.

"What've we done! Poor Mister Quartermain!"

"We must've killed him. And someone must've seen and followed us. Look . . ."

Miss Fern and Miss Roberta peered from the cobwebbed attic window. Below, as if no great tragedy had occurred, the oaks and elms continued to grow in fresh sunlight. A boy strolled by on the sidewalk, turned, strolled by again, looking up.

In the attic the old women peered at each other as if trying to see their faces in a running stream.

"The police!"

But no one hammered the downstairs door and cried, "In the name of the law!"

"Who's that boy down there?"

"Douglas, Douglas Spaulding! Lord, he's come to ask for a ride in our Green Machine. He doesn't know. Our pride has ruined us. Pride and that electrical contraption!"

"That terrible salesman from Gumport Falls. It's his fault, him and his talking."

Talking, talking, like soft rain on a summer roof.

Suddenly it was another day, another noon. They sat with white fans and dishes of cool, trembling lime Jell-O on their arbored porch.

Out of the blinding glare, out of the yellow sun, glittering, splendid as a prince's coach . . .

THE GREEN MACHINE!

It glided. It whispered, an ocean breeze. Delicate as maple leaves, fresher than creek water, it purred with the majesty of cats prowling the noon-tide. In the machine, his Panama hat afloat in Vaseline above his ears, the salesman from Gumport Falls! The machine, with a rubber tread, soft, shrewd, whipped up their scalded white sidewalk, whirred to the lowest porch step, twirled, stopped. The salesman leaped out, blocked off the sun with his Panama. In this small shadow, his smile flashed.

"The name is William Tara! And this——" He pinched a bulb. A seal barked. "—is the horn!" He lifted black satin cushions. "Storage batteries!" A smell of lightning blew on the hot air. "Steering lever! Foot rest! Overhead parasol! Here, *in toto,* is The Green Machine!"

In the dark attic the ladies shuddered, remembering, eyes shut.

"Why didn't we stab him with our darning needles!"

"Shh! Listen."

Someone knocked on the front door downstairs. After a time the knocking stopped. They saw a woman cross the yard and enter the house next door.

"Only Lavinia Nebbs, come with an empty cup, to borrow sugar, I guess."

"Hold me, I'm afraid."

They shut their eyes. The memory-play began again. An old straw hat on an iron trunk was suddenly flourished, it seemed, by the man from Gumport Falls.

"Thanks, I *will* have some iced tea." You could hear the cool liquid shock his stomach, in the silence. Then he turned his gaze upon the old ladies like a doctor with a small light, looking into their eyes and nostrils and mouths. "Ladies, I know you're both vigorous. You *look* it. Eighty years"—he snapped his fingers—"mean nothing to you! But there are times, mind, when you're so busy, busy, you need a friend indeed, a friend in need, and *that* is the two-seater Green Machine."

He fixed his bright, stuffed-fox, green-glass-eyed gaze upon that wonderful merchandise. It stood, smelling new, in the hot sunlight, waiting for them, a parlor chair comfortably put to wheels.

"Quiet as a swan's feather." They felt him breathe softly in their faces. "Listen." They listened. "The storage batteries are fully charged and ready now! Listen! Not a tremor, not a sound. Electric, ladies. You recharge it every night in your garage."

"It couldn't—that is——" The younger sister gulped some iced tea. "It couldn't electrocute us accidently?"

"Perish the thought!"

He vaulted to the machine again, his teeth like those you saw in dental windows, alone, grimacing at you, as you passed by late at night.

"Tea parties!" he waltzed the runabout in a circle. "Bridge clubs. Soirees. Galas. Luncheons. Birthday gatherings! D.A.R. breakfasts." He purred away as if running off forever. He returned in a rubber-tired hush. "Gold Star Mother suppers." He sat primly, corseted by his supple characterization of a woman. "Easy steering. Silent, elegant arrivals and departures. No license needed. On hot days—take the breeze. Ah . . ." He glided by the porch, head back, eyes closed deliciously, hair tousling in the wind thus cleanly sliced through.

He trudged reverently up the porch stairs, hat in hand, turning to gaze at the trial model as at the altar of a familiar church. "Ladies," he said softly, "twenty-five dollars down. Ten dollars a month, for two years."

Fern was first down the steps onto the double seat. She sat apprehensively. Her hand itched. She raised it. She dared tweak the rubber bulb horn.

A seal barked.

Roberta, on the porch, screamed hilariously and leaned over the railing.

The salesman joined their hilarity. He escorted the older sister down the steps, roaring, at the same time taking out his pen and searching in his straw hat for some piece of paper or other.

"And so we bought it!" remembered Miss Roberta, in the attic, horrified at their nerve. "We should've been warned! Always *did* think it looked like a little car off the carnival roller coaster!"

"Well," said Fern defensively, "my hip's bothered me for years, and you always get tired walking. It seemed so refined, so regal. Like in the old days when women wore hoop skirts. They *sailed!* The Green Machine sailed *so* quietly."

Like an excursion boat, wonderfully easy to steer, a baton handle you twitched with your hand, so.

Oh, that glorious and enchanted first week—the magical afternoons of golden light, humming through the shady town on a dreaming, timeless river, seated stiffly, smiling at passing acquaintances, sedately purring out their wrinkled claws at every turn, squeezing a hoarse cry from the black rubber horn at intersections, sometimes letting Douglas or Tom Spaulding or any of the other boys who trotted, chatting, alongside, hitch a little ride. Fifteen slow and pleasurable miles an hour top speed. They came and went through the summer sunlight and shadow, their faces freckled and stained by passing trees, going and coming like an ancient, wheeled vision.

"And then" whispered Fern, "this afternoon! Oh, this afternoon!"

"It was an accident."

"But we ran away, and that's criminal!"

This noon. The smell of the leather cushions under their bodies, the gray perfume smell of their own sachets trailing back as they moved in their silent Green Machine through the small, languorous town.

It happened quickly. Rolling soft onto the sidewalk at noon, because the streets were blistering and fiery, and the only shade was under the lawn trees, they had glided to a blind corner, bulbing their throaty horn. Suddenly, like a jack-in-the-box, Mister Quartermain had tottered from nowhere!

"Look out!" screamed Miss Fern.

"Look out!" screamed Miss Roberta.

"Look out!" cried Mister Quartermain.

The two women grabbed each other instead of the steering stick.

There was a terrible thud. The Green Machine sailed on in the hot daylight, under the shady chestnut trees, past the ripening apple trees. Looking back only once, the two old ladies' eyes filled with faded horror.

The old man lay on the sidewalk, silent.

"And here we are," mourned Miss Fern in the darkening attic. "Oh, why didn't we stop! Why did we run away?"

"Shh!" They both listened.

The rapping downstairs came again.

When it stopped they saw a boy cross the lawn in the dim light. "Just Douglas Spaulding come for a ride again." They both sighed.

The hours passed; the sun was going down.

"We've been up here all afternoon," said Roberta tiredly. "We can't stay in the attic three weeks hiding till everybody forgets."

"We'd starve."

"What'll we do, then? Do you think anyone saw and followed us?" They looked at each other.

"No. Nobody saw."

The town was silent, all the tiny houses putting on lights. There was a smell of watered grass and cooking suppers from below.

"Time to put on the meat," said Miss Fern. "Frank'll be coming home in ten minutes."

"Do we dare go down?"

"Frank'd call the police if he found the house empty. That'd make things worse."

The sun went swiftly. Now they were only two moving things in the musty blackness. "Do you," wondered Miss Fern, "think he's dead?"

"Mister Quartermain?"

A pause. "Yes."

Roberta hesitated. "We'll check the evening paper."

They opened the attic door and looked carefully at the steps leading down. "Oh, if Frank hears about this, he'll take our Green Machine away from us, and it's *so* lovely and nice riding and getting the cool wind and seeing the town."

"We won't tell him."

"Won't we?"

They helped each other down the creaking stairs to the second floor, stopping to listen. . . . In the kitchen they peered at the pantry, peeked out windows with frightened eyes, and finally set to work frying hamburger on the stove. After five minutes of working silence Fern looked sadly over at Roberta and said, "I've been thinking. We're old and feeble and don't like to admit it. We're dangerous. We owe a debt to society for running off——"

"And——?" A kind of silence fell on the frying in the kitchen as the two sisters faced each other, nothing in their hands.

"I think that"—Fern stared at the wall for a long time—"we shouldn't drive the Green Machine ever again."

Roberta picked up a plate and held it in her thin hand. "Not—ever?" she said.

"No."

"But," said Roberta, "we don't have to—to get rid of it, do we? We *can* keep it, can't we?"

Fern considered this. "Yes, I guess we can keep it."

"At least that'll be something. I'll go out now and disconnect the batteries."

Roberta was leaving just as Frank, their younger brother, only fifty-six, entered.

"Hi, sisters!" he cried.

Roberta brushed past him without a word and walked out into the summer dusk. Frank was carrying a newspaper which Fern immediately snatched from him. Trembling, she looked it through and through, and sighing, gave it back to him.

"Saw Doug Spaulding outside just now. Said he had a message for you. Said for you not to worry—he saw everything and everything's all right. What did he mean by that?"

"I'm sure I wouldn't know." Fern turned her back and searched for her handkerchief.

"Oh well, these kids." Frank looked at his sister's back for a long moment, then shrugged.

"Supper almost ready?" he asked pleasantly.

"Yes." Fern set the kitchen table.

There was a bulbing cry from outside. Once, twice, three times—far away.

"What's that?" Frank peered through the kitchen window into the dusk. "What's Roberta up to? Look at her out there, sitting in the Green Machine, poking the rubber horn!"

Once, twice more, in the dusk, softly, like some kind of mournful animal, the bulbing sound was pinched out.

"What's got into *her?*" demanded Frank.

"You just leave her alone!" screamed Fern.

Frank looked surprised.

A moment later Roberta entered quietly, without looking at anyone, and they all sat down to supper.

THE first light on the roof outside; very early morning. The leaves on all the trees tremble with a soft awakening to any breeze the dawn may offer. And then, far off, around a curve of silver track, comes the trolley, balanced on four small steel-blue wheels, and it is painted the color of tangerines. Epaulets of shimmery brass cover it, and pipings of gold; and its chrome bell bings if the ancient motorman taps it with a wrinkled shoe. The numerals on the trolley's front and sides are bright as lemons. Within, its seats prickle with cool green moss. Something like a buggy whip flings up from its roof to brush the spider thread high in the passing trees from which it takes its juice. From every window blows an incense, the all-pervasive blue and secret smell of summer storms and lightning.

Down the long elm-shadowed streets the trolley moves along, the motorman's gray-gloved hand touched gently, timelessly, to the levered controls.

At noon the motorman stopped his car in the middle of the block and leaned out. "Hey!"

And Douglas and Charlie and Tom and all the boys and girls on the block saw the gray glove waving, and dropped from trees and left skip ropes in white snakes on lawns, to run and sit in the green plush seats, and there was no charge. Mr. Tridden, the conductor, kept his glove over the mouth of the money box as he moved the trolley on down the shady block, calling.

"Hey!" said Charlie. "Where we going?"

"Last ride," said Mr. Tridden, eyes on the high electric wire ahead. "No more trolley. Bus starts to run tomorrow. Going to retire me with a pension, they are. So—a free ride for everyone! Watch out!"

He ricocheted the brass handle, the trolley groaned and swung round an endless green curve, and all the time in the world held still, as if only the children and Mr. Tridden and his miraculous machine were riding an endless river, away.

"Last day?" asked Douglas, stunned. "They can't *do* that! It's bad enough the Green Machine is gone, locked up in the garage, and no arguments. And bad enough my new tennis shoes are getting old and slowing down! How'll I get around? But . . . But . . . They *can't* take off the trolley! Why," said Douglas, "no matter how you look at it, a bus ain't a trolley. Don't make the same kind of noise. Don't have tracks or wires, don't throw sparks, don't pour sand on the tracks, don't have the same colors, don't have a bell, don't let down a step like a trolley does!"

"Hey, that's right," said Charlie. "I always get a kick watching a trolley let down the step, like an accordion."

"Sure," said Douglas.

And then they were at the end of the line, the silver tracks, abandoned for eighteen years, ran on into rolling country. In 1910 people took the trolley out to Chessman's Park with vast picnic hampers. The track, never ripped up, still lay rusting among the hills.

"Here's where we turn around," said Charlie.

"Here's where you're wrong!" Mr. Tridden snapped the emergency generator switch. "Now!"

The trolley, with a bump and a sailing glide, swept past the city limits, turned off the street, and swooped downhill through intervals of odorous sunlight and vast acreages of shadow that smelled of toadstools. Here and there creek waters flushed the tracks and sun filtered through trees like green glass. They slid whispering on meadows washed with wild sunflowers past abandoned way stations empty of all

98

save transfer-punched confetti, to follow a forest
stream into a summer country, while Douglas talked.

"Why, just the *smell* of a trolley, that's different.
I been on Chicago busses; they smell funny."

"Trolleys are too slow," said Mr. Tridden. "Going to put busses on. Busses for people and busses
for school."

The trolley whined to a stop. From overhead
Mr. Tridden reached down huge picnic hampers.
Yelling, the children helped him carry the baskets
out by a creek that emptied into a silent lake where
an ancient bandstand stood crumbling into termite
dust.

They sat eating ham sandwiches and fresh strawberries and waxy oranges and Mr. Tridden told them
how it had been twenty years ago, the band playing
on that ornate stand at night, the men pumping air
into their brass horns, the plump conductor flinging
perspiration from his baton, the children and fireflies
running in the deep grass, the ladies with long
dresses and high pompadours treading the wooden
xylophone walks with men in choking collars. There
was the walk now, all softened into a fiber mush by
the years. The lake was silent and blue and serene,
and fish peacefully threaded the bright reeds, and
the motorman murmured on and on, and the children
felt it was some other year, with Mr. Tridden looking
wonderfully young, his eyes lighted like small bulbs,
blue and electric. It was a drifting, easy day, nobody
rushing, and the forest all about, the sun held in one
position, as Mr. Tridden's voice rose and fell, and a
darning needle sewed along the air, stitching, restitch-
ing designs both golden and invisible. A bee settled
into a flower, humming and humming. The trolley
stood like an enchanted calliope, simmering where
the sun fell on it. The trolley was on their hands, a
brass smell, as they ate ripe cherries. The bright odor
of the trolley blew from their clothes on the summer
wind.

A loon flew over the sky, crying.

Somebody shivered.

Mr. Tridden worked on his gloves. "Well, time to go. Parents'll think I stole you all for good."

The trolley was silent and cool dark, like the inside of an ice-cream drugstore. With a soft green rustling of velvet buff, the seats were turned by the quiet children so they sat with their backs to the silent lake, the deserted bandstand and the wooden planks that made a kind of music if you walked down the shore on them into other lands.

Bing! went the soft bell under Mr. Tridden's foot and they soared back over sun-abandoned, withered flower meadows, through woods, toward a town that seemed to crush the sides of the trolley with bricks and asphalt and wood when Mr. Tridden stopped to let the children out in shady streets.

Charlie and Douglas were the last to stand near the opened tongue of the trolley, the folding step, breathing electricity, watching Mr. Tridden's gloves on the brass controls.

Douglas ran his fingers on the green creek moss, looked at the silver, the brass, the wine color of the ceiling.

"Well . . . so long again, Mr. Tridden."

"Good-by, boys."

"See you around, Mr. Tridden."

"See you around."

There was a soft sigh of air; the door collapsed gently shut, tucking up its corrugated tongue. The trolley sailed slowly down the late afternoon, brighter than the sun, all tangerine, all flashing gold and lemon, turned a far corner, wheeling, and vanished, gone away.

"School busses!" Charlie walked to the curb. "Won't even give us a chance to be late to school. Come get you at your front door. Never be late again in all our lives. Think of that nightmare, Doug, just think it all over."

But Douglas, standing on the lawn, was seeing how it would be tomorrow, when the men would pour hot tar over the silver tracks so you would never know a trolley had ever run this way. He knew it would take as many years as he could think of now to forget the tracks, no matter how deeply buried. Some morning in autumn, spring, or winter he knew he'd wake and, if he didn't go near the window, if he just lay deep and snug and warm in his bed, he would hear it, faint and far away.

And around the bend of the morning street, up the avenue, between the even rows of sycamore, elm and maple, in the quietness before the start of living, past his house he would hear the familiar sounds. Like the ticking of a clock, the rumble of a dozen metal barrels rolling, the hum of a single immense dragonfly at dawn. Like a merry-go-round, like a small electrical storm, the color of blue lightning, coming, here, and gone. The trolley's chime! The hiss like a soda-fountain spigot as it let down and took up its step, and the starting of the dream again, as on it sailed along its way, traveling a hidden and buried track to some hidden and buried destination.

. . .

"Kick-the-can after supper?" asked Charlie.
"Sure, said Douglas. "Kick-the-can."

THE facts about John Huff, aged twelve, are
simple and soon stated. He could pathfind more
trails than any Choctaw or Cherokee since time
began, could leap from the sky like a chimpanzee
from a vine, could live underwater two minutes and
slide fifty yards downstream from where you last saw
him. The baseballs you pitched him he hit in the
apple trees, knocking down harvests. He could jump
six-foot orchard walls, swing up branches faster and
come down, fat with peaches, quicker than anyone
else in the gang. He ran laughing. He sat easy. He
was not a bully. He was kind. His hair was dark and
curly and his teeth were white as cream. He remembered the words to all the cowboy songs and
would teach you if you asked. He knew the names of
all the wild flowers and when the moon would rise
and set and when the tides came in or out. He was,
in fact, the only god living in the whole of Green
Town, Illinois, during the twentieth century that
Douglas Spaulding knew of.

And right now he and Douglas were hiking out
beyond town on another warm and marble-round
day, the sky blue blown-glass reaching high, the
creeks bright with mirror waters fanning over white
stones. It was a day as perfect as the flame of a
candle.

Douglas walked through it thinking it would go
on this way forever. The perfection, the roundness,
the grass smell traveled on out ahead as far and fast
as the speed of light. The sound of a good friend
whistling like an oriole, pegging the softball, as you

horse-danced, key-jingled the dusty paths, all of it was complete, everything could be touched; things stayed near, things were at hand and would remain.

It was such a fine day and then suddenly a cloud crossed the sky, covered the sun, and did not move again.

John Huff had been speaking quietly for several minutes. Now Douglas stopped on the path and looked over at him.

"John, say that again."

"You heard me the first time, Doug."

"Did you say you were—going away?"

"Got my train ticket here in my pocket. Whoo-whoo, clang! Shush-shush-shush-shush. Whooooooooo . . ."

His voice faded.

John took the yellow and green train ticket solemnly from his pocket and they both looked at it.

"Tonight!" said Douglas. "My gosh! Tonight we were going to play Red Light, Green Light and Statues! How come, all of a sudden? You been here in Green Town all my life. You just don't pick up and leave!"

"It's my father," said John. "He's got a job in Milwaukee. We weren't sure until today. . . ."

"My gosh, here it is with the Baptist picnic next week and the big carnival Labor Day and Halloween —can't your dad wait till then?"

John shook his head.

"Good grief!" said Douglas. "Let me sit down!"

They sat under an old oak tree on the side of the hill looking back at town, and the sun made large trembling shadows around them; it was cool as a cave in under the tree. Out beyond, in sunlight, the town was painted with heat, the windows all gaping. Douglas wanted to run back in there where the town, by its very weight, its houses, their bulk, might enclose and prevent John's ever getting up and running off.

"But we're friends," Douglas said helplessly.

"We always will be," said John.

"You'll come back to visit every *week* or so, won't you?"

"Dad says only once or twice a year. It's eighty miles."

"Eighty miles ain't far!" shouted Douglas.

"No, it's not far at all," said John.

"My grandma's got a phone. I'll call you. Or maybe we'll all visit up your way, too. That'd be great!"

John said nothing for a long while.

"Well," said Douglas, "let's talk about something."

"What?"

"My gosh, if you're going away, we got a million things to talk about! All the things we would've talked about next month, the month after! Praying mantises, zeppelins, acrobats, sword swallowers! Go on like you was back there, grasshoppers spitting tobacco!"

"Funny thing is I don't feel like talking about grasshoppers."

"You always did!"

"Sure." John looked steadily at the town. "But I guess this just ain't the time."

"John, what's wrong? You look funny. . . ."

John had closed his eyes and screwed up his face. "Doug, the Terle house, upstairs, you know?"

"Sure."

"The colored windowpanes on the little round windows, have they *always* been there?"

"Sure."

"You *positive?*"

"Darned old windows been there since before we were born. Why?"

"I never saw them before today," said John. "On the way walking through town I looked up and there they were. Doug, what was I *doing* all these years I didn't see them?"

"You had other things to do."

"Did I?" John turned and looked in a kind of panic at Douglas. "Gosh, Doug, why should those darn windows scare me? I mean, that's nothing to be scared of, is it? It's just . . ." He floundered. "It's just, if I didn't see these windows until today, what *else* did I miss? And what about all the things I *did* see here in town? Will I be able to remember them when I go away?"

"Anything you want to remember, you remember. I went to camp two summers ago. Up *there* I remembered."

"No, you didn't! You told me. You woke nights and couldn't remember your mother's face."

"*No!*"

"Some nights it happens to me in my own house; scares heck out of me. I got to go in my folks' room and look at their faces while they sleep, to be sure! And I go back to my room and lose it again. Gosh, Doug, oh gosh!" He held onto his knees tight. "Promise me just one thing, Doug. Promise you'll remember me, promise you'll remember my face and everything. Will you promise?"

"Easy as pie. Got a motion-picture machine in my head. Lying in bed nights I can just turn on a light in my head and out it comes on the wall, clear as heck, and there you'll be, yelling and waving at me."

"Shut your eyes, Doug. Now, tell me, what color eyes I got? Don't peek. What color eyes I got?"

Douglas began to sweat. His eyelids twitched nervously. "Aw heck, John, that's not fair."

"Tell me!"

"Brown!"

John turned away. "No, sir."

"What you mean, no?"

"You're not even close!" John closed his eyes.

"Turn around here," said Douglas. "Open up, let me see."

"It's no use," said John. "You forgot already. Just the way I said."

"Turn around here!" Douglas grabbed him by the hair and turned him slowly.

"Okay, Doug."

John opened his eyes.

"Green." Douglas, dismayed, let his hand drop. "Your eyes are green. . . . Well, that's close to brown. Almost hazel!"

"Doug, don't lie to me."

"All right," said Doug quietly. "I won't."

They sat there listening to the other boys running up the hill, shrieking and yelling at them.

They raced along the railroad tracks, opened their lunch in brown-paper sacks, and sniffed deeply of the wax-wrapped deviled-ham sandwiches and green-sea pickles and colored peppermints. They ran and ran again and Douglas bent to scorch his ear on the hot steel rails, hearing trains so far away they were unseen voyagings in other lands, sending Morse-code messages to him here under the killing sun. Douglas stood up, stunned.

"John!"

For John was running, and this was terrible. Because if you ran, time ran. You yelled and screamed and raced and rolled and tumbled and all of a sudden the sun was gone and the whistle was blowing and you were on your long way home to supper. When you weren't looking, the sun got around behind you! The only way to keep things slow was to watch everything and do nothing! You could stretch a day to three days, sure, just by watching!

"John!"

There was no way to get him to help now, save by a trick.

"John, ditch, ditch the others!"

Yelling, Douglas and John sprinted off, kiting the wind downhill, letting gravity work for them, over meadows, around barns until at last the sound of the pursuers faded.

John and Douglas climbed into a haystack which was like a great bonfire crisping under them.

"Let's not do anything," said John.

"Just what I was going to say," said Douglas.

They sat quietly, getting their breath.

There was a small sound like an insect in the hay.

They both heard it, but they didn't look at the sound. When Douglas moved his wrist the sound ticked in another part of the haystack. When he brought his arm around on his lap the sound ticked in his lap. He let his eyes fall in a brief flicker. The watch said three o'clock.

Douglas moved his right hand stealthily to the ticking, pulled out the watch stem. He set the hands back.

Now they had all the time they would ever need to look long and close at the world, feel the sun move like a fiery wind over the sky.

But at last John must have felt the bodiless weight of their shadows shift and lean, and he spoke.

"Doug, what time is it?"

"Two-thirty."

John looked at the sky.

Don't! thought Douglas.

"Looks more like three-thirty, four," said John. "Boy Scout. You learn them things."

Douglas sighed and slowly turned the watch ahead.

John watched him do this, silently. Douglas looked up. John punched him, not hard at all, in the arm.

With a swift stroke, a plunge, a train came and went so quickly the boys all leaped aside, yelling, shaking their fists after it, Douglas and John with them. The train roared down the track, two hundred people in it, gone. The dust followed it a little way toward the south, then settled in the golden silence among the blue rails.

The boys were walking home.

"I'm going to Cincinnati when I'm seventeen and be a railroad fireman," said Charlie Woodman.

"I got an uncle in New York," said Jim. "I'll go there and be a printer."

Doug did not ask the others. Already the trains were chanting and he saw their faces drifting off on back observation platforms, or pressed to windows. One by one they slid away. And then the empty track and the summer sky and himself on another train run in another direction.

Douglas felt the earth move under his feet and saw their shadows move off the grass and color the air.

He swallowed hard, then gave a screaming yell, pulled back his fist, shot the indoor ball whistling in the sky. "Last one home's a rhino's behind!"

They pounded down the tracks, laughing, flailing the air. There went John Huff, not touching the ground at all. And here came Douglas, touching it all the time.

It was seven o'clock, supper over, and the boys gathering one by one from the sound of their house doors slammed and their parents crying to them not to slam the doors. Douglas and Tom and Charlie and John stood among half a dozen others and it was time for hide-and-seek and Statues.

"Just one game," said John. "Then I got to go home. The train leaves at nine. Who's going to be 'it'?"

"Me," said Douglas.

"That's the first time I ever heard of anybody volunteering to be 'it,'" said Tom.

Douglas looked at John for a long moment. "Start running," he cried.

The boys scattered, yelling. John backed away, then turned and began to lope. Douglas counted slowly. He let them run far, spread out, separate each to his own small world. When they had got their momentum up and were almost out of sight he took a deep breath.

"Statues!"

Everyone froze.

Very quietly Douglas moved across the lawn to

where John Huff stood like an iron deer in the twilight.

Far away, the other boys stood hands up, faces grimaced, eyes bright as stuffed squirrels.

But here was John, alone and motionless and no one rushing or making a great outcry to spoil this moment.

Douglas walked around the statue one way, walked around the statue the other way. The statue did not move. It did not speak. It looked at the horizon, its mouth half smiling.

It was like that time years ago in Chicago when they had visited a big place where the carved marble figures were, and his walking around them in the silence. So here was John Huff with grass stains on his knees and the seat of his pants, and cuts on his fingers and scabs on his elbows. Here was John Huff with the quiet tennis shoes, his feet sheathed in silence. There was the mouth that had chewed many an apricot pie come summer, and said many a quiet thing or two about life and the lay of the land. And there were the eyes, not blind like statues' eyes, but filled with molten green-gold. And there the dark hair blowing now north now south or any direction in the little breeze there was. And there the hands with all the town on them, dirt from roads and bark-slivers from trees, the fingers that smelled of hemp and vine and green apple, old coins or pickle-green frogs. There were the ears with the sunlight shining through them like bright warm peach wax and here, invisible, his spearmint-breath upon the air.

"John, now," said Douglas, "don't you move so much as an eyelash. I absolutely command you to stay here and not move at all for the next three hours!"

"Doug . . ."

John's lips moved.

"Freeze!" said Douglas.

John went back to looking at the sky, but he was not smiling now.

"I got to go," he whispered.

"Not a muscle, it's the game!"

"I just got to get home now," said John.

Now the statue moved, took its hands down out of the air and turned its head to look at Douglas. They stood looking at each other. The other kids were putting their arms down, too.

"We'll play one more round," said John, "except this time, I'm 'it.' Run!"

The boys ran.

"Freeze!"

The boys froze, Douglas with them.

"Not a muscle!" shouted John. "Not a hair!"

He came and stood by Douglas.

"Boy, this is the only way to do it," he said.

Douglas looked off at the twilight sky.

"Frozen statues, every single one of you, the next three minutes!" said John.

Douglas felt John walking around him even as he had walked around John a moment ago. He felt John sock him on the arm once, not too hard. "So long," he said.

Then there was a rushing sound and he knew without looking that there was nobody behind him now.

Far away, a train whistle sounded.

Douglas stood that way for a full minute, waiting for the sound of the running to fade, but it did not stop. He's still running away, but he doesn't sound any further off, thought Douglas. Why doesn't he stop running?

And then he realized it was only the sound of his heart in his body.

Stop! He jerked his hand to his chest. Stop running! I don't *like* that sound!

And then he felt himself walking across the lawns among all the other statues now, and whether they, too, were coming to life he did not know. They did not seem to be moving at all. For that matter he himself was only moving from the knees down. The rest of him was cold stone, and very heavy.

Going up the front porch of his house, he turned suddenly to look at the lawns behind him.

The lawns were empty.

A series of rifle shots. Screen doors banged one after the other, a sunset volley, along the street.

Statues are best, he thought. They're the only things you can keep on your lawn. Don't ever let them move. Once you do, you can't do a thing with them.

Suddenly his fist shot out like a piston from his side and it shook itself hard at the lawns and the street and the gathering dusk. His face was choked with blood, his eyes were blazing.

"John!" he cried. "You, John! John, you're my enemy, you hear? You're no friend of mine! Don't come back now, ever! Get away, you! Enemy, you hear? That's what you are! It's all off between us, you're dirt, that's all, dirt! John, you hear me, John!"

As if a wick had been turned a little lower in a great clear lamp beyond the town, the sky darkened still more. He stood on the porch, his mouth gasping and working. His fist still thrust straight out at that house across the street and down the way. He looked at the fist and it dissolved, the world dissolved beyond it.

Going upstairs, in the dark, where he could only feel his face but see nothing of himself, not even his fists, he told himself over and over, I'm mad, I'm angry, I hate him, I'm mad, I'm angry, I hate him!

Ten minutes later, slowly he reached the top of the stairs, in the dark. . . .

"Tom," said Douglas, "just promise me one thing, okay?"

"It's a promise. What?"

"You may be my brother and maybe I hate you sometimes, but stick around, all right?"

"You mean you'll let me follow you and the older guys when you go on hikes?"

"Well . . . sure . . . even that. What I mean is, don't go away, huh? Don't let any cars run over you or fall off a cliff."

"I should say not! Whatta you think I *am*, anyway?"

" 'Cause if worst comes to worst, and both of us are real old—say forty or forty-five some day—we can own a gold mine out West and sit there smoking corn silk and growing beards."

"Growing beards! Boy!"

"Like I say, you stick around and don't let nothing happen."

"You can depend on me," said Tom.

"It's not you I worry about," said Douglas. "It's the way God runs the world."

Tom thought about this for a moment.

"He's all right, Doug," said Tom. "He *tries*."

S HE came out of the bathroom putting iodine on her finger where she had almost lopped it off cutting herself a chunk of cocoanut cake. Just then the mailman came up the porch steps, opened the door, and walked in. The door slammed. Elmira Brown jumped a foot.

"Sam!" she cried. She waved her iodined finger on the air to cool it. "I'm still not used to my husband being a postman. Every time you just walk in, it scares the life out of me!"

Sam Brown stood there with the mail pouch half empty, scratching his head. He looked back out the door as if a fog had suddenly rolled in on a calm sweet summer morn.

"Sam, you're home early," she said.

"Can't stay," he said in a puzzled voice.

"Spit it out, what's wrong?" She came over and looked into his face.

"Maybe nothing, maybe lots. I just delivered some mail to Clara Goodwater up the street. . . ."

"Clara Goodwater!"

"Now don't get your dander up. Books it was, from the Johnson-Smith Company, Racine, Wisconsin. Title of one book . . . let's see now." He screwed up his face, then unscrewed it. "*Albertus Magnus*—that's it. *Being the approved, verified, sympathetic and natural EGYPTIAN SECRETS or . . .*" He peered at the ceiling to summon the lettering. "*White and Black Art for Man and Beast, Revealing the Forbidden Knowledge and Mysteries of Ancient Philosophers!*"

113

"Clara Goodwater's you say?"

"Walking along, I had a good chance to peek at the front pages, no harm in that. 'Hidden Secrets of Life Unveiled by that celebrated Student, Philosopher, Chemist, Naturalist, Psychomist, Astrologer, Alchemist, Metallurgist, Sorcerer, Explanator of the Mysteries of Wizards and Witchcraft, together with recondite views of numerous Arts and Sciences—Obscure, Plain, Practical, etc.' There! By God, I got a head like a box Brownie. Got the words, even if I haven't got the sense."

Elmira stood looking at her iodined finger as if it were pointed at her by a stranger.

"Clara Goodwater," she murmured.

"Looked me right in the eye as I handed it over, said, 'Going to be a witch, first-class, no doubt. Get my diploma in no time. Set up business. Hex crowds and individuals, old and young, big and small.' Then she kinda laughed, put her nose in that book, and went in."

Elmira stared at a bruise on her arm, carefully tongued a loose tooth in her jaw.

A door slammed. Tom Spaulding, kneeling on Elmira Brown's front lawn, looked up. He had been wandering about the neighborhood, seeing how the ants were doing here or there, and had found a particularly good hill with a big hole in which all kinds of fiery bright pismires were tumbling about scissoring the air and wildly carrying little packets of dead grasshopper and infinitesimal bird down into the earth. Now here was something else: Mrs. Brown, swaying on the edge of her porch as if she'd just found out the world was falling through space at sixty trillion miles a second. Behind her was Mr. Brown, who didn't know the miles per second and probably wouldn't care if he did know.

"You, Tom!" said Mrs. Brown. "I need moral support and the equivalent of the blood of the Lamb with me. Come along!"

And off she rushed, squashing ants and kicking

tops off dandelions and trotting big spiky holes in flower beds as she cut across yards.

Tom knelt a moment longer studying Mrs. Brown's shoulder blades and spine as she toppled down the street. He read the bones and they were eloquent of melodrama and adventure, a thing he did not ordinarily connect with ladies, even though Mrs. Brown had the remnants of a pirate's mustache. A moment later he was in tandem with her.

"Mrs. Brown, you sure look mad!"

"You don't know what mad *is*, boy!"

"Watch out!" cried Tom.

Mrs. Elmira Brown fell right over an iron dog lying asleep there on the green grass.

"Mrs. Brown!"

"You see?" Mrs. Brown sat there. "Clara Goodwater did this to me! Magic!"

"Magic?"

"Never mind, boy. Here's the steps. You go first and kick any invisible strings out of the way. Ring that doorbell, but pull your finger off quick, the juice'll burn you to a cinder!"

Tom did not touch the bell.

"Clara Goodwater!" Mrs. Brown flicked the bell button with her iodined finger.

Far away in the cool dim empty rooms of the big old house, a silver bell tinkled and faded.

Tom listened. Still farther away there was a stir of mouselike running. A shadow, perhaps a blowing curtain, moved in a distant parlor.

"Hello," said a quiet voice.

And quite suddenly Mrs. Goodwater was there, fresh as a stick of peppermint, behind the screen.

"Why, hello there, Tom, Elmira. What——"

"Don't rush me! We came over about your practicing to be a full-fledged witch!"

Mrs. Goodwater smiled. "Your husband's not only a mailman, but a guardian of the law. Got a nose out to *here!*"

"He didn't look at no mail."

"He's ten minutes between houses laughing at post cards and tryin' on mail-order shoes."

"It ain't what he seen; it's what you yourself told him about the books you got."

"Just a joke. Goin' to be a witch! I said, and bang! Off gallops Sam, like I'd flung lightning at him. I declare there can't be one wrinkle in that man's brain."

"You talked about your magic other places yesterday——"

"You must mean the Sandwich Club . . ."

"To which I pointedly was *not* invited."

"Why, lady, we thought that was your regular day with your grandma."

"I can always have another Grandma day, if people'd only ask me places."

"All there was to it at the Sandwich Club was me sitting there with a ham and pickle sandwich, and I said right out loud, "At last I'm going to get my witch's diploma. Been studying for years!"

"That's what come back to me over the phone!"

"Ain't modern inventions wonderful!" said Mrs. Goodwater.

"Considering you been president of the Honeysuckle Ladies Lodge since the Civil War, it seems, I'll put it to you bang on the nose, have you used witchcraft all these years to spell the ladies and win the ayes-have-it?"

"Do you doubt it for a moment, lady?" said Mrs. Goodwater.

"Election's tomorrow again, and all I want to know is, you runnin' for another term—and ain't you ashamed?"

"Yes to the first question and no to the second. Lady, look here, I bought those books for my boy cousin, Raoul. He's just ten and goes around looking in hats for rabbits. I told him there's about as much chance finding rabbits in hats as brains in heads of certain people I could name, but look he does and so I got these gifts for him."

"Wouldn't believe you on a stack of Bibles."

"God's truth, anyway. I love to fun about the witch thing. The ladies all yodeled when I explained about my dark powers. Wish you'd been there."

"I'll be there tomorrow to fight you with a cross of gold and all the powers of good I can organize behind me," said Elmira. "Right now, tell me how much other magic junk you got in your house."

Mrs. Goodwater pointed to a side table inside the door.

"I been buyin' all kinds of magic herbs. Smell funny and make Raoul happy. That little sack of stuff, that's called Thisis rue, and this is Sabisse root and that there's Ebon herbs; here's black sulphur, and this they claim is bone dust."

"Bone dust!" Elmira skipped back and kicked Tom's ankle. Tom yelped.

"And here's wormwood and fern leaves so you can freeze shotguns and fly like a bat in your dreams, it says in Chapter X of the little book here. I think it's fine for growing boys' heads to think about things like this. Now, from the look on your face you don't believe Raoul exists. Well, I'll give you his Springfield address."

"Yes," said Elmira, "and the day I write him you'll take the Springfield bus and go to General Delivery and get my letter and write back to me in a boy's hand. I know you!"

"Mrs. Brown, speak up—you want to be president of the Honeysuckle Ladies Lodge, right? You run every year now for ten years. You nominate yourself. And always wind up gettin' *one* vote. Yours. Elmira, if the ladies wanted you they'd landslide you in. But from where I stand looking up the mountain, ain't so much as one pebble come rattlin' down save yours. Tell you what, I'll nominate and vote for you myself come noon tomorrow, how's that?"

"Damned for sure, then," said Elmira. "Last year I got a deathly cold right at election time; couldn't get out and campaign back-fence-to-back-fence. Year before that, broke my leg. Mighty strange." She squinted darkly at the lady behind the screen.

"That's not all. Last month I cut my fingers six times, bruised my knee ten times, fell off my back porch twice, you hear—twice! I broke a window, dropped four dishes, one vase worth a dollar forty-nine at Bixby's, and I'm billin' you for every dropped dish from now on in my house and environs!"

"I'll be poor by Christmas," said Mrs. Goodwater. She opened the screen door and came out suddenly and let the door slam. "Elmira Brown, how old are you?"

"You probably got it written in one of your black books. Thirty-five!"

"Well, when I think of thirty-five years of your life . . ." Mrs. Goodwater pursed her lips and blinked her eyes, counting. "That's about twelve thousand seven hundred and seventy-five days, or counting three of them per day, twelve thousand-odd commotions, twelve thousand much-ados and twelve thousand calamities. It's a full rich life you lead, Elmira Brown. Shake hands!"

"Get away!" Elmira fended her off.

"Why, lady, you're only the second most clumsy woman in Green Town, Illinois. You can't sit down without playing the chair like an accordion. You can't stand up but what you kick the cat. You can't trot across an open meadow without falling into a well. Your life has been one long decline, Elmira Alice Brown, so why not admit it?"

"It wasn't clumsiness that caused my calamities, but you being within a mile of me at those times when I dropped a pot of beans or juiced my finger in the electric socket at home."

"Lady, in a town this size, *everybody's* within a mile of someone at one time or other in the day."

"You admit being around then?"

"I admit being born here, yes, but I'd give anything right now to have been born in Kenosha or Zion. Elmira, go to your dentist and see what he can do about that serpent's tongue in there."

"Oh!" said Elmira. "Oh, oh, oh!"

"You've pushed me too far. I wasn't interested in

witchcraft, but I think I'll just look into this business. Listen here! You're invisible right now. While you stood there I put a spell on you. You're clean out of sight."

"You didn't!"

"Course," admitted the witch, "I never *could* see you, lady."

Elmira pulled out her pocket mirror. "There I am!" She peered closer and gasped. She reached up like someone tuning a harp and plucked a single thread. She held it up, Exhibit A. "I never had a gray hair in my life till this second!"

The witch smiled charmingly. "Put it in a jar of still water, be an angleworm come morning. Oh, Elmira, look at yourself at last, won't you? All these years, blaming others for your own mallet feet and floaty ways! You ever read Shakespeare? There's little stage directions in there: ALARUMS AND EXCURSIONS. That's you, Elmira. Alarums and Excursions! Now get home before I feel the bumps on your head and predict gas at night for you! Shoo!"

She waved her hands in the air as if Elmira were a cloud of things. "My, the flies are thick this summer!" she said.

She went inside and hooked the door.

"The line is drawn, Mrs. Goodwater," Elmira said, folding her arms. "I'll give you one last chance. Withdraw from the candidacy of the Honeysuckle Lodge or face me face-to-face tomorrow when I run for office and wrest it from you in a fair fight. I'll bring Tom here with me. An innocent good boy. And innocence and good will win the day."

"I wouldn't count on me being innocent, Mrs. Brown," said the boy. "My mother says——"

"Shut up, Tom, good's good! You'll be there on my right hand, boy."

"Yes'm," said Tom.

"If, that is," said Elmira, "I can live through the night with this lady making wax dummies of me—shoving rusty needles through the very heart and soul of them. If you find a great big fig in my bed all shriveled up come sunrise, Tom, you'll know who picked the fruit in the vineyard. And look to see Mrs. Goodwater president till she's a hundred and ninety-five years old."

"Why, lady," said Mrs. Goodwater, "I'm three hundred and five *now*. Used to call me SHE in the old days." She poked her fingers at the street. "Abra-cadabra-zimmity-ZAM! How's *that?*"

Elmira ran down off the porch.

"Tomorrow!" she cried.

"Till then, lady!" said Mrs. Goodwater.

Tom followed Elmira, shrugging and kicking ants off the sidewalk as he went.

Running across a driveway, Elmira screamed.

"Mrs. Brown!" cried Tom.

A car backing out of a garage ran right over Elmira's right big toe.

Mrs. Elmira Brown's foot hurt her in the middle of the night, so she got up and went down to the kitchen and ate some cold chicken and made a neat, painfully accurate list of things. First, illnesses in the past year. Three colds, four mild attacks of indigestion, one seizure of bloat, arthritis, lumbago, what she imagined to be gout, a severe bronchial cough, incipient asthma, and spots on her arms, plus an abscessed semicircular canal which made her reel like a drunken moth some days, backache, head pains, and nausea. Cost of medicine: *ninety-eight dollars and seventy-eight cents.*

Secondly, things broken in the house during the twelve months just past; two lamps, six vases, ten dishes, one soup tureen, two windows, one chair, one sofa cushion, six glasses, and one crystal chandelier prism. Total cost: *twelve dollars and ten cents.*

Thirdly, her pains this very night. Her toe hurt from being run over. Her stomach was upset. Her back was stiff, her legs were pulsing with agony. Her eyeballs felt like wads of blazing cotton. Her tongue tasted like a dust mop. Her ears were belling and ringing away. Cost? She debated, going back to bed.

Ten thousand dollars in personal suffering.

"Try to settle this out of court!" she said half aloud.

"Eh?" said her husband, awake.

She lay down in bed. "I simply refuse to die."

"Beg pardon?" he said.

"I won't die!" she said, staring at the ceiling.

"That's what I always claimed," said her husband, and turned over to snore.

In the morning Mrs. Elmira Brown was up early and down to the library and then to the drugstore and back to the house where she was busy mixing all kinds of chemicals when her husband, Sam came home with an empty mail pouch at noon.

"Lunch's in the icebox." Elmira stirred a green-looking porridge in a large glass.

"Good Lord, what's that?" asked her husband. "Looks like a milk shake been left out in the sun for forty years. Got kind of a fungus on it."

"Fight magic with magic."

"You goin' to *drink that?*"

"Just before I go up into the Honeysuckle Ladies Lodge for the big doings."

Samual Brown sniffed the concoction. "Take my advice. Get up those steps first, *then* drink it. What's in it?"

"Snow from angels' wings, well, really menthol, to cool hell's fires that burn you, it says in this book I got at the library. The juice of a fresh grape off the vine, for thinking clear sweet thoughts in the face of dark visions, it says. Also red rhubarb, cream of tartar, white sugar, white of eggs, spring water and clover buds with the strength of the good earth in them. Oh, I could go on all day. It's here in the list, good against bad, white against black. I can't lose!"

"Oh, you'll win, all right," said her husband. "But will you *know* it?"

"Think good thoughts. I'm on my way to get Tom for my charm."

"Poor boy," said her husband. "Innocent, like you

say, and about to be torn limb from limb, bargain-basement day at the Honeysuckle Lodge."

"Tom'll survive," said Elmira, and, taking the bubbling concoction with her, hid inside a Quaker Oats box with the lid on, went out the door without catching her dress or snagging her new ninety-eight-cent stockings. Realizing this, she was smug all the way to Tom's house where he waited for her in his white summer suit as she had instructed.

"Phew!" said Tom. "What you got in that box?"

"Destiny," said Elmira.

"I sure hope so," said Tom, walking about two paces ahead of her.

The Honeysuckle Ladies Lodge was full of ladies looking in each other's mirrors and tugging at their skirts and asking to be sure their slips weren't showing.

At one o'clock Mrs. Elmira Brown came up the steps with a boy in white clothes. He was holding his nose and screwing up one eye so he could only half see where he was going. Mrs. Brown looked at the crowd and then at the Quaker Oats box and opened the top and looked in and gasped, and put the top back on without drinking any of that stuff in there. She moved inside the hall and with her moved a rustling as of taffeta, all the ladies whispering in a tide after her.

She sat down in back with Tom, and Tom looked more miserable than ever. The one eye he had open looked at the crowd of ladies and shut up for good. Sitting there, Elmira got the potion out and drank it slowly down.

At one-thirty, the president, Mrs. Goodwater, banged the gavel and all but two dozen of the ladies quit talking.

"Ladies," she called out over the summer sea of silks and laces, capped here and there with white or gray, "it's election time. But before we start, I believe Mrs. Elmira Brown, wife of our eminent graphologist ——"

A titter ran through the room.

"What's graphologist?" Elmira elbowed Tom twice.

"I don't know," whispered Tom fiercely, eyes shut, feeling that elbow come out of darkness at him.

"—wife, as I say, of our eminent handwriting expert, Samuel Brown . . . (more laughter) . . . of the U.S. Postal Service," continued Mrs. Goodwater. "Mrs. Brown wants to give us some opinions. Mrs. Brown?"

Elmira stood up. Her chair fell over backward and snapped shut like a bear trap on itself. She jumped an inch off the floor and teetered on her heels, which gave off cracking sounds like they would fall to dust any moment. "I got plenty to say," she said, holding the empty Quaker Oats box in one hand with a Bible. She grabbed Tom with the other and plowed forward, hitting several people's elbows and muttering to them, "Watch what you're doing! Careful, you!" to reach the platform, turn, and knock a glass of water dripping over the table. She gave Mrs. Goodwater another bristly scowl when this happened and let her mop it up with a tiny handkerchief. Then with a secret look of triumph, Elmira drew forth the empty philter glass and held it up, displaying it for Mrs. Goodwater and whispering, "You know what was in this? It's inside me, now, lady. The charmed circle surrounds me. No knife can cleave, no hatchet break through."

The ladies, all talking, did not hear.

Mrs. Goodwater nodded, held up her hands, and there was silence.

Elmira held tight to Tom's hand. Tom kept his eyes shut, wincing.

"Ladies," Elmira said, "I sympathize with you. I know what you've been through these last ten years. I know why you voted for Mrs. Goodwater here. You've got boys, girls, and men to feed. You've got budgets to follow. You couldn't afford to have your milk sour, your bread fall, or your cakes as flat as wheels. You didn't want mumps, chicken pox, and whooping cough in your house all in three weeks.

You didn't want your husband crashing his car or electrocuting himself on the high-tension wires outside town. But now all of that's over. You can come out in the open now. No more heartburns or backaches, because I've brought the good word and we're going to exorcise this witch we've got here!"

Everybody looked around but didn't see any witch.

"I mean your *president!*" cried Elmira.

"*Me!*" Mrs. Goodwater waved at everyone.

"Today," breathed Elmira, holding onto the desk for support, "I went to the library. I looked up counteractions. How to get rid of people who take advantage of others, how to make witches leave off and go. And I found a way to fight for all our rights. I can feel the power growing. I got the magic of all kinds of good roots and chemicals in me. I got . . ." She paused and swayed. She blinked once. "I got cream of tartar and . . . I got . . . white hawkweed and milk soured in the light of the moon and . . ." She stopped and thought for a moment. She shut her mouth and a tiny sound came from deep inside her and worked up through to come out the corners of her lips. She closed her eyes for a moment to see where the strength was.

"Mrs. Brown, you feelin' all right?" asked Mrs. Goodwater.

"Feelin' fine!" said Mrs. Brown slowly. "I put in some pulverized carrots and parsley root, cut fine; juniper berry . . ."

Again she paused as if a voice had said STOP to her and she looked out across all those faces.

The room, she noticed, was beginning to turn slowly, first from left to right, then right to left.

"Rosemary roots and crowfoot flower . . ." she said rather dimly. She let go of Tom's hand. Tom opened one eye and looked at her.

"Bay leaves, nasturtium petals . . ." she said.

"Maybe you better sit down," said Mrs. Goodwater.

One lady at the side went and opened a window.

"Dry betel nuts, lavender and crab-apple seed," said Mrs. Brown and stopped. "Quick now, let's have the election. Got to have the votes. I'll tabulate."

"No hurry, Elmira," said Mrs. Goodwater.

"Yes, there is." Elmira took a deep trembling breath. "Remember, ladies, no more fear. Do like you always wanted to do. Vote for me, and . . ." The room was moving again, up and down. "Honesty in government. All those in favor of Mrs. Goodwater for president say 'Aye.' "

"Aye," said the whole room.

"All those in favor of Mrs. Elmira Brown?" said Elmira in a faint voice.

She swallowed.

After a moment she spoke, alone.

"Aye," she said.

She stood stunned on the rostrum.

A silence filled the room from wall to wall. In that silence Mrs. Elmira Brown made a croaking sound. She put her hand on her throat. She turned and looked dimly at Mrs. Goodwater, who now very casually drew forth from her purse a small wax doll in which were a number of rusted thumbtacks.

"Tom," said Elmira, "show me the way to the ladies' room."

"Yes'm."

They began to walk and then hurry and then run. Elmira ran on ahead, through the crowd, down the aisle. . . . She reached the door and started left.

"No, Elmira, right, right!" cried Mrs. Goodwater.

Elmira turned left and vanished.

There was a noise like coal down a chute.

"Elmira!"

The ladies ran around like a girl's basketball team, colliding with each other.

Only Mrs. Goodwater made a straight line.

She found Tom looking down the stair well, his hands clenched to the banister.

125

"Forty steps!" he moaned. "Forty steps to the ground!"

Later on and for months and years after it was told how like an inebriate Elmira Brown negotiated those steps touching every one on her long way down. It was claimed that when she began the fall she was sick to unconsciousness and that this made her skeleton rubber, so she kind of rolled rather than ricocheted. She landed at the bottom, blinking and feeling better, having left whatever it was that had made her uneasy all along the way. True, she was so badly bruised she looked like a tattooed lady. But, no, not a wrist was sprained or an ankle twisted. She held her head funny for three days, kind of peering out of the sides of her eyeballs instead of turning to look. But the important thing was Mrs. Goodwater at the bottom of the steps, pillowing Elmira's head on her lap and dropping tears on her as the ladies gathered hysterically.

"Elmira, I promise, Elmira, I swear, if you just live, if you don't die, you hear me, Elmira, listen! I'll use my magic for nothing but good from now on. No more black, nothing but white magic. The rest of your life, if I have my way, no more falling over iron dogs, tripping on sills, cutting fingers, or dropping downstairs for you! Elysium, Elmira, Elysium, I promise! If you just live! Look, I'm pulling the tacks out of the doll! Elmira, speak to me! Speak now and sit up! And come upstairs for another vote. President, I promise, president of the Honeysuckle Ladies Lodge, by acclamation, won't we, ladies?"

At this all the ladies cried so hard they had to lean on each other.

Tom, upstairs, thought this meant death down there.

He was halfway down when he met the ladies coming back up, looking like they had just wandered out of a dynamite explosion.

"Get out of the way, boy!"

First came Mrs. Goodwater, laughing and crying.

Next came Mrs. Elmira Brown, doing the same.

And after the two of them came all the one hundred twenty-three members of the lodge, not knowing if they'd just returned from a funeral or were on their way to a ball.

He watched them pass and shook his head.

"Don't need me no more," he said. "No more at all."

So he tiptoed down the stairs before they missed him, holding tight to the rail all the way.

For what it's worth," said Tom, "there's the whole thing in a nutshell. The ladies carrying on like crazy. Everybody standing around blowing their noses. Elmira Brown sitting there at the bottom of the steps, nothing broke, her bones made out of Jell-O, I suspect, and the witch sobbin' on her shoulder, and then all of them goin' upstairs suddenly laughing. Cry-yi, you figure it out. I got out of there fast!"

Tom loosened his shirt and took off his tie.

"Magic, you say?" asked Douglas.

"Magic six ways from Sunday."

"You believe it?"

"Yes I do and no I don't."

"Boy, this town is full of stuff!" Douglas peered off at the horizon where clouds filled the sky with immense shapes of old gods and warriors. "Spells and wax dolls and needles and elixirs, you said?"

"Wasn't much as an elixir, but awful fine as an upchuck. Blap! Wowie!" Tom clutched his stomach and stuck out his tongue.

"Witches . . ." said Douglas. He squinted his eyes mysteriously.

A ND then there is that day when all around, all around you hear the dropping of the apples, one by one, from the trees. At first it is one here and one there, and then it is three and then it is four and then nine and twenty, until the apples plummet like rain, fall like horse hoofs in the soft, darkening grass, and you are the last apple on the tree; and you wait for the wind to work you slowly free from your hold upon the sky, and drop you down and down. Long before you hit the grass you will have forgotten there ever was a tree, or other apples, or a summer, or green grass below. You will fall in darkness. . . .

"No!"

Colonel Freeleigh opened his eyes quickly, sat erect in his wheel chair. He jerked his cold hand out to find the telephone. It was still there! He crushed it against his chest for a moment, blinking.

"I don't like that dream," he said to his empty room.

At last, his fingers trembling, he lifted the receiver and called the long-distance operator and gave her a number and waited, watching the bedroom door as if at any moment a plague of sons, daughters, grandsons, nurses, doctors, might swarm in to seize away this last vital luxury he permitted his failing senses. Many days, or was it years, ago, when his heart had thrust like a dagger through his ribs and flesh, he had heard the boys below . . . their names, what were they? Charles, Charlie, Chuck, yes! And Douglas! And Tom! He remembered! Calling his name far down the hall, but the door being locked in their faces, the boys turned away. You can't be excited, the doctor said. No visitors, no visitors, no visitors. And he heard the boys moving across the street, he saw them, he waved. And they waved back. "Colonel . . . Colonel . . ." And now he sat alone with the little gray toad of a heart flopping weakly here or there in his chest from time to time.

"Colonel Freeleigh," said the operator. "Here's your call. Mexico City. Erickson 3899."

And now the far away but infinitely clear voice: "Bueno."

"Jorge!" cried the old man.

"Señor Freeleigh! Again? This costs money."

"Let it cost! You know what to do."

"Sí. The window?"

"The window, Jorge, if you please."

"A moment," said the voice.

And, thousands of miles away, in a southern land, in an office in a building in that land, there was the sound of footsteps retreating from the phone. The old man leaned forward, gripping the receiver tight to his wrinkled ear that ached with waiting for the next sound.

The raising of a window.

Ah, sighed the old man.

The sounds of Mexico City on a hot yellow noon rose through the open window into the waiting phone. He could see Jorge standing there holding the mouthpiece out, out into the bright day.

"Señor . . ."

"No, no, please. Let me *listen*."

He listened to the hooting of many metal horns, the squealing of brakes, the calls of vendors selling red-purple bananas and jungle oranges in their stalls. Colonel Freeleigh's feet began to move, hanging from the edge of his wheel chair, making the motions of a man walking. His eyes squeezed tight. He gave a series of immense sniffs, as if to gain the odors of meats hung on iron hooks in sunshine, cloaked with flies like a mantle of raisins; the smell of stone alleys wet with morning rain. He could feel the sun burn his spiny-bearded cheek, and he was twenty-five years old again, walking, walking, looking, smiling, happy to be alive, very much alert, drinking in colors and smells.

A rap on the door. Quickly he hid the phone under his lap robe.

The nurse entered. "Hello," she said. "Have you been good?"

"Yes." The old man's voice was mechanical. He could hardly see. The shock of a simple rap on the door was such that part of him was still in another city, far removed. He waited for his mind to rush home—it must be here to answer questions, act sane, be polite.

"I've come to check your pulse."

"Not now!" said the old man.

"You're not going anywhere, are you?" She smiled.

He looked at the nurse steadily. He hadn't been anywhere in ten years.

"Give me your wrist."

Her fingers, hard and precise, searched for the sickness in his pulse like a pair of calipers.

"What've you been doing to *excite* yourself?" she demanded.

"Nothing."

Her gaze shifted and stopped on the empty phone table. At that instant a horn sounded faintly, two thousand miles away.

She took the receiver from under the lap robe and held it before his face. "Why do you do this to yourself? You promised you wouldn't. That's how you hurt yourself in the first place, isn't it? Getting excited, talking too much. Those boys up here jumping around——"

"They sat quietly and listened," said the colonel. "And I told them things they'd never heard. The buffalo, I told them, the bison. It was worth it. I don't care. I was in a pure fever and I was alive. It doesn't matter if being so alive kills a man; it's better to have the quick fever every time. Now give me that phone. If you won't let the boys come up and sit politely I can at least talk to someone outside the room."

"I'm sorry, Colonel. Your grandson will have to know about this. I prevented his having the phone taken out last week. Now it looks like I'll let him go ahead."

"This is *my* house, my phone. I pay your salary!" he said.

"To make you well, not get you excited." She wheeled his chair across the room. "To bed with you now, young man!"

From bed he looked back at the phone and kept looking at it.

"I'm going to the store for a few minutes," the nurse said. "Just to be sure you don't use the phone again, I'm hiding your wheel chair in the hall."

She wheeled the empty chair out the door. In the downstairs entry, he heard her pause and dial the extension phone.

Was she phoning Mexico City? he wondered. She wouldn't dare!

The front door shut.

He thought of the last week here, alone, in his room, and the secret, narcotic calls across continents, an isthmus, whole jungle countries of rain forest, blue-orchid plateaus, lakes and hills . . . talking . . . talking . . . to Buenos Aires . . . and . . . Lima . . . Rio de Janeiro . . .

He lifted himself in the cool bed. Tomorrow the telephone gone! What a greedy fool he had been! He slipped his brittle ivory legs down from the bed, marveling at their desiccation. They seemed to be things which had been fastened to his body while he slept one night, while his younger legs were taken off and burned in the cellar furnace. Over the years, they had destroyed all of him, removing hands, arms, and legs and leaving him with substitutes as delicate and useless as chess pieces. And now they were tampering with something more intangible—the memory; they were trying to cut the wires which led back into another year.

He was across the room in a stumbling run. Grasping the phone, he took it with him as he slid down the wall to sit upon the floor. He got the long-distance operator, his heart exploding within him, faster and faster, a blackness in his eyes. "Hurry, hurry!"

He waited.

"Bueno?"

"Jorge, we were cut off."

"You must not phone again, Señor," said the faraway voice. "Your nurse called me. She says you are very ill. I must hang up."

"No, Jorge! Please!" the old man pleaded. "One last time, listen to me. They're taking the phone out tomorrow. I can never call you again."

Jorge said nothing.

The old man went on. "For the love of God, Jorge! For friendship, then, for the old days! You don't know what it means. You're my age, but you can *move!* I haven't moved anywhere in ten years."

He dropped the phone and had trouble picking it up, his chest was so thick with pain. "Jorge! You *are* still there, aren't you?"

"This will be the last time?" said Jorge.

"I promise!"

The phone was laid on a desk thousands of miles away. Once more, with that clear familiarity, the footsteps, the pause, and, at last, the raising of the window.

"*Listen,*" whispered the old man to himself.

And he heard a thousand people in another sunlight, and the faint, tinkling music of an organ grinder playing "La Marimba"—oh, a lovely, dancing tune.

With eyes tight, the old man put up his hand as if to click pictures of an old cathedral, and his body was heavier with flesh, younger, and he felt the hot pavement underfoot.

He wanted to say, "You're still there, aren't you?

All of you people in that city in the time of the early siesta, the shops closing, the little boys crying *loteria nacional para hoy!* to sell lottery tickets. You are all there, the people in the city. I can't believe I was ever among you. When you are away from a city it becomes a fantasy. Any town, New York, Chicago, with its people, becomes improbable with distance. Just as I am improbable here, in Illinois, in a small town by a quiet lake. All of us improbable to one another because we are not present to one another. And so it is good to hear the sounds, and know that Mexico City is still there and the people moving and living. . . ."

He sat with the receiver tightly pressed to his ear.

And at last, the clearest, most improbable sound of all—the sound of a green trolley car going around a corner—a trolley burdened with brown and alien and beautiful people, and the sound of other people running and calling out with triumph as they leaped up and swung aboard and vanished around a corner on the shrieking rails and were borne away in the sun-blazed distance to leave only the sound of *tortillas* frying on the market stoves, or was it merely the ever rising and falling hum and burn of static quivering along two thousand miles of copper wire. . . .

The old man sat on the floor.

Time passed.

A downstairs door opened slowly. Light footsteps came in, hesitated, then ventured up the stairs. Voices murmured.

"We shouldn't be here!"

"He phoned me, I tell you. He needs visitors bad. We can't let him down."

"He's sick!"

"Sure! But he said to come when the nurse's out. We'll only stay a second, say hello, and . . ."

The door to the bedroom moved wide. The three boys stood looking in at the old man seated there on the floor.

"Colonel Freeleigh?" said Douglas softly.

There was something in his silence that made them all shut up their mouths.

They approached, almost on tiptoe.

Douglas, bent down, disengaged the phone from the old man's now quite cold fingers. Douglas lifted the receiver to his own ear, listened. Above the static he heard a strange, a far, a final sound.

Two thousand miles away, the closing of a window.

"**B**OOM!" said Tom. "Boom. Boom. Boom."

He sat on the Civil War cannon in the courthouse square. Douglas, in front of the cannon, clutched his heart and fell down on the grass. But he did not get up; he just lay there, his face thoughtful.

"You look like you're going to get out the old pencil any second now," said Tom.

"Let me think!" said Douglas, looking at the cannon. He rolled over and gazed at the sky and the trees above him. "Tom, it just hit me."

"What?"

"Yesterday Ching Ling Soo died. Yesterday the Civil War ended right here in this town forever. Yesterday Mr. Lincoln died right here and so did General Lee and General Grant and a hundred thousand others facing north and south. And yesterday afternoon, at Colonel Freeleigh's house, a herd of buffalo-bison as big as all Green Town, Illinois, went off the cliff into nothing at all. Yesterday a whole lot of dust settled for good. And I didn't even appreciate it at the time. It's awful, Tom, it's awful! What we going to do without all those soldiers and Generals Lee and Grant and Honest Abe; what we going to do without Ching Ling Soo? I never dreamed so many people could die so fast, Tom. But they did. They sure did!"

Tom sat astride the cannon, looking down at his brother as his voice trailed away.

"You got your tablet with you?"

Douglas shook his head.

"Better get home and put all that down before you forget it. It ain't every day you got half the population of the world keeling over on you."

Douglas sat up and then stood up. He walked across the courthouse lawn slowly, chewing his lower lip.

"Boom," said Tom quietly. "Boom. Boom!"

Then he raised his voice:

"Doug! I killed you three times, crossing the grass! Doug, you hear me? Hey, Doug! Okay. All right for you." He lay down on the cannon and sighted along the crusted barrel. He squinted one eye. "Boom!" he whispered at that dwindling figure. "Boom!"

"T HERE!"
"Twenty-nine!"
"There!"
"Thirty!"
"There!"
"Thirty-one!"

The lever plunged. The tin caps, crushed atop the filled bottles, flickered bright yellow. Grandfather handed the last bottle to Douglas.

"Second harvest of the summer. June's on the shelf. Here's July. Now, just-August up ahead."

Douglas raised the bottle of warm dandelion wine but did not set it on the shelf. He saw the other numbered bottles waiting there, one like another, in no way different, all bright, all regular, all self-contained.

There's the day I found I was alive, he thought, and why isn't it brighter than the others?

There's the day John Huff fell off the edge of the world, gone; why isn't it darker than the others?

Where, where all the summer dogs leaping like dolphins in the wind-braided and unbraided tides of wheat? Where lightning smell of Green Machine or trolley? Did the wine remember? It did not! Or seemed not, anyway.

Somewhere, a book said once, all the talk ever talked, all the songs ever sung, still lived, had vibrated way out in space and if you could travel to Far Centauri you could hear George Washington talking in his sleep or Caesar surprised at the knife in his back. So much for sounds. What about light then?

138

All things, once seen, they didn't just die, that *couldn't* be. It must be then that somewhere, searching the world, perhaps in the dripping multiboxed honeycombs where light was an amber sap stored by pollen-fired bees, or in the thirty thousand lenses of the noon dragonfly's gemmed skull you might find all the colors and sights of the world in any one year. Or pour one single drop of this dandelion wine beneath a microscope and perhaps the entire world of July Fourth would firework out in Vesuvius showers. This he would have to believe.

And yet . . . looking here at this bottle which by its number signalized the day when Colonel Freeleigh had stumbled and fallen six feet into the earth, Douglas could not find so much as a gram of dark sediment, not a speck of the great flouring buffalo dust, not a flake of sulphur from the guns at Shiloh.

• • •

"August up ahead," said Douglas. "Sure. But the way things are going, there'll be no machines, no friends, and darn few dandelions for the last harvest."

"Doom. Doom. You sound like a funeral bell tolling," said Grandfather. "Talk like that is worse than swearing. I won't wash out your mouth with soap, however. A thimbleful of dandelion wine is indicated. Here, now, swig it down. What's it taste like?"

"I'm a fire-eater! Whoosh!"

"Now upstairs, run three times around the block, do five somersets, six pushups, climb two trees, and you'll be concertmaster instead of chief mourner. Get!"

On his way, running, Douglas thought, *Four* pushups, *one* tree, and *two* somersets will *do* it!

A ND out there in the middle of the first day of August, just getting into his car, was Bill Forrester, who shouted he was going downtown for some extraordinary ice cream or other and would anyone join him? So, not five minutes later, jiggled and steamed into a better mood, Douglas found himself stepping in off the fiery pavements and moving through the grotto of soda-scented air, of vanilla freshness at the drugstore, to sit at the snow-marble fountain with Bill Forrester. They then asked for a recital of the most unusual ices and when the fountain man said, "Old fashioned lime-vanilla ice . . ."

"That's it!" said Bill Forrester.

"Yes, sir!" said Douglas.

And, while waiting, they turned slowly on their rotating stools. The silver spigots, the gleaming mirrors, the hushed whirl-around ceiling fans, the green shades over the small windows, the harp-wire chairs, passed under their moving gaze. They stopped turning. Their eyes had touched upon the face and form of Miss Helen Loomis, ninety-five years old, ice-cream spoon in hand, ice cream in mouth.

"Young man," she said to Bill Forrester, "you are a person of taste and imagination. Also, you have the will power of ten men; otherwise you would not dare veer away from the common flavors listed on the menu and order, straight out, without quibble or reservation, such an unheard-of thing as lime-vanilla ice."

He bowed his head solemnly to her.

"Come sit with me, both of you," she said. "We'll

140

talk of strange ice creams and such things as we seem to have a bent for. Don't be afraid; I'll foot the bill."

Smiling, they carried their dishes to her table and sat.

"You look like a Spaulding," she said to the boy. "You've got your grandfather's head. And you, you're William Forrester. You write for the *Chronicle*, a good enough column. I've heard more about you than I'd care to tell."

"I know you," said Bill Forrester. "You're Helen Loomis." He hesitated, then continued. "I was in love with you once," he said.

"Now that's the way I like a conversation to open." She dug quietly at her ice cream. "That's grounds for another meeting. No—don't tell me where or when or how you were in love with me. We'll save that for next time. You've taken away my appetite with your talk. Look there now! Well, I must get home anyway. Since you're a reporter, come for tea tomorrow between three and four; it's just possible I can sketch out the history of this town, since it was a trading post, for you. And, so we'll both have something for our curiosity to chew on, Mr. Forrester, you remind me of a gentleman I went with seventy, yes, seventy years ago."

She sat across from them and it was like talking with a gray and lost quivering moth. The voice came from far away inside the grayness and the oldness, wrapped in the powders of pressed flowers and ancient butterflies.

"Well." She arose. "Will you come tomorrow?"

"I most certainly will," said Bill Forrester.

And she went off into the town on business, leaving the young boy and the young man there, looking after her, slowly finishing their ice cream.

William Forrester spent the next morning checking some local news items for the paper, had time after lunch for some fishing in the river outside town, caught only some small fish which he threw back happily, and, without thinking about it, or at least not

141

noticing that he had thought about it, at three o'clock he found his car taking him down a certain street. He watched with interest as his hands turned the steering wheel and motored him up vast circular drive where he stopped under an ivy-covered entry. Letting himself out, he was conscious of the fact that his car was like his pipe—old, chewed-on, unkempt in this huge green garden by this freshly painted, three-story Victorian house. He saw a faint ghostlike movement at the far end of the garden, heard a whispery cry, and saw that Miss Loomis was there, removed across time and distance, seated alone, the tea service glittering its soft silver surfaces, waiting for him.

"This is the first time a woman has ever been ready and waiting," he said, walking up. "It is also," he admitted, "the first time in my life I have been on time for an appointment."

"Why is that?" she asked, propped back in her wicker chair.

"I don't know," he admitted.

"Well." She started pouring tea. "To start things off, what do you think of the world?"

"I don't know anything."

"The beginning of wisdom, as they say. When you're seventeen you know everything. When you're *twenty*-seven if you *still* know everything you're still seventeen."

"You seem to have learned quite a lot over the years."

"It is the privilege of old people to seem to know everything. But it's an act and a mask, like every other act and mask. Between ourselves, we old ones wink at each other and smile, saying, How do you like *my* mask, *my* act, *my* certainty? Isn't life a play? Don't I play it well?"

They both laughed quietly. He sat back and let the laughter come naturally from his mouth for the first time in many months. When they quieted she held her teacup in her two hands and looked into it. "Do you know, it's lucky we met so late. I wouldn't have wanted you to meet me when I was twenty-one and full of foolishness."

"They have special laws for pretty girls twenty-one."

"So you think I was pretty?"

He nodded good-humoredly.

"But how can you tell?" she asked. "When you meet a dragon that has eaten a swan, do you guess by the few feathers left around the mouth? That's what it is—a body like this is a dragon, all scales and folds. So the dragon ate the white swan. I haven't seen her for years. I can't even remember what she looks like. I *feel* her, though. She's safe inside, still alive; the essential swan hasn't changed a feather. Do you know, there are some mornings in spring or fall, when I wake and think, I'll run across the fields into the woods and pick wild strawberries! Or I'll swim in the lake, or I'll dance all night tonight until dawn! And then, in a rage, discover I'm in this old and ruined dragon. I'm the princess in the crumbled tower, no way out, waiting for her Prince Charming."

"You should have written books."

"My dear boy, I *have* written. What else was there for an old maid? I was a crazy creature with a headful of carnival spangles until I was thirty, and then the only man I ever really cared for stopped waiting and married someone else. So in spite, in anger at myself, I told myself I deserved my fate for not having married when the best chance was at hand. I started traveling. My luggage was snowed under blizzards of travel stickers. I have been alone in Paris, alone in Vienna, alone in London, and, all in all, it is very much like being alone in Green Town, Illinois. It is, in essence, being alone. Oh, you have plenty of time to think, improve your manners, sharpen your conversations. But I sometimes think I could easily trade a verb tense or a curtsy for some company that would stay over for a thirty-year weekend."

They drank their tea.

143

"Oh, such a rush of self-pity," she said good-naturedly. "About yourself, now. You're thirty-one and still not married?"

"Let me put it this way," he said. "Women who act and think and talk like you are rare."

"My," she said seriously, "you mustn't expect young women to talk like me. That comes later. They're much too young, first of all. And secondly, the average man runs helter-skelter the moment he finds anything like a brain in a lady. You've probably met quite a few brainy ones who hid it most successfully from you. You'll have to pry around a bit to find the odd beetle. Lift a few boards."

They were laughing again.

"I shall probably be a meticulous old bachelor," he said.

"No, no, you mustn't do that. It wouldn't be right. You shouldn't even be here this afternoon. This is a street which ends only in an Egyptian pyramid. Pyramids are all very nice, but mummies are hardly fit companions. Where would you like to go, what would you really like to do with your life?"

"See Istanbul, Port Said, Nairobi, Budapest. Write a book. Smoke too many cigarettes. Fall off a cliff, but get caught in a tree halfway down. Get shot at a few times in a dark alley on a Moroccan midnight. Love a beautiful woman."

"Well, I don't think I can provide them all," she said. "But I've traveled and I can tell you about many of those places. And if you'd care to run across my front lawn tonight about eleven and if I'm still awake, I'll fire off a Civil War musket at you. Will that satisfy your masculine urge for adventure?"

"That would be just fine."

"Where would you like to go first? I can take you there, you know. I can weave a spell. Just name it. London? Cairo? Cairo makes your face turn on like a light. So let's go to Cairo. Just relax now. Put some of that nice tobacco in that pipe of yours and sit back."

He sat back, lit his pipe, half smiling, relaxing,

and listened, and she began to talk. "Cairo . . ." she said.

The hour passed in jewels and alleys and winds from the Egyptian desert. The sun was golden and the Nile was muddy where it lapped down to the deltas, and there was someone very young and very quick at the top of the pyramid, laughing, calling to him to come on up the shadowy side into the sun, and he was climbing, she putting her hand down to help him up the last step, and then they were laughing on camel back, loping toward the great stretched bulk of the Sphinx, and late at night, in the native quarter, there was the tinkle of small hammers on bronze and silver, and music from some stringed instruments fading away and away and away. . . .

William Forrester opened his eyes. Miss Helen Loomis had finished the adventure and they were home again, very familiar to each other, on the best of terms, in the garden, the tea cold in the silver pourer, the biscuits dried in the latened sun. He sighed and stretched and sighed again.

"I've never been so comfortable in my life."

"Nor I."

"I've kept you late. I should have gone an hour ago."

"You know I love every minute of it. But what you should see in an old silly woman . . ."

He lay back in his chair and half closed his eyes and looked at her. He squinted his eyes so the merest filament of light came through. He tilted his head ever so little this way, then that.

"What are you doing?" she asked uncomfortably.

He said nothing, but continued looking.

"If you do this just right," he murmured, "you can adjust, make allowances. . . ." To himself he was thinking, You can erase lines, adjust the time factor, turn back the years.

Suddenly he started.

"What's wrong?" she asked.

But then it was gone. He opened his eyes to catch it. That was a mistake. He should have stayed back, idling, erasing, his eyes gently half closed.

"For just a moment," he said, "I saw it."

"Saw what?"

"The swan, of course," he thought. His mouth must have pantomimed the words.

The next instant she was sitting very straight in her chair. Her hands were in her lap, rigid. Her eyes were fixed upon him and as he watched, feeling helpless, each of her eyes cupped and brimmed itself full.

"I'm sorry," he said, "terribly sorry."

"No, don't be." She held herself rigid and did not touch her face or her eyes; her hands remained, one atop the other, holding on. "You'd better go now. Yes, you may come tomorrow, but go now, please, and don't say any more."

He walked off through the garden, leaving her by her table in the shade. He could not bring himself to look back.

Four days, eight days, twelve days passed, and he was invited to teas, to suppers, to lunches. They sat talking through the long green afternoons—they talked of art, of literature, of life, of society and politics. They ate ice creams and squabs and drank good wines.

"I don't care what anyone says," she said. "And people are saying things, aren't they?"

He shifted uneasily.

"I knew it. A woman's never safe, even when ninety-five, from gossip."

"I could stop visiting."

"Oh, no," she cried, and recovered. In a quieter voice she said, "You know you can't do that. You know you don't care what they think, do you? So long as we know it's all right?"

"I don't care," he said.

"Now"—she settled back—"let's play our game. Where shall it be this time? Paris? I think Paris."

"Paris," he said, nodding quietly.

"Well," she began, "it's the year 1885 and we're boarding the ship in New York harbor. There's our luggage, here are our tickets, there goes the sky line. Now we're at sea. Now we're coming into Marseilles. . . ."

Here she was on a bridge looking into the clear waters of the Seine, and here he was, suddenly, a moment later, beside her, looking down at the tides of summer flowing past. Here she was with an apéritif in her talcum-white fingers, and here he was, with amazing quickness, bending toward her to tap her wineglass with his. His face appeared in mirrored halls at Versailles, over steaming *smörgasbörds* in Stockholm, and they counted the barber poles in the Venice canals. The things she had done alone, they were now doing together.

In the middle of August they sat staring at one another one late afternoon.

"Do you realize," he said, "I've seen you nearly every day for two and a half weeks?"

"Impossible!"

"I've enjoyed it immensely."

"Yes, but there are so many young girls . . ."

"You're everything they are not—kind, intelligent, witty."

"Nonsense. Kindness and intelligence are the preoccupations of age. Being cruel and thoughtless is far more fascinating when you're twenty." She paused and drew a breath. "Now, I'm going to embarrass you. Do you recall that first afternoon we met in the soda fountain, you said that you had had some degree of—shall we say affection for me at one time? You've purposely put me off on this by never mentioning it again. Now I'm forced to ask you to explain the whole uncomfortable thing."

He didn't seem to know what to say. "That's embarrassing," he protested.

"Spit it out!"

"I saw your picture once, years ago."

"I never let my picture be taken."

"This was an old one, taken when you were twenty."

"Oh, that. It's quite a joke. Each time I give to a charity or attend a ball they dust that picture off and print it. Everyone in town laughs; even *I.*"

"It's cruel of the paper."

"No. I told them, If you want a picture of me, use the one taken back in 1853. Let them remember me that way. Keep the lid down, in the name of the good Lord, during the service."

"I'll tell you all about it." He folded his hands and looked at them and paused a moment. He was remembering the picture now and it was very clear in his mind. There was time, here in the garden to think of every aspect of the photograph and of Helen Loomis, very young, posing for her picture the first time, alone and beautiful. He thought of her quiet, shyly smiling face.

It was the face of spring, it was the face of summer, it was the warmness of clover breath. Pomegranate glowed in her lips, and the noon sky in her eyes. To touch her face was that always new experience of opening your window one December morning, early, and putting out your hand to the first white cool powdering of snow that had come, silently, with no announcement, in the night. And all of this, this breath-warmness and plum-tenderness was held forever in one miracle of photographic chemistry which no clock winds could blow upon to change one hour or one second; this fine first cool white snow would never melt, but live a thousand summers.

That was the photograph; that was the way he knew her. Now he was talking again, after the remembering and the thinking over and the holding of the picture in his mind. "When I first saw that picture—it was a simple, straightforward picture with a simple hairdo—I didn't know it had been taken that long ago. The item in the paper said something about

Helen Loomis marshalling the Town Ball that night. I tore the picture from the paper. I carried it with me all that day. I intended going to the ball. Then, late in the afternoon, someone saw me looking at the picture, and told me about it. How the picture of the beautiful girl had been taken so long ago and used every year since by the paper. And they said I shouldn't go to the Town Ball that night, carrying that picture and looking for you."

They sat in the garden for a long minute. He glanced over at her face. She was looking at the farthest garden wall and the pink roses climbing there. There was no way to tell what she was thinking. Her face showed nothing. She rocked for a little while in her chair and then said softly, "Shall we have some more tea? There you are."

They sat sipping the tea. Then she reached over and patted his arm. "Thank you."

"For what?"

"For wanting to come to find me at the dance, for clipping out my picture, for everything. Thank you so very much."

They walked about the garden on the paths.

"And now," she said, "it's my turn. Do you remember, I mentioned a certain young man who once attended me, seventy years ago? Oh, he's been dead fifty years now, at least, but when he was very young and very handsome he rode a fast horse off for days, or on summer nights over the meadows around town. He had a healthy, wild face, always sunburned, his hands were always cut and he fumed like a stovepipe and walked as if he were going to fly apart; wouldn't keep a job, quit those he had when he felt like it, and one day he sort of rode off away from me because I was even wilder than he and wouldn't settle down, and that was that. I never thought the day would come when I would see him alive again. But you're pretty much alive, you spill ashes around like he did, you're clumsy and graceful combined, I know everything you're going to do before you do it, but after you've done it I'm always surprised. Reincarna-

149

tion's a lot of milk-mush to me, but the other day I felt, What if I called Robert, Robert, to you on the street, would William Forrester turn around?"

"I don't know," he said.

"Neither do I. That's what makes life interesting."

August was almost over. The first cool touch of autumn moved slowly through the town and there was a softening and the first gradual burning fever of color in every tree, a faint flush and coloring in the hills, and the color of lions in the wheat fields. Now the pattern of days was familiar and repeated like a penman beautifully inscribing again and again, in practice, a series of *l*'s and *w*'s and *m*'s, day after day the line repeated in delicate rills.

William Forrester walked across the garden one early August afternoon to find Helen Loomis writing with great care at the tea table.

She put aside her pen and ink.

"I've been writing you a letter," she said.

"Well, my being here saves you the trouble."

"No, this is a special letter. Look at it." She showed him the blue envelope, which she now sealed and pressed flat. "Remember how it looks. When you receive this in the mail, you'll know I'm dead."

"That's no way to talk, is it?"

"Sit down and listen to me."

He sat.

"My dear William," she said, under the parasol shade. "In a few days I will be dead. No." She put up her hand. "I don't want you to say a thing. I'm not afraid. When you live as long as I've lived you lose that, too. I never liked lobster in my life, and mainly because I'd never tried it. On my eightieth birthday I tried it. I can't say I'm greatly excited over lobster still, but I have no doubt as to its taste now, and I don't fear it. I dare say death will be a lobster, too, and I can come to terms with it." She motioned with her hands. "But enough of that. The important thing is that I shan't be seeing you again.

There will be no services. I believe that a woman who has passed through that particular door has as much right to privacy as a woman who has retired for the night."

"You can't predict death," he said at last.

"For fifty years I've watched the grandfather clock in the hall, William. After it is wound I can predict to the hour when it will stop. Old people are no different. They can feel the machinery slow down and the last weights shift. Oh, please don't look that way—please don't."

"I can't help it," he said.

"We've had a nice time, haven't we? It has been very special here, talking every day. It was that much-overburdened and worn phrase referred to as a 'meeting of the minds.'" She turned the blue envelope in her hands. "I've always known that the quality of love was the mind, even though the body sometimes refuses this knowledge. The body lives for itself. It lives only to feed and wait for the night. It's essentially nocturnal. But what of the mind which is born of the sun, William, and must spend thousands of hours of a lifetime awake and aware? Can you balance off the body, that pitiful, selfish thing of night against a whole lifetime of sun and intellect? I don't know. I only know there has been your mind here and my mind here, and the afternoons have been like none I can remember. There is still so much to talk about, but we must save it for another time."

"We don't seem to have much time now."

"No, but perhaps there *will* be another time. Time is so strange and life is twice as strange. The cogs miss, the wheels turn, and lives interlace too early or too late. I lived too long that much is certain. And you were born either too early or too late. It was a terrible bit of timing. But perhaps I am being punished for being a silly girl. Anyway, the next spin around, wheels might function right again. Meantime you must find a nice girl and be married and be happy. But you must promise me one thing."

"Anything."

"You must promise me not to live to be too old, William. If it is at all convenient, die before you're fifty. It may take a bit of doing. But I advise this simply because there is no telling when another Helen Loomis might be born. It would be dreadful, wouldn't it, if you lived on to be very, very old and some afternoon in 1999 walked down Main Street and saw me standing there, aged twenty-one, and the whole thing out of balance again? I don't think we could go through any more afternoons like these we've had, no matter how pleasant, do you? A thousand gallons of tea and five hundred biscuits is enough for one friendship. So you must have an attack of pneumonia some time in about twenty years. For I don't know how long they let you linger on the other side. Perhaps they send you back immediately. But I shall do my best, William, really I shall. And everything put right and in balance, do you know what might happen?"

"You tell me."

"Some afternoon in 1985 or 1990 a young man named Tom Smith or John Green or a name like that, will be walking downtown and will stop in the drugstore and order, appropriately, a dish of some unusual ice cream. A young girl the same age will be sitting there and when she hears the name of that ice cream, something will happen. I can't say what or how. *She* won't know why or how, assuredly. Nor will the young man. It will simply be that the name of that ice cream will be a very good thing to both of them. They'll talk. And later, when they know each other's names, they'll walk from the drugstore together."

She smiled at him.

"This is all very neat, but forgive an old lady for tying things in neat packets. It's a silly trifle to leave you. Now let's talk of something else. What shall we talk about? Is there any place in the world we haven't traveled to yet? Have we been to Stockholm?"

"Yes, it's a fine town."

"Glasgow? Yes? Where then?"

"Why not Green Town, Illinois?" he said. "Here.

152

We haven't really visited our own town together at all."

She settled back, as did he, and she said, "I'll tell you how it was, then, when I was only nineteen, in this town, a long time ago. . . ."

It was a night in winter and she was skating lightly over a pond of white moon ice, her image gliding and whispering under her. It was a night in summer in this town of fire in the air, in the cheeks, in the heart, your eyes full of the glowing and shutting-off color of fireflies. It was a rustling night in October, and there she stood, pulling taffy from a hook in the kitchen, singing, and there she was, running on the moss by the river, and swimming in the granite pit beyond town on a spring night, in the soft deep warm waters, and now it was the Fourth of July with rockets slamming the sky and every porch full of now red-fire, now blue-fire, now white-fire faces, hers dazzling bright among them as the last rocket died.

"Can you see all these things?" asked Helen Loomis. "Can you see me doing them and being with them?"

"Yes," said William Forrester, eyes closed. "I can see you."

"And then," she said, "and then . . ."

Her voice moved on and on as the afternoon grew late and the twilight deepened quickly, but her voice moved in the garden and anyone passing on the road, at a far distance, could have heard its moth sound, faintly, faintly. . . .

Two days later William Forrester was at his desk in his room when the letter came. Douglas brought it upstairs and handed it to Bill and looked as if he knew what was in it.

William Forrester recognized the blue envelope, but did not open it. He simply put it in his shirt pocket, looked at the boy for a moment, and said, "Come on, Doug; my treat."

They walked downtown, saying very little, Douglas preserving the silence he sensed was necessary. Autumn, which had threatened for a time, was gone. Summer was back full, boiling the clouds and scouring the metal sky. They turned in at the drugstore and sat at the marble fountain. William Forrester took the letter out and laid it before him and still did not open it.

He looked out at the yellow sunlight on the concrete and on the green awnings and shining on the gold letters of the window signs across the street, and he looked at the calendar on the wall. August 27, 1928. He looked at his wrist watch and felt his heart beat slowly, saw the second hand of the watch moving moving with no speed at all, saw the calendar frozen there with its one day seeming forever, the sun nailed to the sky with no motion toward sunset whatever. The warm air spread under the sighing fans over his head. A number of women laughed by the open door and were gone through his vision, which was focused beyond them at the town itself and the high courthouse clock. He opened the letter and began to read.

He turned slowly on the revolving chair. He tried the words again and again, silently, on his tongue, and at last spoke them aloud and repeated them.

"A dish of lime-vanilla ice," he said. "A dish of lime-vanilla ice."

D OUGLAS and Tom and Charlie came panting along the unshaded street.

"Tom, answer me true, now."

"Answer what true?"

"What ever happened to happy endings?"

"They got them on shows at Saturday matinees."

"Sure, but what about life?"

"All I know is I feel good going to bed nights, Doug. That's a happy ending once a day. Next morning I'm up and maybe things go bad. But all I got to do is remember that I'm going to bed that night and just lying there a while makes everything okay."

"I'm talking about Mr. Forrester and old Miss Loomis."

"Nothing we can do; she's dead."

"I know! But don't you figure someone slipped up there?"

"You mean about him thinking she was the same age as her picture and her a trillion years old all the time? No, sir, I think it's swell!"

"Swell, for gosh sakes?"

"The last few days when Mr. Forrester told me a little here or a little there and I finally put it all together—boy, did I bawl my head off. I don't even know why. I wouldn't change one bit of it. If you changed it, what would we have to talk about? Noth-

"You just won't admit you like crying, too. You cry just so long and everything's fine. And there's your happy ending. And you're ready to go back out and walk around with folks again. And it's the *start* of gosh-knows-what-all! Any time now, Mr. Forrester

155

will think it over and see it's just the only way and have a good cry and then look around and see it's morning again, even though it's five in the afternoon."

"That don't sound like no happy ending to me."

"A good night's sleep, or a ten-minute bawl, or a pint of chocolate ice cream, or all three together, is good medicine, Doug. You listen to Tom Spaulding, M.D."

"Shut up, you guys," said Charlie. "We're almost there!"

They turned a corner.

Deep in winter they had looked for bits and pieces of summer and found it in furnace cellars or in bonfires on the edge of frozen skating ponds at night. Now, in summer, they went searching for some little bit, some piece of the forgotten winter.

Rounding the corner, they felt a continual light rain spray down from a vast brick building to refresh them as they read the sign they knew by heart, the sign which showed them what they'd come searching for:

Summer's Ice House.

Summer's Ice House on a summer day! They said the words, laughing, and moved to peer into that tremendous cavern where in fifty, one-hundred, and two-hundred-pound chunks, the glaciers, the icebergs, the fallen but not forgotten snows of January slept in ammoniac steams and crystal drippings.

"Feel that," sighed Charlie Woodman. "What more could you ask?"

For the winter breath was exhaled again and again about them as they stood in the glary day, smelling the wet wood platform with the perpetual mist shimmering in rainbows down from the ice machinery above.

They chewed icicles that froze their fingers so they had to grip the ice in handkerchiefs and suck the linen.

"All that steam, all that fog," whispered Tom. "The Snow Queen. Remember that story? Nobody believes in that stuff, Snow Queens, now. So don't be surprised if this is where she came to hide out because nobody believes in her anymore."

They looked and saw the vapors rise and drift in long swathes of cool smoke.

"No," said Charlie. "You know who lives here? Only one guy. A guy who gives you goose-pimples just to think of him." Charlie dropped his voice very low. "The Lonely One."

"The Lonely One?"

"Born, raised, and *lives* here! All that winter, Tom, all that cold, Doug! Where else would he come from to make us shiver the hottest nights of the year? Don't it *smell* like him? You know darn well it does. The Lonely One . . . the Lonely One . . ."

The mists and vapors curled in darkness.

Tom screamed.

"It's okay, Doug." Charlie grinned. "I just dropped a little bitty hunk of ice down Tom's back, is all."

THE courthouse clock chimed seven times. The echoes of the chimes faded.

Warm summer twilight here in upper Illinois country in this little town deep far away from everything, kept to itself by a river and a forest and a meadow and a lake. The sidewalks still scorched. The stores closing and the streets shadowed. And there were two moons; the clock moon with four faces in four night directions above the solemn black courthouse, and the real moon rising in vanilla whiteness from the dark east.

In the drugstore fans whispered in the high ceiling. In the rococo shade of porches, a few invisible people sat. Cigars glowed pink, on occasion. Screen doors whined their springs and slammed. On the purple bricks of the summer-night streets, Douglas Spaulding ran; dogs and boys followed after.

"Hi, Miss Lavinia!"

The boys loped away. Waving after them quietly, Lavinia Nebbs sat all alone with a tall cool lemonade in her white fingers, tapping it to her lips, sipping, waiting.

"Here I am, Lavinia."

She turned and there was Francine, all in snow white, at the bottom steps of the porch, in the smell of zinnias and hibiscus.

Lavinia Nebbs locked her front door and, leaving her lemonade glass half empty on the porch, said, "It's a fine night for the movie."

They walked down the street.

"Where you going, girls?" cried Miss Fern and Miss Roberta from their porch over the way.

Lavinia called back through the soft ocean of darkness: "To the Elite Theater to see CHARLIE CHAPLIN!"

"Won't catch us out on no night like this," wailed Miss Fern. "Not with the Lonely One strangling women. Lock ourselves up in our closet with a gun."

"Oh, bosh!" Lavinia heard the old women's door bang and lock, and she drifted on, feeling the warm breath of summer night shimmering off the oven-baked sidewalks. It was like walking on a hard crust of freshly warmed bread. The heat pulsed under your dress, along your legs, with a stealthy and not un-pleasant sense of invasion.

"Lavinia, you don't believe all that about the Lonely One, do you?"

"Those women like to see their tongues dance."

"Just the same, Hattie McDollis was killed two months ago, Roberta Ferry the month before, and now Elizabeth Ramsell's disappeared. . . ."

"Hattie McDollis was a silly girl, walked off with a traveling man, I bet."

"But the others, all of them, strangled, their tongues sticking out their mouths, they say."

They stood upon the edge of the ravine that cut the town half in two. Behind them were the lit houses and music, ahead was deepness, moistness, fireflies and dark.

"Maybe we shouldn't go to the show tonight," said Francine. "The Lonely One might follow and kill us. I don't like that ravine. Look at it, will you!"

Lavinia looked and the ravine was a dynamo that never stopped running, night or day; there was a great moving hum, a bumbling and murmuring of creature, insect, or plant life. It smelled like a green-house, of secret vapors and ancient, washed shales and quicksands. And always the black dynamo hum-ming, with sparkles like great electricity where fire-flies moved on the air.

159

"It won't be *me* coming back through this old ravine tonight late, so darned late; it'll be you, Lavinia, you down the steps and over the bridge and maybe the Lonely One there."

"Bosh!" said Lavinia Nebbs.

"It'll be you alone on the path, listening to your shoes, not me. You all alone on the way back to your house. Lavinia, don't you get lonely living in that house?"

"Old maids love to live alone." Lavinia pointed at the hot shadowy path leading down into the dark. "Let's take the short cut."

"I'm afraid!"

"It's early. Lonely One won't be out till late." Lavinia took the other's arm and led her down and down the crooked path into the cricket warmth and frog sound and mosquito-delicate silence. They brushed through summer-scorched grass, burs prickling at their bare ankles.

"Let's run!" gasped Francine.

"No!"

They turned a curve in the path—and there it was.

In the singing deep night, in the shade of warm trees, as if she had laid herself out to enjoy the soft stars and the easy wind, her hands at either side of her like the oars of a delicate craft, lay Elizabeth Ramsell!

Francine screamed.

"Don't scream!" Lavinia put out her hands to hold onto Francine, who was whimpering and choking. "Don't! Don't!"

The woman lay as if she had floated there, her face moonlit, her eyes wide and like flint, her tongue sticking from her mouth.

"She's dead!" said Francine. "Oh, she's dead, dead! She's dead!"

Lavinia stood in the middle of a thousand warm shadows with the crickets screaming and the frogs loud.

"We'd better get the police," she said at last.

"Hold me, Lavinia, hold me, I'm cold, oh, I've never been so cold in all my life!"

Lavinia held Francine and the policemen were brushing through the crackling grass, flashlights ducked about, voices mingled, and the night grew toward eight-thirty.

"It's like December. I need a sweater," said Francine, eyes shut, against Lavinia.

The policeman said, "I guess you can go now, ladies. You might drop by the station tomorrow for a little more questioning."

Lavinia and Francine walked away from the police and the sheet over the delicate thing upon the ravine grass.

Lavinia felt her heart going loudly in her and she was cold, too, with a February cold; there were bits of sudden snow all over her flesh, and the moon washed her brittle fingers whiter, and she remembered doing all the talking while Francine just sobbed against her.

A voice called from far off, "You want an escort, ladies?"

"No, we'll make it," said Lavinia to nobody, and they walked on. They walked through the nuzzling, whispering ravine, the ravine of whispers and clicks, the little world of investigation growing small behind them with its lights and voices.

"I've never seen a dead person before," said Francine.

Lavinia examined her watch as if it was a thousand miles away on an arm and wrist grown impossibly distant. "It's only eight-thirty. We'll pick up Helen and get on to the show."

"The show!" Francine jerked.

"It's what we need. We've got to forget this. It's not good to remember. If we went home now we'd remember. We'll go to the show as if nothing happened."

"Lavinia, you don't *mean* it!"

"I never meant anything more in my life. We need to laugh now and forget."

"But Elizabeth's back there—your friend, my friend——"

"We can't help her; we can only help ourselves. Come on."

They started up the ravine side, on the stony path, in the dark. And suddenly there, barring their way, standing very still in one spot, not seeing them, but looking on down at the moving lights and the body and listening to the official voices, was Douglas Spaulding.

He stood there, white as a mushroom, with his hands at his sides, staring down into the ravine.

"Get home!" cried Francine.

He did not hear.

"You!" shrieked Francine. "Get home, get out of this place, you hear? Get home, get home, get *home!*"

Douglas jerked his head, stared at them as if they were not there. His mouth moved. He gave a bleating sound. Then, silently, he whirled about and ran. He ran silently up the distant hills into the warm darkness.

Francine sobbed and cried again and, doing this, walked on with Lavinia Nebbs.

"There you are! I thought you ladies'd never come!" Helen Greer stood tapping her foot atop her porch steps. "You're only an hour late, that's all. What happened?"

"We——" started Francine.

Lavinia clutched her arm tight. "There was a commotion. Somebody found Elizabeth Ramsell in the ravine."

"Dead? Was she—dead?"

Lavinia nodded. Helen gasped and put her hand to her throat. "Who found her?"

Lavinia held Francine's wrist firmly. "We don't know."

The three young women stood in the summer night looking at each other. "I've got a notion to go in the house and lock the doors," said Helen at last.

But finally she went to get a sweater, for though

it was still warm, she, too, complained of the sudden winter night. While she was gone Francine whispered frantically, "Why didn't you *tell* her?"

"Why upset her?" said Lavinia. "Tomorrow. Tomorrow's plenty of time."

The three women moved along the street under the black trees, past suddenly locked houses. How soon the news had spread outward from the ravine, from house to house, porch to porch, telephone to telephone. Now, passing, the three women felt eyes looking out at them from curtained windows as locks rattled into place. How strange the popsicle, the vanilla night, the night of close-packed ice cream, of mosquito-lotioned wrists, the night of running children suddenly veered from their games and put away behind glass, behind wood, the popsicles in melting puddles of lime and strawberry where they fell when the children were scooped indoors. Strange the hot rooms with the sweating people pressed tightly back into them behind the bronze knobs and knockers. Baseball bats and balls lay upon the unfootprinted lawns. A half-drawn, white-chalk game of hopscotch lay on the broiled, steamed sidewalk. It was as if someone had predicted freezing weather a moment ago.

"We're crazy being out on a night like this," said Helen.

"Lonely One won't kill three ladies," said Lavinia. "There's safety in numbers. And besides, it's too soon. The killings always come a month separated."

A shadow fell across their terrified faces. A figure loomed behind a tree. As if someone had struck an organ a terrible blow with his fist, the three women gave off a scream, in three different shrill notes.

"Got you!" roared a voice. The man plunged at them. He came into the light, laughing. He leaned against a tree, pointing at the ladies weakly, laughing again.

"Hey! I'm the Lonely One!" said Frank Dillon.

"Frank Dillon!"

"Frank!"

"Frank," said Lavinia, "if you ever do a childish thing like that again, may someone riddle you with bullets!"

"What a thing to do!"

Francine began to cry hysterically.

Frank Dillon stopped smiling. "Say, I'm sorry."

"Go away!" said Lavinia. "Haven't you heard about Elizabeth Ramsell—found dead in the ravine? You running around scaring women! Don't speak to us again!"

"Aw, now——"

They moved. He moved to follow.

"Stay right there, Mr. Lonely One, and scare yourself. Go take a look at Elizabeth Ramsell's face and see if it's funny. Good night!" Lavinia took the other two on along the street of trees and stars, Francine holding a kerchief to her face.

"Francine, it was only a joke." Helen turned to Lavinia. "Why's she crying so hard?"

"We'll tell you when we get downtown. We're going to the show no matter what! Enough's enough. Come on now, get your money ready, we're almost there!"

The drugstore was a small pool of sluggish air which the great wooden fans stirred in tides of arnica and tonic and soda-smell out onto the brick streets.

"I need a nickel's worth of green peppermint chews," said Lavinia to the druggist. His face was set and pale, like all the faces they had seen on the half-empty streets. "For eating in the show," said Lavinia as the druggist weighed out a nickel's worth of the green candy with a silver shovel.

"You sure look pretty tonight, ladies. You looked cool this afternoon, Miss Lavinia, when you was in for a chocolate soda. So cool and nice that someone asked after you."

"Oh?"

"Man sitting at the counter—watched you walk out. Said to me, 'Say, who's that?' Why, that's Lavinia

164

Nebbs, prettiest maiden lady in town, I said. 'She's beautiful,' he said. 'Where does she live?'" Here the druggist paused uncomfortably.

"You didn't!" said Francine. "You didn't give him her address, I hope? You didn't!"

"I guess I didn't think. I said, 'Oh, over on Park Street, you know, near the ravine.' A casual remark. But now, tonight, them finding the body, I heard a minute ago, I thought, My God, what've I done!" He handed over the package, much too full.

"You fool!" cried Francine, and tears were in her eyes.

"I'm sorry. Course, maybe it was nothing."

Lavinia stood with the three people looking at her, staring at her. She felt nothing. Except, perhaps, the slightest prickle of excitement in her throat. She held out her money automatically.

"There's no charge on those peppermints," said the druggist, turning to shuffle some papers.

"Well, I know what I'm going to do right now!" Helen stalked out of the drugshop. "I'm calling a taxi to take us all home. I'll be no part of a hunting party for you, Lavinia. That man was up to no good. Asking about you. You want to be dead in the ravine next?"

"It was just a man," said Lavinia, turning in a slow circle to look at the town.

"So is Frank Dillon a man, but maybe he's the Lonely One."

Francine hadn't come out with them, they noticed, and turning, they found her arriving. "I made him give me a description—the druggist. I made him tell what the man looked like. A stranger," she said, "in a dark suit. Sort of pale and thin."

"We're all overwrought," said Lavinia. "I simply won't take a taxi if you get one. If I'm the next victim, let me *be* the next. There's all too little excitement in life, especially for a maiden lady thirty-three years old, so don't you mind if I enjoy it. Anyway, it's silly; I'm not beautiful."

"Oh, but you are, Lavinia; you're the loveliest lady in town, now that Elizabeth is——" Francine stopped. "You keep men off at a distance. If you'd only relax, you'd been married years ago!"

"Stop sniveling, Francine! Here's the theater box office, I'm paying forty-one cents to see Charlie Chaplin. If you two want a taxi, go on. I'll sit alone and go home alone."

"Lavinia, you're crazy; we can't let you do that——"

They entered the theater.

The first showing was over, intermission was on, and the dim auditorium was sparsely populated. The three ladies sat halfway down front, in the smell of ancient brass polish, and watched the manager step through the worn red velvet curtains to make an announcement.

"The police have asked us to close early tonight so everyone can be out at a decent hour. Therefore we are cutting our short subjects and running our feature again immediately. The show will be over at eleven. Everyone is advised to go straight home. Don't linger on the streets."

"That means us, Lavinia!" whispered Francine.

The lights went out. The screen leaped to life.

"Lavinia," whispered Helen.

"What?"

"As we came in, a man in a dark suit, across the street, crossed over. He just walked down the aisle and is sitting in the row behind us."

"Oh, Helen!"

"Right behind us?"

One by one the three women turned to look.

They saw a white face there, flickering with unholy light from the silver screen. It seemed to be all men's faces hovering there in the dark.

"I'm going to get the manager!" Helen was gone up the aisle. "Stop the film! Lights!"

"Helen, come back!" cried Lavinia, rising.

They tapped their empty soda glasses down, each with a vanilla mustache on their upper lip, which they found with their tongues, laughing.

"You see how silly?" said Lavinia. "All that riot for nothing. How embarrassing."

"I'm sorry," said Helen faintly.

The clock said eleven-thirty now. They had come out of the dark theater, away from the fluttering rush of men and women hurrying everywhere, nowhere, on the street while laughing at Helen. Helen was trying to laugh at herself.

"Helen, when you ran up that aisle crying, 'Lights!' I thought I'd *die!* That *poor* man!"

"The theater manager's brother from Racine!"

"I apologized," said Helen, looking up at the great fan still whirling, whirling the warm late night air, stirring, restirring the smells of vanilla, raspberry, peppermint and Lysol.

"We shouldn't have stopped for these sodas. The police warned——"

"Oh, bosh the police," laughed Lavinia. "I'm not afraid of anything. The Lonely One is a million miles away now. He won't be back for weeks and the police'll get him then, just wait. Wasn't the film wonderful?"

"Closing up, ladies." The druggist switched off the lights in the cool white-tiled silence.

Outside, the streets were swept clean and empty of cars or trucks or people. Bright lights still burned in the small store windows where the warm wax dummies lifted pink wax hands fired with blue-white diamond rings, or flourished orange wax legs to reveal hosiery. The hot blue-glass eyes of the mannequins watched as the ladies drifted down the empty river bottom street, their images shimmering in windows like blossoms seen under darkly moving waters.

"Do you suppose if we screamed they'd do anything?"

"Who?"

"The dummies, the window people."

"Oh, Francine."

"Well..."

There were a thousand people in the windows, stiff and silent, and three people on the street, the echoes following like gunshots from store fronts across the way when they tapped their heels on the baked pavement.

A red neon sign flickered dimly, buzzed like a dying insect, as they passed.

Baked and white, the long avenues lay ahead. Blowing and tall in a wind that touched only their leafy summits, the trees stood on either side of the three small women. Seen from the courthouse peak, they appeared like three thistles far away.

"First, we'll walk you home, Francine."

"No, I'll walk *you* home."

"Don't be silly. You live way out at Electric Park. If you walked me home you'd have to come back across the ravine alone, yourself. And if so much as a leaf fell on you, you'd drop dead."

Francine said, "I can stay the night at your house. You're the *pretty* one!"

And so they walked, they drifted like three prim clothes forms over a moonlit sea of lawn and concrete, Lavinia watching the black trees flit by each side of her, listening to the voices of her friends murmuring, trying to laugh; and the night seemed to quicken, they seemed to run while walking slowly, everything seemed fast and the color of hot snow.

"Let's sing," said Lavinia.

They sang, "Shine On, Shine On, Harvest Moon . . ."

They sang sweetly and quietly, arm in arm, not looking back. They felt the hot sidewalk cooling underfoot, moving, moving.

"Listen!" said Lavinia.

They listened to the summer night. The summer-night crickets and the far-off tone of the courthouse clock making it eleven forty-five.

*"Listen!"*

Lavinia listened. A porch swing creaked in the dark and there was Mr. Terle, not saying anything to anybody, alone on his swing, having a last cigar. They saw the pink ash swinging gently to and fro.

Now the lights were going, going, gone. The little house lights and big house lights and yellow lights and green hurricane lights, the candles and oil lamps and porch lights, and everything felt locked up in brass and iron and steel, everything, thought Lavinia, is boxed and locked and wrapped and shaded. She imagined the people in their moonlit beds. And their breathing in the summer-night rooms, safe and together. And here we are, thought Lavinia, our footsteps on along the baked summer evening sidewalk. And above us the lonely street lights shining down, making a drunken shadow.

"Here's your house, Francine. Good night."

"Lavinia, Helen, stay here tonight. It's late, almost midnight now. You can sleep in the parlor. I'll make hot chocolate—it'll be such fun!" Francine was holding them both now, close to her.

"No, thanks," said Lavinia.

And Francine began to cry.

"Oh, not again, Francine," said Lavinia.

"I don't want you dead," sobbed Francine, the tears running straight down her cheeks. "You're so fine and nice, I want you alive. Please, oh, please!"

"Francine, I didn't know how much this has done to you. I promise I'll phone when I get home."

"Oh, will you?"

"And tell you I'm safe, yes. And tomorrow we'll have a picnic lunch at Electric Park. With ham sandwiches I'll make myself, how's that? You'll see, I'll live forever!"

"You'll phone, then?"

"I promised, didn't I?"

"Good night, good night!" Rushing upstairs, Francine whisked behind a door, which slammed to be snap-bolted tight on the instant.

"Now," said Lavinia to Helen, "I'll walk *you* home."

The courthouse clock struck the hour. The sounds blew across a town that was empty, emptier than it had ever been. Over empty streets and empty lots and empty lawns the sound faded.

"Nine, ten, eleven, twelve," counted Lavinia, with Helen on her arm.

"Don't you feel funny?" asked Helen.

"How do you mean?"

"When you think of us being out here on the sidewalks, under the trees, and all those people safe behind locked doors, lying in their beds. We're practically the only walking people out in the open in a thousand miles, I bet."

The sound of the deep warm dark ravine came near.

In a minute they stood before Helen's house, looking at each other for a long time. The wind blew the odor of cut grass between them. The moon was sinking in a sky that was beginning to cloud. "I don't suppose it's any use asking you to stay, Lavinia?"

"I'll be going on."

"Sometimes——"

"Sometimes what?"

"Sometimes I think people *want* to die. You've acted odd all evening."

"I'm just not afraid," said Lavinia. "And I'm curious, I suppose. And I'm using my head. Logically, the Lonely One can't be around. The police and all."

"The police are home with their covers up over their ears."

"Let's just say I'm enjoying myself, precariously, but safely. If there was any real chance of anything happening to me, I'd stay here with you, you can be sure of that."

"Maybe part of you doesn't want to live anymore."

"You and Francine. Honestly!"

"I feel so guilty. I'll be drinking some hot cocoa just as you reach the ravine bottom and walk on the bridge."

"Drink a cup for me. Good night."

Lavinia Nebbs walked alone down the midnight street, down the late summer-night silence. She saw houses with the dark windows and far away she heard a dog barking. In five minutes, she thought, I'll be safe at home. In five minutes I'll be phoning silly little Francine. I'll——"

She heard the man's voice.

A man's voice singing far away among the trees.

"Oh, give me a June night, the moonlight and you . . ."

She walked a little faster.

The voice sang, "In my arms . . . with all your charms . . ."

Down the street in the dim moonlight a man walked slowly and casually along.

I can run knock on one of these doors, thought Lavinia, if I must.

"Oh, give me a June night," sang the man, and he carried a long club in his hand. "The moonlight and you. Well, look who's *here!* What a time of night for you to be out, Miss Nebbs!"

"Officer Kennedy!"

And that's who it was, of course.

"I'd better see you home!"

"Thanks, I'll make it."

"But you live across the ravine. . . ."

Yes, she thought, but I won't walk through the ravine with any man, not even an officer. How do I know who the Lonely One is? "No," she said, "I'll hurry."

"I'll wait right here," he said. "If you need any help, give a yell. Voices carry good here. I'll come running."

"Thank you."

She went on, leaving him under a light, humming to himself, alone.

Here I am, she thought.

The ravine.

She stood on the edge of the one hundred and thirteen steps that went down the steep hill and then across the bridge seventy yards and up the hills leading to Park Street. And only one lantern to see by. Three minutes from now, she thought, I'll be putting my key in my house door. Nothing can happen in just one hundred eighty seconds.

She started down the long dark-green steps into the deep ravine.

"One, two, three, four, five, six, seven, eight, nine, ten steps," she counted in a whisper.

She felt she was running, but she was not running.

"Fifteen, sixteen, seventeen, eighteen, nineteen, twenty steps," she breathed.

"One fifth of the way!" she announced to herself.

The ravine was deep, black and black, black! And the world was gone behind, the world of safe people in bed, the locked doors, the town, the drugstore, the theater, the lights, everything was gone. Only the ravine existed and lived, black and huge, about her.

"Nothing's happened, has it? No one around, is there? Twenty-four, twenty-five steps. Remember that old ghost story you told each other when you were children?"

She listened to her shoes on the steps.

"The story about the dark man coming in your house and you upstairs in bed. And now he's at the first step coming up to your room. And now he's at the second step. And now he's at the third step and the fourth step and the fifth! Oh, how you used to laugh and scream at that story! And now the horrid dark man's at the twelfth step and now he's opening the door of your room and now he's standing by your bed. 'I GOT YOU!'"

She screamed. It was like nothing she'd ever heard, that scream. She had never screamed that loud in her life. She stopped, she froze, she clung to the wooden banister. Her heart exploded in her. The sound of the terrified beating filled the universe.

"There, *there!*" she screamed to herself. "At the bottom of the steps. A man, under the light! No, now he's gone! He was *waiting* there!"

She listened.

Silence.

The bridge was empty.

Nothing, she thought, holding her heart. Nothing. Fool! That story I told myself. How silly. What shall I do?

Her heartbeats faded.

Shall I call the officer—did he hear me scream?

She listened. Nothing. Nothing.

I'll go the rest of the way. That silly story.

She began again, counting the steps.

"Thirty-five, thirty-six, careful, don't fall. Oh, I am a fool. Thirty-seven steps, thirty-eight, nine and forty, and two makes forty-two—almost halfway."

She froze again.

Wait, she told herself.

She took a step. There was an echo.

She took another step.

Another echo. Another step, just a fraction of a moment later.

"Someone's following me," she whispered to the ravine, to the black crickets and dark-green hidden frogs and the black stream. "Someone's on the steps behind me. I don't dare turn around."

Another step, another echo.

"Every time I take a step, they take one."

A step and an echo.

Weakly she asked of the ravine, "Officer Kennedy, is that *you?*"

The crickets were still.

The crickets were *listening*. The night was listening to *her*. For a change, all of the far summer-night meadows and close summer-night trees were suspending motion; leaf, shrub, star, and meadow grass ceased their particular tremors and were listening to Lavinia Nebbs's heart. And perhaps a thousand miles away, across locomotive-lonely country, in an empty way station, a single traveler reading a dim newspaper under a solitary naked bulb, might raise up his head, listen, and think, What's that? and decide, Only a woodchuck, surely, beating on a hollow log. But it was Lavinia Nebbs, it was most surely the heart of Lavinia Nebbs.

Silence. A summer-night silence which lay for a thousand miles, which covered the earth like a white and shadowy sea.

Faster, faster! She went down the steps.

Run!

She heard music. In a mad way, in a silly way, she heard the great surge of music that pounded at her, and she realized as she ran, as she ran in panic and terror, that some part of her mind was dramatizing, borrowing from the turbulent musical score of some private drama, and the music was rushing and pushing her now, higher and higher, faster, faster, plummeting and scurrying, down, and down into the pit of the ravine.

Only a little way, she prayed. One hundred eight, nine, one hundred ten steps! The bottom! Now, run! Across the bridge!

She told her legs what to do, her arms, her body, her terror; she advised all parts of herself in this white and terrible moment, over the roaring creek waters, on the hollow, thudding, swaying, almost alive, resilient bridge planks she ran, followed by the wild footsteps behind, behind, with the music following, too, the music shrieking and babbling.

He's following, don't turn, don't look, if you see him, you'll not be able to move, you'll be so frightened. Just run, run!

She ran across the bridge.

Oh, God, God, please, please let me get up the hill! Now up, the path, now between the hills, oh God, it's dark, and everything so far away. If I screamed now it wouldn't help; I can't scream anyway. Here's the top of the path, here's the street, oh, God, please let me be safe, if I get home safe I'll never go out alone; I was a fool, let me admit it, I was a fool, I didn't know what terror was, but if you let me get home from this I'll never go without Helen or Francine again! Here's the street. Across the street!

She crossed the street and rushed up the sidewalk.

Oh God, the porch! My house! Oh God, please

give me time to get inside and lock the door and I'll be safe!

And there—silly thing to notice—why did she notice, instantly, no time, no time—but there it was anyway, flashing by—there on the porch rail, the half-filled glass of lemonade she had abandoned a long time, a year, half an evening ago! The lemonade glass sitting calmly, imperturbably there on the rail . . . and . . .

She heard her clumsy feet on the porch and listened and felt her hands scrabbling and ripping at the lock with the key. She heard her heart. She heard her inner voice screaming.

The key fit.

Unlock the door, quick, quick!

The door opened.

Now, inside. Slam it!

She slammed the door.

"Now lock it, bar it, lock it!" she gasped wretchedly.

"Lock it, tight, *tight!*"

The door was locked and bolted tight.

The music stopped. She listened to her heart again and the sound of it diminishing into silence.

Home! Oh God, safe at home! Safe, safe and safe at home! She slumped against the door. Safe, safe. Listen. Not a sound. Safe, safe, oh thank God, safe at home. I'll never go out at night again. I'll stay home. I won't go over that ravine again ever. Safe, oh safe, safe home, so good, so good, safe! Safe inside, the door locked. Wait.

Look out the window.

She looked.

Why, there's no one there at all! Nobody. There was nobody following me at all. Nobody running after me. She got her breath and almost laughed at herself. It stands to *reason.* If a man *had* been following me, he'd have *caught* me! I'm not a fast runner. . . . There's no one on the porch or in the yard. How silly of me. I wasn't running from anything. That ravine's as safe as anyplace. Just the same, it's nice to be home. Home's the really good warm place, the only place to be.

She put her hand out to the light switch and stopped.

"What?" she asked. "What, *What?*"

Behind her in the living room, someone cleared his throat.

**G**OOD grief, they ruin everything!"

"Don't take it so hard, Charlie."

"Well, what's we going to talk about now? It's no use talking the Lonely One if he ain't even alive! It's not scary anymore!"

"Don't know about you, Charlie," said Tom. "I'm going back to Summer's Ice House and sit in the door and pretend he's alive and get cold all up and down my spine."

"That's cheating."

"You got to take your chills where you can find them, Charlie."

Douglas did not listen to Tom and Charlie. He looked at Lavinia Nebbs's house and spoke, almost to himself.

"I was there last night in the ravine. I saw it. I saw everything. On my way home I cut across here. I saw that lemonade glass right on the porch rail, half empty. Thought I'd like to drink it. Like to drink it, I thought. I was in the ravine and I was here, right in the middle of it all."

Tom and Charlie, in turn, ignored Douglas.

"For that matter," said Tom. "I don't really think the Lonely One is dead."

"You were here this morning when the ambulance came to bring that man out on the stretcher, weren't you?"

"Sure," said Tom.

"Well, *that* was the Lonely One, dumb! Read the papers! After ten long years escaping, old Lavinia

Nebbs up and stabbed him with a handy pair of sewing scissors. I wish she'd minded her own business."

"You want she'd laid down and let him squeeze her windpipe?"

"No, but the least she could've done is gallop out of the house and down the street screaming 'Lonely One! Lonely One!' long enough to give him a chance to beat it. This town used to have some good stuff in it up until about twelve o'clock last night. From here on, we're vanilla junket."

"Let me say it for the last time, Charlie; I figure the Lonely One ain't dead. I saw his face, you saw his face, Doug saw his face, didn't you, Doug?"

"What? Yes. I think so. Yes."

"Everybody saw his face. Answer me this, then: Did it *look* like the Lonely One to you?"

"I . . ." said Douglas, and stopped.

The sun buzzed in the sky for about five seconds.

"My gosh . . ." whispered Charlie at last.

Tom waited, smiling.

"It didn't look like the Lonely One at all," gasped Charlie. "It looked like a *man*."

"Right, yes, sir, a plain everyday man, who wouldn't pull the wings off even so much as a fly, Charlie, a fly! The least the Lonely One would do if he was the Lonely One is look like the Lonely One, right? Well, he looked like the candy butcher down front the Elite Theater nights."

"What you think he was, a tramp coming through town, got in what he thought was an empty house, and got killed by Miss Nebbs?"

"Sure!"

"Hold on, though. None of us know what the Lonely One should look like. There're no pictures. Only people ever saw him wound up dead."

"You know and Doug knows and I know what he looks like. He's got to be tall, don't he?"

"Sure . . ."

"And he's got to be pale, don't he?"

"Pale, that's right."

"And skinny like a skeleton and have long dark hair, don't he?"

"That's what I always said."

"And big eyes bulging out, green eyes like a cat?"

"That's him to the t."

"Well, then." Tom snorted. "You saw that poor guy they lugged out of the Nebbs's place a couple hours ago. What was he?"

"Little and red-faced and kind of fat and not much hair and what there was was sandy. Tom, you hit on it! Come on! Call the guys! You go tell them like you told me! The Lonely One ain't dead. He'll still be out lurkin' around tonight."

"Yeah," said Tom, and stopped, suddenly thoughtful.

"Tom, you're a pal, you got a real brain. None of us would've saved the day this way. The summer was sure going bad up to this very minute. You got your thumb in the dike just in time. August won't be a *total* loss. Hey, kids!"

And Charlie was off, waving his arms, yelling.

Tom stood on the sidewalk in front of Lavinia Nebbs's house, his face pale.

"My gosh!" he whispered. "What've I gone and done *now?*"

He turned to Douglas.

"I say, Doug, what've I gone and done now?"

Douglas was staring at the house. His lips moved.

"I was there, last night, in the ravine. I saw Elizabeth Ramsell. I came by here last night on the way home. I saw the lemonade glass there on the rail. Just last night it was. I could drink that, I thought . . . I could drink that. . . ."

S HE was a woman with a broom or a dustpan or a washrag or a mixing spoon in her hand. You saw her cutting piecrust in the morning, humming to it, or you saw her setting out the baked pies at noon or taking them in, cool, at dusk. She rang porcelain cups like a Swiss bell ringer, to their place. She glided through the halls as steadily as a vacuum machine, seeking, finding, and setting to rights. She made mirrors of every window, to catch the sun. She strolled but twice through any garden, trowel in hand, and the flowers raised their quivering fires upon the warm air in her wake. She slept quietly and turned no more than three times in a night, as relaxed as a white glove to which, at dawn, a brisk hand will return. Waking, she touched people like pictures, to set their frames straight.

But, now . . . ?

"Grandma," said everyone. "Great-grandma."

Now it was as if a huge sum in arithmetic were finally drawing to an end. She had stuffed turkeys, chickens, squabs, gentlemen, and boys. She had washed ceilings, walls, invalids, and children. She had laid linoleum, repaired bicycles, wound clocks, stoked furnaces, swabbed iodine on ten thousand grievous wounds. Her hands had flown all around about and down, gentling this, holding that, throwing baseballs, swinging bright croquet mallets, seeding black earth, or fixing covers over dumplings, ragouts, and children wildly strewn by slumber. She had pulled down shades, pinched out candles, turned switches, and—grown old. Looking back on thirty billions of things started, carried, finished and done, it all summed up, totaled out; the last decimal was placed, the final zero swung slowly into line. Now, chalk in hand, she stood back from life a silent hour before reaching for the eraser.

"Let me see now," said Great-grandma. "Let me see . . ."

With no fuss or further ado, she traveled the house in an ever-circling inventory, reached the stairs at last, and, making no special announcement, she took herself up three flights to her room where, silently, she laid herself out like a fossil imprint under the snowing cool sheets of her bed and began to die.

Again the voices:

"Grandma! Great-grandma!"

The rumor of what she was doing dropped down the stair well, hit, and spread ripples through the rooms, out doors and windows and along the street of elms to the edge of the green ravine.

"Here now, here!"

The family surrounded her bed.

"Just let me lie," she whispered.

Her ailment could not be seen in any microscope; it was a mild but ever-deepening tiredness, a dim weighing of her sparrow body; sleepy, sleepier, sleepiest.

As for her children and her children's children— it seemed impossible that with such a simple act, the most leisurely act in the world, she could cause such apprehension.

"Great-grandma, now listen—what you're doing is no better than breaking a lease. This house will fall down without you. You must give us at least a year's notice!"

Great-grandma opened one eye. Ninety years gazed calmly out at her physicians like a dust-ghost from a high cupola window in a fast-emptying house. "Tom . . . ?"

The boy was sent, alone, to her whispering bed.

"Tom," she said, faintly, far away, "in the Southern Seas there's a day in each man's life when he knows it's time to shake hands with all his friends and say good-by and sail away, and he does, and it's natural—it's just his time. That's how it is today. I'm so like you sometimes, sitting through Saturday matinees until nine at night when we send your dad to bring you home. Tom, when the time comes that the same cowboys are shooting the same Indians on the same mountaintop, then it's best to fold back the seat and head for the door, with no regrets and no walking backward up the aisle. So, I'm leaving while I'm still happy and still entertained."

Douglas was summoned next to her side.

"Grandma, who'll shingle the roof next spring?"

Every April for as far back as there were calendars, you thought you heard woodpeckers tapping the housetop. But no, it was Great-grandma somehow transported, singing, pounding nails, replacing shingles, high in the sky!

"Douglas," she whispered, "don't ever let anyone do the shingles unless it's fun for them."

"Yes'm."

"Look around come April, and say, 'Who'd like to fix the roof?' And whichever face lights up is the face you want, Douglas. Because up there on that roof you can see the whole town going toward the country and the country going toward the edge of the earth and the river shining, and the morning lake, and birds on the trees down under you, and the best of the wind all around above. Any one of those should be enough to make a person climb a weather vane some spring sunrise. It's a powerful hour, if you give it half a chance...."

Her voice sank to a soft flutter.

Douglas was crying.

She roused herself again. "Now, why are you doing that?"

"Because," he said, "you won't be here tomorrow."

She turned a small hand mirror from herself to the boy. He looked at her face and himself in the mirror and then at her face again as she said, "Tomorrow morning I'll get up at seven and wash behind my ears; I'll run to church with Charlie Woodman; I'll picnic at Electric Park; I'll swim, run barefoot, fall out of trees, chew spearmint gum. . . . Douglas, Douglas, for shame! You cut your fingernails, don't you?"

"Yes'm."

"And you don't yell when your body makes itself over every seven years or so, old cells dead and new ones added to your fingers and your heart. You don't mind that, do you?"

"No'm."

"Well, consider then, boy. Any man saves finger-nail clippings is a fool. You ever see a snake bother to keep his peeled skin? That's about all you got here today in this bed is fingernails and snake skin. One good breath would send me up in flakes. Important thing is not the me that's lying here, but the me that's sitting on the edge of the bed looking back at me, and the me that's downstairs cooking supper, or out in the garage under the car, or in the library reading. All the new parts, they count. I'm not really dying today. No person ever died that had a family. I'll be around a long time. A thousand years from now a whole township of my offspring will be biting sour apples in the gumwood shade. That's my answer to anyone asks big questions! Quick now, send in the rest!"

At last the entire family stood, like people seeing someone off at the rail station, waiting in the room.

"Well," said Great-grandma, "there I am. I'm not humble, so it's nice seeing you standing around my bed. Now next week there's late gardening and closet-cleaning and clothes-buying for the children to do. And since that part of me which is called, for convenience, Great-grandma, won't be here to step it along, those others parts of me called Uncle Bert and Leo and Tom and Douglas, and all the other names, will have to take over, each to his own."

"Yes, Grandma."

"I don't want any Halloween parties here tomorrow. Don't want anyone saying anything sweet about me; I said it all in my time and my pride. I've tasted every victual and danced every dance; now there's one last tart I haven't bit on, one tune I haven't whistled. But I'm not afraid. I'm truly curious. Death won't get a crumb by my mouth I won't keep and savor. So don't you worry over me. Now, all of you go, and let me find my sleep. . . ."

Somewhere a door closed quietly.

"That's better." Alone, she snuggled luxuriously down through the warm snowbank of linen and wool, sheet and cover, and the colors of the patchwork quilt were bright as the circus banners of old time. Lying there, she felt as small and secret as on those mornings eighty-some-odd years ago when, wakening, she comforted her tender bones in bed.

A long time back, she thought, I dreamed a dream, and was enjoying it so much when someone wakened me, and that was the day when I was born. And now? Now, let me see . . . She cast her mind back. Where was I? she thought. Ninety years . . . how to take up the thread and the pattern of that lost dream again? She put out a small hand. *There* . . . Yes, that was it. She smiled. Deeper in the warm snow hill she turned her head upon her pillow. That was better. Now, yes, now she saw it shaping in her mind quietly, and with a serenity like a sea moving along an endless and self-refreshing shore. Now she let the old dream touch and lift her from the snow and drift her above the scarce-remembered bed.

Downstairs, she thought, they are polishing the silver, and rummaging the cellar, and dusting in the halls. She could hear them living all through the house.

"It's all right," whispered Great-grandma, as the dream floated her. "Like everything else in this life, it's fitting."

And the sea moved her back down the shore.

"A GHOST!" cried Tom.

"No," said a voice. "Just me."

The ghastly light flowed into the dark apple-scented bedroom. A quart-size Mason jar, seemingly suspended upon space, flickered many twilight-colored flakes of light on and off. In this pallid illumination Douglas's eyes shone pale and solemn. He was so tan his face and hands were dissolved in darkness and his nightgown seemed a disembodied spirit.

"My gosh!" hissed Tom. "Two dozen, three dozen fireflies!"

"Shh, for cry-yi!"

"What you got 'em for?"

"We got caught reading nights with flashlights under our sheets, right? So, nobody'll suspect an old jar of fireflies; folks'll think it's just a night museum."

"Doug, you're a genius!"

But Douglas did not answer. Very gravely he placed the intermittently signaling light source upon the night table and picked up his pencil and began to write large and long on his tablet. With the fireflies burning, dying, burning, dying, and his eyes glinting with three dozen fugitive bits of pale green color, he block printed for ten and then twenty minutes, aligning and realigning, writing and rewriting the facts that he had gathered all too swiftly during the season. Tom watched, hypnotized by the small bonfire of insects leaping and furling within the jar, until he froze, sleeping, raised on elbow, while Douglas wrote on. He summed it all up on a final page:

## YOU CAN'T DEPEND ON *THINGS*
## BECAUSE...

*... like machines, for instance, they fall apart or rust or rot, or maybe never get finished at all ... or wind up in garages ...*
*... like tennis shoes, you can only run so far, so fast, and then the earth's got you again ...*
*... like trolleys. Trolleys, big as they are, always come to the end of the line ...*

## YOU CAN'T DEPEND ON *PEOPLE*
## BECAUSE...

*... they go away.*
*... strangers die.*
*... people you know fairly well die.*
*... friends die.*
*... people* murder *people, like in books.*
*... your own folks can die.*

*So...!*
He held onto a double fistful of breath, let it hiss out slow, grabbed more breath, and let it whisper through his tight-gritted teeth.

SO. He finished in huge heavily blocked capitals.

SO IF TROLLEYS AND RUNABOUTS AND FRIENDS AND NEAR FRIENDS CAN GO AWAY FOR A WHILE OR GO AWAY FOREVER, OR RUST, OR FALL APART OR DIE, AND IF PEOPLE CAN BE MURDERED, AND IF SOMEONE LIKE GREAT-GRANDMA, WHO WAS GOING TO LIVE FOREVER, CAN DIE ... IF ALL OF THIS IS TRUE ... THEN ... I, DOUGLAS SPAULDING, SOME DAY ... MUST ...

But the fireflies, as if extinguished by his somber thoughts, had softly turned themselves off.

I can't write any more, anyway, thought Douglas. I won't write any more. I won't, I won't finish it tonight.

He looked over at Tom asleep on his upraised elbow and hand. He touched Tom's wrist and Tom collapsed into a sighing ruin, back upon the bed.

Douglas picked up the Mason jar with the cold dark lumps in it and the cool lights flicked on again, as if given life by his hand. He lifted the Mason jar to where it shone fitfully on his summing-up. The final words waited to be written. But he went instead to the window and pushed the screen frame out. He unscrewed the top of the jar and tilted the fireflies in a pale shower of sparks down the windless night. They found their wings and flew away.

Douglas watched them go. They departed like the pale fragments of a final twilight in the history of a dying world. They went like the few remaining shreds of warm hope from his hand. They left his face and his body and the space inside his body to darkness. They left him empty as the Mason jar which now, without knowing that he did so, he took back into bed with him, when he tried to sleep. . . .

**T**HERE she sat in her glass coffin, night after night, her body melted by the carnival blaze of summer, frozen in the ghost winds of winter, waiting with her sickle smile and carved, hooked, and wax-pored nose hovering above her pale pink and wrinkled wax hands poised forever above the ancient fanned-out deck of cards. The Tarot Witch. A delicious name. The Tarot Witch. You thrust a penny in the silver slot and far away below, behind, inside, machinery groaned and cogged, levers stroked, wheels spun. And in her case the witch raised up her glittery face to blind you with a single needle stare. Her implacable left hand moved down to stroke and fritter enigmatic tarot-card skulls, devils, hanging men, hermits, cardinals and clowns, while her head hung close to delve your misery or murder, hope or health, your rebirths each morning and death's renewals by night. Then she spidered a calligrapher's pen across the back of a single card and let it titter down the chute into your hands. Whereupon the witch, with a last veiled glimmer of her eyes, froze back in her eternal caul for weeks, months, years, awaiting the next copper penny to revive her from oblivion. Now, waxen dead, she suffered the two boys' approach.

Douglas fingerprinted the glass.

"There she is."

"It's a wax dummy," said Tom. "Why do you want me to see her?"

"All the time asking why!" yelled Douglas. "Because, *that's* why, because!"

Because . . . the arcade lights dimmed . . . because . . .

One day you discover you are alive.

Explosion! Concussion! Illumination! Delight!

You laugh, you dance around, you shout.

But, not long after, the sun goes out. Snow falls, but no one sees it, on an August noon.

At the cowboy matinee last Saturday a man had dropped down dead on the white-hot screen. Douglas had cried out. For years he had seen billions of cowboys shot, hung, burned, destroyed. But now, this one particular man . . .

He'll never walk, run, sit, laugh, cry, won't do anything ever, thought Douglas. Now he's turning cold. Douglas's teeth chattered, his heart pumped sludge in his chest. He shut his eyes and let the convulsion shake him.

He had to get away from these other boys because they weren't thinking about death, they just laughed and yelled at the dead man as if he still lived. Douglas and the dead man were on a boat pulling away, with all the others left behind on the bright shore, running, jumping, hilarious with motion, not knowing that the boat, the dead man and Douglas were going, going, and now gone into darkness. Weeping, Douglas ran to the lemon-smelling men's room where, sick, it seemed a fire hydrant churned three times from his throat.

And waiting for the sickness to pass he thought: All the people I know who died this summer! Colonel Freeleigh, dead! I didn't know it before; why? Great-grandma, dead, too. Really-truly. Not only that but . . . He paused. Me! No, they can't kill me! Yes, said a voice, yes, any time they want to they can, no matter how you kick or scream, they just put a big hand over you and you're still. . . . I don't want to die! Douglas screamed, without a sound. You'll have to anyway, said the voice, you'll have to anyway. . . .

The sunlight outside the theater blazed down upon unreal street, unreal buildings, and people moving slowly, as if under a bright and heavy ocean of pure burning gas and him thinking that now, now at last he must go home and finish out the final line in his nickel tablet: SOME DAY, I, DOUGLAS SPAULD-ING, MUST DIE. . . .

It had taken him ten minutes to get up enough courage to cross the street, his heart slowing, and there was the arcade and he saw the strange wax witch back where she had always hidden in cool dusty shadow with the Fates and Furies tucked under her fingernails. A car passing flashed an explosion of light through the arcade, jumping the shadows, making it seem that the wax woman nodded swiftly for him to enter.

And he had gone in at the witch's summoning and come forth five minutes later, certain of survival. Now, he must show Tom. . . .

"She looks almost alive," said Tom.

"She *is* alive. I'll show you."

He shoved a penny in the slot.

Nothing happened.

Douglas yelled across the arcade at Mr. Black, the proprietor, seated on an upended soda-pop crate uncorking and taking a swig from a three-quarters empty bottle of brown-yellow liquid.

"Hey, something's wrong with the witch!"

Mr. Black shuffled over, his eyes half closed, his breath sharp and strong. "Something's wrong with the pinball, wrong with the peep show, wrong with the ELECTROCUTE YOURSELF FOR A PENNY machine." He struck the case. "Hey, in there! Come alive!" The witch sat unperturbed. "Costs me more to fix her each month than she earns." Mr. Black reached behind the case and hung a sign "OUT OF ORDER" over her face. "She ain't the only thing's out of order. Me, you, this town, this country, the whole world! To hell with it!" He shook his fist at the woman. "The junk heap for you, you hear me, the junk heap!" He walked off and plunged himself down on the soda-pop crate to feel the coins in his money apron again, like it was his stomach giving him pain.

"She just can't—oh, she can't be out of order," said Douglas, stricken.

"She's old," said Tom. "Grandpa says she was here when he was a boy and before. So it's bound to be some day she'd konk out and . . ."

"Come on now," whispered Douglas. "Oh, please, please, write so Tom can see!"

He shoved another coin stealthily into the machine. "Please . . ."

The boys pressed the glass, their breath made cumulus clouds on the pane.

Then, deep inside the box, a whisper, a whir.

And slowly, the witch's head rose up and looked at the boys and there was something in her eyes that froze them as her hand began to scrabble almost frantically back and forth upon the tarots, to pause, hurry on, return. Her head bent down, one hand came to rest and a shuddering shook the machine as the other hand wrote, paused, wrote, and stopped at last with a paroxysm so violent the glass in the case chimed. The witch's face bent in a rigid mechanical misery, almost fisted into a ball. Then the machinery gasped and a single cog slipped and a tiny tarot card tickled down the flue into Douglas's cupped hands.

"She's alive! She's working again!"

"What's the card say, Doug?"

"It's the same one she wrote for me last Saturday! Listen . . ."

And Douglas read:

*"Hey, nonny no!*
*Men are fools that wish to die!*
*Is't not fine to dance and sing*
*When the bells of death do ring?*
*Is't not fine to swim in wine,*
*And turn upon the toe,*
*And sing Hey, nonny no!*
*When the winds blow and the seas flow?*
*Hey, nonny no!"*

"Is that *all* it says?" said Tom.

"At the bottom is a message: 'PREDICTION: A long life and a lively one.'"

"That's more like it! Now how about one for me?"

Tom put his coin in. The witch shuddered. A card fell into his hand.

"Last one off the premises is the witch's behind," said Tom calmly.

They ran out so fast, the proprietor gasped and clutched forty-five copper pennies in one fist, thirty-six in the other.

Outside in the glare of the uneasy street lights Douglas and Tom made a terrible discovery.

The tarot card was empty, there was no message.

"That can't be!"

"Don't get excited, Doug. It's just a plain old card; we only lost a penny."

"It's not a plain old card, it's more than a penny, it's life and death."

Under the fluttering moth light in the street Douglas's face was milky as he stared at the card and turned it, rustling, trying somehow to put words on it.

"She ran out of ink."

"She *never* runs out of ink!"

He looked at Mr. Black sitting there finishing off his bottle and cursing, not knowing how lucky he was, living in the arcade. Please, he thought, don't let the arcade fall apart, too. Bad enough that friends disappeared, people were killed and buried in the real world, but let the arcade run along the way it was, please, please. . . .

Now Douglas knew why the arcade had drawn him so steadily this week and drew him still tonight. For there was a world completely set in place, predictable, certain, sure, with its bright silver slots, its terrible gorilla behind glass forever stabbed by waxen hero to save still more waxen heroine, and then the flipping waterfalling chitter of Keystone Kops on eternal photographic spindles set spiraling in darkness by Indian-head pennies under naked bulb light. The Kops, forever in collision or near-collision with train, truck, streetcar, forever gone off piers in oceans which did not drown, because there they rushed to collide again with train, truck, streetcar, dive off old and beautifully familiar pier. Worlds within worlds, the penny peek shows which you cranked to repeat old rites and formulas. There, when you wished, the Wright Brothers sailed sandy winds at Kittyhawk, Teddy Roosevelt exposed his dazzling teeth, San Francisco was built and burned, burned and built, as long as sweaty coins fed self-satisfied machines.

Douglas looked around at this night town, where anything at all might happen now, a minute from now. Here, by night or day, how few the slots to shove your money in, how few the cards delivered to your hand for reading, and, if read, how few made sense. Here in the world of people you might give time, money, and prayer with little or no return.

But there in the arcade you could hold lightning with the CAN YOU TAKE IT? electrical machine when you pried its chromed handles apart as the power wasp-stung, sizzled, sewed your vibrant fingers. You punched a bag and saw how many hundred pounds of sinew were available in your arm to strike the world if it need be struck. There grip a robot's hand to Indian-wrestle out your fury and light the bulbs half up a numbered chart where fireworks at the summit proved your violence supreme.

In the arcade, then, you did this and this, and that and that occurred. You came forth in peace as from a church unknown before.

And now? Now?

The witch moving but silent, and perhaps soon dead in her crystal coffin. He looked at Mr. Black droning there, defying all worlds, even his own. Someday the fine machinery would rust from lack of loving care, the Keystone Kops freeze forever half in, half out of the lake, half caught, half struck by loco-motive; the Wright Brothers never get their kite machine off the ground. . . .

"Tom," Douglas said, "we got to sit in the library and figure this thing out."

They moved on down the street, the white unwritten card passing between them.

They sat inside the library in the lidded green light and then they sat outside on the carved stone lion, dangling their feet over its back, frowning.

"Old man Black, all the time screaming at her, threatening to kill her."

"You can't kill what's never lived, Doug."

"He treats the witch like she's alive or was once alive, or something. Screaming at her, so maybe she's finally given up. Or maybe she hasn't given up at all, but's taken a secret way to warn us her life's in danger. Invisible ink. Lemon juice, maybe! There's a message here she didn't want Mr. Black to see, in case he looked while we were in his arcade. Hold on! I got some matches."

"Why would she write us, Doug?"

"Hold the card. Here!" Douglas struck a match and ran it under the card.

"Ouch! The words ain't on my fingers, Doug, so keep the match away."

"There!" cried Douglas. And there it was, a faint spidery scrawl which began to shape itself in a spiral of incredible corkscrew calligrapher's letters, dark on light . . . a word, two words, three . . .

"The card, it's on fire!"

Tom yelled and let it drop.

"Stomp on it!"

But by the time they had jumped up to smash their feet on the stony spine of the ancient lion, the card was a black ruin.

"Doug! Now we'll never know what it said!"

Douglas held the flaking warm ashes in the palm of his hand. "No, I saw. I remember the words."

The ashes blew about in his fingers, whispering.

"You remember in that Charlie Chase Comedy last spring where the Frenchman was drowning and kept yelling something in French which Charlie

Chase couldn't figure. *Secours, Secours!* And someone told Charlie what it meant and he jumped in and saved the man. Well, on this card, with my own eyes, I saw it. *Secours!*"

"Why would she write it in French?"

"So Mr. Black wouldn't know, dumb!"

"Doug, it was just an old watermark coming out when you scorched the card. . . ." Tom saw Douglas's face and stopped. "Okay, don't look mad. It was 'sucker' or whatever. But there were other words. . . ."

"Mme. Tarot, it said. Tom, I got it now! Mme. Tarot's real, lived a long time ago, told fortunes. I saw her picture once in the encyclopedia. People came from all over Europe to see her. Well, don't you figure it now yourself? Think, Tom, think!"

Tom sat back down on the lion's back, looking along the street to where the arcade lights flickered.

"That's not the *real* Mrs. Tarot?"

"Inside that glass box, under all that red and blue silk and all that old half-melted wax, sure! Maybe a long time ago someone got jealous or hated her and poured wax over her and kept her prisoner forever and she's passed down the line from villain to villain and wound up here, centuries later, in Green Town, Illinois—working for Indian-head pennies instead of the crown heads of Europe!"

"Villains? Mr. Black?"

"Name's Black, shirt's black, pants're black, tie's black. Movie villains wear black, don't they?"

"But why didn't she yell last year, the year before?"

"Who knows, every night for a hundred years she's been writing messages in lemon juice on cards, but everybody read her regular message, nobody thought, like us, to run a match over the back to bring out the *real* message. Lucky I know what *secours* means."

"Okay, she said 'Help!' Now what?"

"We save her, of course."

"Steal her out from under Mr. Black's nose, huh? And wind up witches ourselves in glass boxes with wax poured on our faces the next ten thousand years."

"Tom, the library's here. We'll arm ourselves with spells and magic philters to fight Mr. Black."

"There's only one magic philter will fix Mr. Black," said Tom. "Soon's he gets enough pennies any one evening, he—well, let's see." Tom drew some coins from his pocket. "This just might do it. Doug, you go read the books. I'll run back and look at the Keystone Kops fifteen times; I never get tired. By the time you meet me at the arcade, it might be the old philter will be working for us."

"Tom, I hope you know what you're doing."

"Doug, you want to rescue this princess or not?"

Douglas whirled and plunged.

Tom watched the library doors wham shut and settle. Then he leaped over the lion's back and down into the night. On the library steps, the ashes of the tarot card fluttered, blew away.

The arcade was dark; inside, the pinball machines lay dim and enigmatic as dust scribblings in a giant's cave. The peep shows stood with Teddy Roosevelt and the Wright Brothers faintly smirking or just cranking up a wooden propeller. The witch sat in her case, her waxen eyes cauled. Then, suddenly, one eye glittered. A flashlight bobbed outside through the dusty arcade windows. A heavy figure lurched against the locked door, a key scrabbled into the lock. The door slammed open, stayed open. There was a sound of thick breathing.

"It's only me, old girl," said Mr. Black, swaying.

Outside on the street, coming along with his nose in a book, Douglas found Tom hiding in a door nearby.

"Shh!" said Tom. "It worked. The Keystone Kops, fifteen times; and when Mr. Black heard me drop all that money in, his eyes popped, he opened the machine, took out the pennies, threw me out and went across to the speak-easy for the magic philter."

Douglas crept up and peered into the shadowy

arcade and saw the two gorilla figures there, one not moving at all, the wax heroine in his arms, the other one standing stunned in the middle of the room, weaving slightly from side to side.

"Oh, Tom," whispered Douglas, "you're a genius. He's just *full* of magic philter, ain't he?"

"You can say *that* again. What did *you* find out?"

Douglas tapped the book and talked in a low voice. "Mme. Tarot, like I said, told all about death and destiny and stuff in rich folks' parlors, but she made one mistake. She predicted Napoleon's defeat and death to his *face!* So . . ."

Douglas's voice faded as he looked again through the dusty window at that distant figure seated quietly in her crystal case.

"*Secours,*" murmured Douglas. "Old Napoleon just called in Mme. Tussaud's waxworks and had them drop the Tarot Witch alive in boiling wax, and now . . . now . . ."

"Watch out, Doug, Mr. Black, in there! He's got a club or something!"

This was true. Inside, cursing horribly, the huge figure of Mr. Black lurched. In his hand a camping knife seethed on the air six inches from the witch's face.

"He's picking on her because she's the only human-looking thing in the whole darn joint," said Tom. "He won't do her no harm. He'll fall over any second and sleep it off."

"No, sir," said Douglas. "He knows she warned us and we're coming to rescue her. He doesn't want us revealing his guilty secret, so maybe tonight he's going to destroy her once and for all."

"How could he know she warned us? We didn't even know ourselves till we got away from here."

"He made her tell, put coins in the machine; that's one thing she can't lie on, the cards, all them tarot skulls and bones. She just can't help telling the truth and she gave him a card, sure, with two little knights on it, no bigger than kids, you see? That's us, clubs in our hands, coming down the street."

"One last time!" cried Mr. Black from the cave inside. "I'm puttin' the coin in. One last time now, dammit, tell me! Is this damn arcade ever goin' to make money or do I declare bankruptcy? Like all women; sit there, cold fish, while a man starves! Gimme the card. There! Now, let me see." He held the card up to the light.

"Oh, my gosh!" whispered Douglas. "Get ready."

"No!" cried Mr. Black. "Liar! Liar! Take that!" He smashed his fist through the case. Glass exploded in a great shower of starlight, it seemed, and fell away in darkness. The witch sat naked, in the open air, reserved and calm, waiting for the second blow.

"No!" Douglas plunged through the door. "Mr. Black!"

"Doug!" cried Tom.

Mr. Black wheeled at Tom's shout. He raised the knife blindly in the air as if to strike. Douglas froze. Then, eyes wide, lids blinking once, Mr. Black turned perfectly so he fell with his back toward the floor and took what seemed a thousand years to strike, his flashlight flung from his right hand, the knife scuttling away like a silverfish from the left.

Tom moved slowly in to look at the long-strewn figure in the dark. "Doug, is he dead?"

"No, just the shock of Mme. Tarot's predictions. Boy, he's got a scalded look. Horrible, that's what the cards must have been."

The man slept noisily on the floor.

Douglas picked up the strewn tarot cards, put them, trembling, in his pocket. "Come on, Tom, let's get her out of here before it's too late."

"Kidnap her? You're crazy!"

"You wanna be guilty of aiding and abetting an even worse crime? Murder, for instance?"

"For gosh sakes, you can't kill a darn old dummy!"

But Doug was not listening. He had reached through the open case and now, as if she had waited for too many years, the wax Tarot Witch with a rustling sigh, leaned forward and fell slowly slowly down into his arms.

The town clock struck nine forty-five. The moon was high and filled all the sky with a warm but wintry light. The sidewalk was solid silver on which black shadows moved. Douglas moved with the thing of velvet and fairy wax in his arms, stopping to hide in pools of shadow under trembling trees, alone. He listened, looking back. A sound of running mice. Tom burst around the corner and pulled up beside him.

"Doug, I stayed behind. I was afraid Mr. Black was, well . . . then he began to come alive . . . swearing. . . . Oh, Doug, if he catches you with his dummy! What will our folks think? Stealing!"

"Quiet!"

They listened to the moonlit river of street behind them. "Now, Tom, you can come help me rescue her, but you can't if you say 'dummy' or talk loud or drag along as so much dead weight."

"I'll help!" Tom assumed half the weight. "My gosh, she's light!"

"She was real young when Napoleon . . ." Douglas stopped. "Old people are heavy. That's how you tell."

"But why? Tell me why all this running around for her, Doug. Why?"

Why? Douglas blinked and stopped. Things had gone so fast, he had run so far and his blood was so high, he had long since forgotten why. Only now, as they moved again along the sidewalk, shadows like black butterflies on their eyelids, the thick smell of dusty wax on their hands, did he have time to reason why, and, slowly, speak of it, his voice was strange as moonlight.

"Tom, a couple weeks ago, I found out I was alive. Boy, did I hop around. And then, just last week in the movies, I found out I'd have to die someday. I never thought of that, really. And all of a sudden it was like knowing the Y.M.C.A. was going to be shut up forever—or school, which isn't so bad as we like to think, being over for good, and all the peach trees outside town shriveling up and the ravine being filled in and no place to play ever again and me sick in bed for as long as I could think and everything dark, and I got scared. So, I don't know; what I want to do is this: help Mme. Tarot. I'll hide her a few weeks or months while I look up in the black-magic books at the library how to undo spells and get her out of the wax to run around in the world again after all this time. And she'll be so grateful, she'll lay out the cards with all those devils and cups and swords and bones on them and tell me what sump holes to walk around and when to stay in bed on certain Thursday afternoons. I'll live forever, or next thing to it."

"You don't believe that."

"Yes, I do, or most of it. Watch it now, here's the ravine. We'll cut down through by the dump heap, and . . ."

Tom stopped. Douglas had stopped him. The boys did not turn, but they heard the heavy clubbing blows of feet behind them, each one like a shotgun set off in the bed of a dry lake not far away. Someone was shouting and cursing.

"Tom, you let him follow you!"

As they ran a giant hand lifted and tossed them aside, and Mr. Black was there laying to left and right and the boys, crying out, on the grass, saw the raving man, spittle showering the air from his biting teeth and widened lips. He held the witch by her neck and one arm and glared with fiery eyes down on the boys.

"This is mine! To do with like I want! What you mean, taking her? Caused all my trouble—money, business, everything. Here's what I think of her!"

"No!" shouted Douglas.

But like a great iron catapult, the huge arms hoisted the figure up against the moon and flourished and wheeled the fragile body upon the stars and let it fly out with a curse and a rustling wind down the air into the ravine to tumble and take avalanches of junk with her into white dust and cinders.

"No!" said Douglas, sitting there, looking down. "NO!"

The big man toppled on the rim of the hill, gasping. "You just thank God it wasn't you I did that to!" He moved unsteadily away, falling once, getting up, talking to himself, laughing, swearing, then gone.

Douglas sat on the edge of the ravine and wept. After a long while he blew his nose. He looked at Tom.

"Tom, it's late. Dad'll be out walking, looking for us. We should've been home an hour ago. Run back along Washington Street, get Dad and bring him here."

"You're not going down in that ravine?"

"She's city property now, on the trash dump, and nobody cares what happens, not even Mr. Black. Tell Dad what he's coming here for and he don't have to be seen coming home with me and her. I'll take her the back way around and nobody'll ever know."

"She won't be no good to you now, her machinery all busted."

"We can't leave her out in the rain, don't you see, Tom?"

"Sure."

Tom moved slowly off.

Douglas let himself down the hill, walking in piles of cinder and old paper and tin cans. Halfway down he stopped and listened. He peered at the multicolored dimness, the great landslide below. "Mme. Tarot?" he almost whispered. "Mme. Tarot?"

At the bottom of the hill in the moonlight he thought he saw her white wax hand move. It was a piece of white paper blowing. But he went toward it anyway....

The town clock struck midnight. The house lights around were mostly turned out. In the workshop garage the two boys and the man stood back

201

from the witch, who now sat, rearranged and at peace, in an old wicker chair before an oilcloth-covered card table, upon which were spread, in fantastic fans of popes and clowns and cardinals and deaths and suns and comets, the tarot cards upon which one wax hand touched.

Father was speaking.

". . . know how it is. When I was a boy, when the circus left town I ran around collecting a million posters. Later it was breeding rabbits, and magic. I built illusions in the attic and couldn't get them out." He nodded to the witch. "Oh, I remember she told my fortune once, thirty years ago. Well, clean her up good, then come in to bed. We'll build her a special case Saturday." He moved out the garage door but stopped when Douglas spoke softly.

"Dad. Thanks. Thanks for the walk home. Thanks."

"Heck," said Father, and was gone.

The two boys left alone with the witch looked at each other. "Gosh, right down the main street we go, all four of us, you, me, Dad, the witch! Dad's one in a million!"

"Tomorrow," said Douglas, "I go down and buy the rest of the machine from Mr. Black, for ten bucks, or he'll throw it out."

"Sure." Tom looked at the old woman there in the wicker chair. "Boy, she sure looks alive. I wonder what's inside."

"Little tiny bird bones. All that's left of Mme. Tarot after Napoleon——"

"No machinery at all? Why don't we just cut her open and see?"

"Plenty of time for that, Tom."

"When?"

"Well, in a year, two years, when I'm fourteen or fifteen, then's the time to do it. Right now I don't want to know nothing except she's here. And tomorrow I get to work on the spells to let her escape forever. Some night you'll hear that a strange, beautiful Italian girl was seen downtown in a summer dress, buying a ticket for the East and everyone saw her at the station and saw her on the train as it pulled out and everyone said she was the prettiest girl they ever saw, and when you hear that, Tom—and believe me, the news will get around fast! nobody knowing *where* she came from or *where* she went—then you'll know I worked the spell and set her free. And then, as I said, a year, two years from now, on that night when that train pulls out, it'll be the time when we can cut through the wax. With her gone, you're liable to find nothing but little cogs and wheels and stuff inside her. That's how it is."

Douglas picked up the witch's hand and moved it over the dance of life, the frolic of bone-white death, the dates and dooms, the fates and follies, tapping, touching, whispering her worn-down fingernails. Her face tilted with some secret equilibrium and looked at the boys and the eyes flashed bright in the raw bulb light, unblinking.

"Tell your fortune, Tom?" asked Douglas quietly.

"Sure."

A card fell from the witch's voluminous sleeve.

"Tom, you see that? A card, hidden away, and now she throws it out at us!" Douglas held the card to the light. "It's blank. I'll put it in a matchbox full of chemicals during the night. Tomorrow we'll open the box and there the message'll be!"

"What'll it say?"

Douglas closed his eyes the better to see the words.

"It'll say. 'Thanks from your humble servant and grateful friend, Mme. Floristan Mariani Tarot, the Chiromancer, Soul Healer, and Deep-Down Diviner of Fates and Furies.'"

Tom laughed and shook his brother's arm.

"Go on, Doug, what else, what else?"

"Let me see . . . And it'll say, 'Hey nonny no! . . . is't not fine to dance and sing? . . . when the bells of death do ring . . . and turn upon the toe . . . and sing Hey nonny no!' And it'll say, 'Tom and Douglas Spaulding, everything you wish for, all your life through, you'll get . . .' And it'll say that we'll live forever, you and me, Tom, we'll live forever. . . ."

"All that on just this one card?"

"All that, every single bit of it, Tom."

In the light of the electric bulb they bent, the two boys' heads down, the witch's head down, staring and staring at the beautiful blank but promising white card, their bright eyes sensing each and every incredibly hidden word that would soon rise up from pale oblivion.

"Hey," said Tom in the softest of voices.

And Douglas repeated in a glorious whisper, "Hey . . ."

FAINTLY, the voice chanted under the fiery green trees at noon.

"... nine, ten, eleven, twelve ..."

Douglas moved slowly across the lawn. "Tom, what you counting?"

"... thirteen, fourteen, shut up, sixteen, seventeen, cicadas, eighteen, nineteen ... !"

"Cicadas?"

"Oh hell!" Tom unsqueezed his eyes. "Hell, hell, hell!"

"Better not let people hear you swearing."

"Hell, hell, hell is a place!" Tom cried. "Now I got to start all over. I was counting the times the cicadas buzz every fifteen seconds." He held up his two dollar watch. "You time it, then add thirty-nine and you get the temperature at that very moment." He looked at the watch, one eye shut, tilted his head and whispered again, "One, two, three ... !"

Douglas turned his head slowly, listening. Somewhere in the burning bone-colored sky a great copper wire was strummed and shaken. Again and again the piercing metallic vibrations, like charges of raw electricity, fell in paralyzing shocks from the stunned trees.

"Seven!" counted Tom. "Eight."

Douglas walked slowly up the porch steps. Painfully he peered into the hall. He stayed there a moment, then slowly he stepped back out on the porch and called weakly to Tom. "It's exactly eighty-seven degrees Fahrenheit."

"—twenty-seven, twenty-eight—"

"Hey, Tom, you hear me?"

"I hear you—thirty, thirty-one! Get away! Two, three, thirty-four!"

"You can stop counting now, right inside on that old thermometer it's eighty-seven and going up, without the help of no katydids."

"Cicadas! Thirty-nine, forty! Not katydids! Forty-two!"

"Eighty-seven degrees, I thought you'd like to know."

"Forty-five, that's inside, not outside! Forty-nine, fifty, fifty-one! Fifty-two, fifty-three! Fifty-three plus thirty-nine is—ninety-two degrees!"

"Who says?"

"I say! Not eighty-seven degrees Fahrenheit! But ninety-two degrees Spaulding!"

"You and who else?"

Tom jumped up and stood red-faced, staring at the sun. "Me and the cicadas, that's who! Me and the cicadas! You're out-numbered! Ninety-two, ninety-two, ninety-two degrees Spaulding, by gosh!"

They both stood looking at the merciless unclouded sky like a camera that has broken and stares, shutter wide, at a motionless and stricken town dying in a fiery sweat.

Douglas shut his eyes and saw two idiot suns dancing on the reverse side of the pinkly translucent lids.

"One ... two ... three ..."

Douglas felt his lips move.

"... four ... five ... six ..."

This time the cicadas sang even faster.

FROM noontime to sundown, from midnight to sunrise, one man, one horse, and one wagon were known to all twenty-six thousand three hundred forty-nine inhabitants of Green Town, Illinois.

In the middle of the day, for no reason quickly apparent, children would stop still and say:

"Here comes Mr. Jonas!"

"Here comes Ned!"

"Here comes the wagon!"

Older folks might peer north or south, east or west and see no sign of the man named Jonas, the horse named Ned, or the wagon which was a Conestoga of the kind that bucked the prairie tides to beach on the wilderness.

But then if you borrowed the ear of a dog and tuned it high and stretched it taut you could hear, miles and miles across the town a singing like a rabbi in the lost lands, a Moslem in a tower. Always, Mr. Jonas's voice went clear before him so people had a half an hour, an hour, to prepare for his arrival. And by the time his wagon appeared, the curbs were lined by children, as for a parade.

So here came the wagon and on its high board seat under a persimmon-colored umbrella, the reins like a stream of water in his gentle hands, was Mr. Jonas, singing.

*"Junk! Junk!*
*No, sir, not Junk!*
*Junk! Junk!*
*No, ma'am, not Junk!*

*Bricabracs, brickbats!*
*Knitting needles, knick-knacks!*
*Kickshaws! Curios!*
*Camisoles! Cameos!*
*But . . . Junk!*
*Junk!*
*No, sir, not . . . Junk!"*

As anyone could tell who had heard the songs Mr. Jonas made up as he passed, he was no ordinary junkman. To all appearances, yes, the way he dressed in tatters of moss-corduroy and the felt cap on his head, covered with old presidential campaign buttons going back before Manila Bay. But he was unusual in this way: not only did he tread the sunlight, but often you could see him and his horse swimming along the moonlit streets, circling and recircling by night the islands, the blocks where all the people lived he had known all of his life. And in that wagon he carried things he had picked up here and there and carried for a day or a week or a year until someone wanted and needed them. Then all they had to say was, "I want that clock," or "How about the mattress?" And Jonas would hand it over, take no money, and drive away, considering the words for another tune.

So it happened that often he was the only man alive in all Green Town at three in the morning and often people with headaches, seeing him amble by with his moon-shimmered horse, would run out to see if by chance he had aspirin, which he did. More than once he had delivered babies at four in the morning and only then had people noticed how incredibly clean his hands and fingernails were—the hands of a rich man who had another life somewhere they could not guess. Sometimes he would drive people to work downtown, or sometimes, when men could not sleep, go up on their porch and bring cigars and sit with them and smoke and talk until dawn.

Whoever he was or whatever he was and no matter how different and crazy he seemed, he was not crazy. As he himself had often explained gently, he had tired of business in Chicago many years before and looked around for a way to spend the rest of his life. Couldn't stand churches, though he appreciated their ideas, and having a tendency toward preaching and decanting knowledge, he bought the horse and wagon and set out to spend the rest of his life seeing to it that one part of town had a chance to pick over what the other part of town had cast off. He looked upon himself as a kind of process, like osmosis, that made various cultures within the city limits available one to another. He could not stand waste, for he knew that one man's junk is another man's luxury.

So adults, and especially children, clambered up to peer over into the vast treasure horde in the back of the wagon.

"Now, remember," said Mr. Jonas, "you can have what you want if you really want it. The test is, ask yourself, Do I want it with all my heart? Could I live through the day without it? If you figure to be dead by sundown, grab the darned thing and run. I'll be happy to let you have whatever it is."

And the children searched the vast heaps of parchments and brocades and bolts of wallpaper and marble ash trays and vests and roller skates and great fat overstuffed chairs and end tables and crystal chandeliers. For a while you just heard whispering and rattling and tinkling. Mr. Jonas watched, comfortably puffing on his pipe, and the children knew he watched. Sometimes their hands reached out for a game of checkers or a string of beads or an old chair, and just as they touched it they looked up and there were Mr. Jonas's eyes gently questioning them. And they pulled their hand away and looked further on. Until at last each of them put their hand on a single item and left it there. Their faces came up and this time their faces were so bright Mr. Jonas had to laugh. He put up his hand as if to fend off the brightness of their faces from his eyes. He covered his eyes for a moment. When he did this, the children yelled their thanks, grabbed their roller skates or clay tiles or bumbershoots and, dropping off, ran.

And the children came back in a moment with something of their own in their hands, a doll or a game they had grown tired of, something the fun had gone out of, like the flavor from gum, and now it was time for it to pass on to some other part of town where, seen for the first time, it would be revivified and would revivify others. These tokens of exchange were shyly dropped over the rim of the wagon down into unseen riches and then the wagon was trundling on, flickering light on its great spindling sunflower wheels and Mr. Jonas singing again . . .

> *"Junk! Junk!*
> *No, sir, not Junk!*
> *No, ma'am, not Junk!"*

until he was out of sight and only the dogs, in the shadow pools under trees, heard the rabbi in the wilderness, and twitched their tails . . .

". . . junk . . ."
Fading.
". . . junk . . ."
A whisper.
". . . junk . . ." Gone.
And the dogs asleep.

THE sidewalks were haunted by dust ghosts all night as the furnace wind summoned them up, swung them about, and gentled them down in a warm spice on the lawns. Trees, shaken by the footsteps of late-night strollers, sifted avalanches of dust. From midnight on, it seemed a volcano beyond the town was showering red-hot ashes everywhere, crusting slumberless night watchmen and irritable dogs. Each house was a yellow attic smoldering with spontaneous combustion at three in the morning.

Dawn, then, was a time where things changed element for element. Air ran like hot spring waters nowhere, with no sound. The lake was a quantity of steam very still and deep over valleys of fish and sand held baking under its serene vapors. Tar was poured licorice in the streets, red bricks were brass and gold, roof tops were paved with bronze. The high-tension wires were lightning held forever, blazing, a threat above the unslept houses.

The cicadas sang louder and yet louder.

The sun did not rise, it overflowed.

In his room, his face a bubbled mass of perspiration, Douglas melted on his bed.

"Wow," said Tom, entering. "Come on, Doug. We'll drown in the river all day."

Douglas breathed out. Douglas breathed in. Sweat trickled down his neck.

"Doug, you awake?"

The slightest nod of the head.

"You don't feel good, huh? Boy, this house'll burn

down today." He put his hand on Douglas's brow. It was like touching a blazing stove lid. He pulled his fingers away, startled. He turned and went downstairs.

"Mom," he said, "Doug's really sick."

His mother, taking eggs out of the icebox, stopped, let a quick look of concern cross her face, put the eggs back, and followed Tom upstairs.

Douglas had not moved so much as a finger.

The cicadas were screaming now.

At noon, running as if the sun were after him to smash him to the ground, the doctor pulled up on the front porch, gasping, his eyes weary already, and gave his bag to Tom.

At one o'clock the doctor came out of the house, shaking his head. Tom and his mother stood behind the screen door, as the doctor talked in a low voice, saying over and over again he didn't know, he didn't know. He put his Panama hat on his head, gazed at the sunlight blistering and shriveling the trees overhead, hesitated like a man plunging into the outer rim of hell, and ran again for his car. The exhaust of the car left a great pall of blue smoke in the pulsing air for five minutes after he was gone.

Tom took the ice pick in the kitchen and chipped a pound of ice into prisms which he carried upstairs. Mother was sitting on the bed and the only sound in the room was Douglas breathing in steam and breathing out fire. They put the ice in handkerchiefs on his face and along his body. They drew the shades and made the room like a cave. They sat there until two o'clock, bringing up more ice. Then they touched Douglas's brow again and it was like a lamp that had burned all night. After touching him you looked at your fingers to make sure they weren't seared to the bone.

Mother opened her mouth to say something, but the cicadas were so loud now they shook dust down from the ceiling.

Inside redness, inside blindness, Douglas lay listening to the dim piston of his heart and the muddy ebb and flow of the blood in his arms and legs.

His lips were heavy and would not move. His thoughts were heavy and barely ticked like seed pellets falling in an hourglass slow one by falling one. Tick.

Around a bright steel corner of rail a trolley swung, throwing a crumbling wave of sizzling sparks, its clamorous bell knocking ten thousand times until it blended with the cicadas. Mr. Tridden waved. The trolley stormed around a corner like a cannonade and dissolved. Mr. Tridden!

*Tick*. A pellet fell. *Tick*.

"Chug-a-chug-ding! Woo-woooo!"

On the roof top a boy locomoted, pulling an invisible whistle string, then froze into a statue. "John! John Huff, you! Hate you, John! John, we're pals! Don't hate you, no."

John fell down the elm-tree corridor like someone falling down an endless summer well, dwindling away.

Tick. John Huff. Tick. Sand pellet dropping. Tick. John . . .

Douglas moved his head flat over, crashing on the white white terribly white pillow.

The ladies in the Green Machine sailed by in a sound of black seal barking, lifting hands as white as doves. They sank into the lawn's deep waters, their gloves still waving to him as the grass closed over. . . .

Miss Fern! Miss Roberta!

Tick . . . Tick . . .

And quickly then from a window across the way Colonel Freeleigh leaned out with the face of a clock, and buffalo dust sprang up in the street. Colonel Freeleigh spanged and rattled, his jaw fell open, a mainspring shot out and dangled on the air instead of his tongue. He collapsed like a puppet on the sill, one arm still waving. . . .

Mr. Auffmann rode by in something that was

bright and something like the trolley and the green electric runabout; and it trailed glorious clouds and it put out your eyes like the sun. "Mr. Auffmann, did you invent it?" he cried. "Did you finally build the Happiness Machine?"

But then he saw there was no bottom to the machine. Mr. Auffmann ran along on the ground, carrying the whole incredible frame from his shoulders.

"Happiness, Doug, here goes happiness!" And he went the way of the trolley, John Huff, and the dove-fingered ladies.

Above on the roof a tapping sound. Tap-rap-bang. Pause. Tap-rap-bang. Nail and hammer. Hammer and nail. A bird choir. And an old woman singing in a frail but hearty voice.

> *"Yes, we'll gather at the river . . . river . . . river*
> *. . .*
> *Yes, we'll gather at the river . . .*
> *That flows by the throne of God . . ."*

"Grandma! Great-grandma!"
Tap, softly, tap. Tap, softly, tap.
". . . river . . . river . . ."
And now it was only the birds picking up their tiny feet and putting them down again on the roof. Rattle-rattle. Scratch. Peep. Peep. Soft. Soft.
". . . river . . ."
Douglas took one breath and let it all out at once, wailing.

He did not hear his mother run into the room.

A fly, like the burning ash of a cigarette, fell upon his senseless hand, sizzled, and flew away.

Four o'clock in the afternoon. Flies dead on the pavement. Dogs wet mops in their kennels. Shadows herded under trees. Downtown stores shut up and locked. The lake shore empty. The lake full of thousands of people up to their necks in the warm but soothing water.

Four-fifteen. Along the brick streets of town the junk wagon moved, with Mr. Jonas singing on it.

Tom, driven out of the house by the scorched look on Douglas's face, walked slowly down to the curb as the wagon stopped.

"Hi, Mr. Jonas."

"Hello, Tom."

Tom and Mr. Jonas were alone on the street with all that beautiful junk in the wagon to look at and neither of them looking at it. Mr. Jonas didn't say anything right away. He lit his pipe and puffed it, nodding his head as if he knew before he asked, that something was wrong.

"Tom?" he said.

"It's my brother," said Tom. "It's Doug."

Mr. Jonas looked up at the house.

"He's sick," said Tom. "He's dying!"

"Oh, now, that can't be so," said Mr. Jonas, scowling around at the very real world where nothing that vaguely looked like death could be found on this quiet day.

"He's dying," said Tom. "And the doctor doesn't know what's wrong. The heat, he said, nothing but the heat. Can that be, Mr. Jonas? Can the heat kill people, even in a dark room?"

"Well," said Mr. Jonas and stopped.

For Tom was crying now.

"I always thought I hated him . . . that's what I thought . . . we fight half the time . . . I guess I did hate him . . . sometimes . . . but now . . . now. Oh, Mr. Jonas, if only . . ."

"If only what, boy?"

"If only you had something in this wagon would help. Something I could pick and take upstairs and make him okay."

Tom cried again.

Mr. Jonas took out his red bandanna handkerchief and handed it to Tom. Tom wiped his nose and eyes with the handkerchief.

"It's been a tough summer," Tom said. "Lots of things have happened to Doug."

"Tell me about them," said the junkman.

"Well," said Tom, gasping for breath, not quite done crying yet, "he lost his best aggie for one, a real beaut. And on top of that somebody stole his catcher's mitt, it cost a dollar ninety-five. Then there was the bad trade he made of his fossil stones and shell collection with Charlie Woodman for a Tarzan clay statue you got by saving up macaroni box tops. Dropped the Tarzan statue on the sidewalk second day he had it."

"That's a shame," said the junkman and really saw all the pieces on the cement.

"Then he didn't get the book of magic tricks he wanted for his birthday, got a pair of pants and a shirt instead. That's enough to ruin the summer right there."

"Parents sometimes forget how it is," said Mr. Jonas.

"Sure," Tom continued in a low voice, "then Doug's genuine set of Tower-of-London manacles left out all night and rusted. And worst of all, I grew one inch taller, catching up with him almost."

"Is that all?" asked the junkman quietly.

"I could think of ten dozen other things, all as bad or worse. Some summers you get a run of luck like that. It's been silverfish getting in his comics collection or mildew in his new tennis shoes ever since Doug got out of school."

"I remember years like that," said the junkman. He looked off at the sky and there were all the years.

"So there you are, Mr. Jonas. That's it. That's why he's dying. . . ."

Tom stopped and looked away.

"Let me think," said Mr. Jonas.

"Can you help, Mr. Jonas? *Can* you?"

Mr. Jonas looked deep in the big old wagon and shook his head. Now, in the sunlight, his face looked tired and he was beginning to perspire. Then he peered into the mounds of vases and peeling lamp shades and marble nymphs and satyrs made of greening copper. He sighed. He turned and picked up the reins and gave them a gentle shake. "Tom," he said, looking at the horse's back, "I'll see you later. I got to plan. I got to look around and come again after supper. Even then, who knows? Until then . . ." He reached down and picked up a little set of Japanese wind-crystals. "Hang these in his upstairs window. They make a nice cool music!"

Tom stood with the wind-crystals in his hands as the wagon rolled away. He held them up and there was no wind, they did not move. They could not make a sound.

Seven o'clock. The town resembled a vast hearth over which the shudderings of heat moved again and again from the west. Charcoal-colored shadows quivered outward from every house, every tree. A redhaired man moved along below. Tom, seeing him illumined by the dying but ferocious sun, saw a torch proudly carrying itself, saw a fiery fox, saw the devil marching in his own country.

At seven-thirty Mrs. Spaulding came out of the back door of the house to empty some watermelon rinds into the garbage pail and saw Mr. Jonas standing there.

"How is the boy?" said Mr. Jonas.

Mrs. Spaulding stood there for a moment, a response trembling on her lips.

"May I see him, please?" said Mr. Jonas.

Still she could say nothing.

"I know the boy well," he said. "Seen him most every day of his life since he was out and around. I've something for him in the wagon."

"He's not——" She was going to say "conscious," but she said, "awake. He's not awake, Mr. Jonas. The doctor said he's not to be disturbed. Oh, we don't know *what's* wrong!"

"Even if he's not 'awake,'" said Mr. Jonas, "I'd like to talk to him. Sometimes the things you hear in your sleep are more important, you listen better, it gets through."

"I'm sorry, Mr. Jonas, I just can't take the chance." Mrs. Spaulding caught hold of the screen-door handle and held fast to it. "Thanks. Thank you, anyway, for coming by."

"Yes, ma'am," said Mr. Jonas.

He did not move. He stood looking up at the window above. Mrs. Spaulding went in the house and shut the screen door.

Upstairs, on his bed, Douglas breathed.

It was a sound like a sharp knife going in and out, in and out, of a sheath.

At eight o'clock the doctor came and went again shaking his head, his coat off, his tie untied, looking as if he had lost thirty pounds that day. At nine o'clock Tom and Mother and Father carried a cot outside and brought Douglas down to sleep in the yard under the apple tree where, if there might be a wind, it would find him sooner than in the terrible rooms above. Then they went back and forth until eleven o'clock, when they set the alarm clock to wake them at three and chip more ice to refill the packs.

The house was dark and still at last, and they slept.

At twelve thirty-five, Douglas's eyes flinched.

The moon had begun to rise.

And far away a voice began to sing.

It was a high sad voice rising and falling. It was a clear voice and it was in tune. You could not make out the words.

The moon came over the edge of the lake and looked upon Green Town, Illinois, and saw it all and showed it all, every house, every tree, every pre-historic-remembering dog twitching in his simple dreams.

And it seemed that the higher the moon the nearer and louder and clearer the voice that was singing.

And Douglas turned in his fever and sighed.

Perhaps it was an hour before the moon spilled all its light upon the world, perhaps less. But the voice was nearer now and a sound like the beating of a heart which was really the motion of a horse's hoofs on the brick streets muffled by the hot thick foliage of the trees.

And there was another sound like a door slowly opening or closing, squeaking, squealing softly from time to time. The sound of a wagon.

And down the street in the light of the risen moon came the horse pulling the wagon and the wagon riding the lean body of Mr. Jonas easy and casual on the high seat. He wore his hat as if he were still out under the summer sun and he moved his hands on occasion to ripple the reins like a flow of water on the air above the horse's back. Very slowly the wagon moved down the street with Mr. Jonas singing, and in his sleep Douglas seemed for a moment to stop breathing and listen.

"Air, air . . . who will buy this air. . . . Air like water and air like ice . . . buy it once and you'll buy it twice . . . here's the April air . . . here's an autumn breeze . . . here's papaya wind from the Antilles. . . . Air, air, sweet pickled air . . . fair . . . rare . . . from everywhere . . . bottled and capped and scented with thyme, all that you want of air for a dime!"

At the end of this the wagon was at the curb. And someone stood in the yard, treading his shadow, carrying two beetle-green bottles which glittered like cats' eyes. Mr. Jonas looked at the cot there and called the boy's name once, twice, three times, softly. Mr. Jonas swayed in indecision, looked at the bottles he carried, made his decision, and moved forward stealthily to sit on the grass and look at this boy crushed down by the great weight of summer.

"Doug," he said, "you just lie quiet. You don't have to say anything or open your eyes. You don't even have to pretend to listen. But inside there, I know you hear me, and it's old Jonas, your friend. Your friend," he repeated and nodded.

He reached up and picked an apple off the tree, turned it round, took a bite, chewed, and continued.

"Some people turn sad awfully young," he said.

"No special reason, it seems, but they seem almost to be born that way. They bruise easier, tire faster, cry quicker, remember longer and, as I say, get sadder younger than anyone else in the world. I know, for I'm one of them."

He took another bite of the apple and chewed it.

"Well, now, where are we?" he asked.

"A hot night, not a breath stirring, in August," he answered himself. "Killing hot. And a long summer it's been and too much happening, eh? Too much. And it's getting on toward one o'clock and no sign of a wind or rain. And in a moment now I'm going to get up and go. But when I go, and remember this clearly, I will leave these two bottles here upon your bed. And when I've gone I want you to wait a little while and then slowly open your eyes and sit up and reach over and drink the contents of these bottles. Not with your mouth, no. Drink with your nose. Tilt the bottles, uncork them, and let what is in them go right down into your head. Read the labels first, of course. But here, let me read them for you."

He lifted one bottle into the light.

"'GREEN DUSK FOR DREAMING BRAND PURE NORTHERN AIR,'" he read. "'Derived from the atmosphere of the white Arctic in the spring of 1900, and mixed with the wind from the upper Hudson Valley in the month of April, 1910, and containing particles of dust seen shining in the sunset of one day in the meadows around Grinnell, Iowa, when a cool air rose to be captured from a lake and a little creek and a natural spring.'

"Now the small print," he said. He squinted. "'Also containing molecules of vapor from menthol, lime, papaya, and watermelon and all other water-smelling, cool-savored fruits and trees like camphor and herbs like wintergreen and the breath of a rising wind from the Des Plaines River itself. Guaranteed most refreshing and cool. To be taken on summer nights when the heat passes ninety.'"

He picked up the other bottle.

"This one the same, save I've collected a wind

from the Aran Isles and one from off Dublin Bay with salt on it and a strip of flannel fog from the coast of Iceland."

He put the two bottles on the bed.

"One last direction." He stood by the cot and leaned over and spoke quietly. "When you're drinking these, remember: It was bottled by a friend. The S. J. Jonas Bottling Company, Green Town, Illinois —August, 1928. A vintage year, boy . . . a vintage year."

A moment later there was the sound of reins slapping the back of the horse in the moonlight, and the rumble of the wagon down the street and away.

After a moment Douglas's eyes twitched and, very slowly, opened.

"Mother!" whispered Tom. "Dad! Doug, it's Doug! He's going to be well. I just went down to check and—come *on!*"

Tom ran out of the house. His parents followed.

Douglas was asleep as they approached. Tom motioned to his parents, smiling wildly. They bent over the cot.

A single exhalation, a pause, a single exhalation, a pause, as the three bent there.

Douglas's mouth was slightly open and from his lips and from the thin vents of his nostrils, gently there rose a scent of cool night and cool water and cool white snow and cool green moss, and cool moonlight on silver pebbles lying at the bottom of a quiet river and cool clear water at the bottom of a small white stone well.

It was like holding their heads down for a brief moment to the pulse of an apple-scented fountain flowing cool up into the air and washing their faces.

They could not move for a long time.

THE next morning was a morning of no caterpillars. The world that had been full to bursting with tiny bundles of black and brown fur trundling on their way to green leaf and tremulous grass blade, was suddenly empty. The sound that was no sound, the billion footfalls of the caterpillars stomping through their own universe, died. Tom, who said he could hear that sound, precious as it was, looked with wonder at a town where not a single bird's mouthful stirred. Too, the cicadas had ceased.

Then, in the silence, a great sighing rustle began and they knew then why the absence of caterpillar and abrupt silence of cicada.

Summer rain.

The rain began light, a touch. The rain increased and fell heavily. It played the sidewalks and roofs like great pianos.

And upstairs, Douglas, inside again, like a fall of snow in his bed, turned his head and opened his eyes to see the freshly falling sky and slowly slowly twitch his fingers toward his yellow nickel pad and yellow Ticonderoga pencil. . . .

THERE was a great flurry of arrival. Somewhere trumpets were shouting. Somewhere rooms were teeming with boarders and neighbors having afternoon tea. An aunt had arrived and her name was Rose and you could hear her voice clarion clear above the others, and you could imagine her warm and huge as a hothouse rose, exactly like her name, filling any room she sat in. But right now, to Douglas, the voice, the commotion, were nothing at all. He had come from his own house, and now stood outside Grandma's kitchen door just as Grandma, having excused herself from the chicken squabble in the parlor, whisked into her own domain and set about making supper. She saw him standing there, opened the screen door for him, kissed his brow, brushed his pale hair back from his eyes, looked him straight on in the face to see if the fever had fallen to ashes and, seeing that it had, went on, singing, to her work.

Grandma, he had often wanted to say, Is this where the world began? For surely it had begun in no other than a place like this. The kitchen, without doubt, was the center of creation, all things revolved about it; it was the pediment that sustained the temple.

Eyes shut to let his nose wander, he snuffed deeply. He moved in the hell-fire steams and sudden baking-powder flurries of snow in this miraculous climate where Grandma, with the look of the Indies in her eyes and the flesh of two firm warm hens in her bodice, Grandma of the thousand arms, shook, bast-

223

ed, whipped, beat, minced, diced, peeled, wrapped, salted, stirred.

Blind, he touched his way to the pantry door. A squeal of laughter rang from the parlor, teacups tinkled. But he moved on into the cool underwater green and wild-persimmon country where the slung and hanging odor of creamy bananas ripened silently and bumped his head. Gnats fizzed angrily about vinegar cruets and his ears.

He opened his eyes. He saw bread waiting to be cut into slices of warm summer cloud, doughnuts strewn like clown hoops from some edible game. The faucets turned on and off in his cheeks. Here on the plum-shadowed side of the house with maple leaves making a creek-water running in the hot wind at the window he read spice-cabinet names.

How do I thank Mr. Jonas, he wondered, for what he's done? How do I thank him, how pay him back? No way, no way at all. You just can't pay. What then? What? Pass it on somehow, he thought, pass it on to someone else. Keep the chain moving. Look around, find someone, and pass it on. That was the only way. . . .

"Cayenne, marjoram, cinnamon."

The names of lost and fabulous cities through which storms of spice bloomed up and dusted away.

He tossed the cloves that had traveled from some dark continent where once they had spilled on milk marble, jack-stones for children with licorice hands.

And looking at one single label on a jar, he felt himself gone round the calendar to that private day this summer when he had looked at the circling world and found himself at its center.

The word on the jar was RELISH.

And he was glad he had decided to live.

RELISH! What a special name for the minced pickle sweetly crushed in its white-capped jar. The man who had named it, what a man he must have been. Roaring, stamping around, he must have tromped the joys of the world and jammed them in this jar and writ in a big hand, shouting, RELISH!

For its very sound meant rolling in sweet fields with roistering chestnut mares, mouths bearded with grass, plunging your head fathoms deep in trough water so the sea poured cavernously through your head. REL-ISH!

He put out his hand. And here was—SAVORY.

"What's Grandma cooking for dinner tonight?" said Aunt Rose's voice from the real world of after-noon in the parlor.

"No one knows what Grandma cooks," said Grandfather, home from the office early to tend this immense flower, "until we sit at table. There's always mystery, always suspense."

"Well, I always like to know what I'm going to eat," cried Aunt Rose, and laughed. The chandelier prisms in the dining room rang with pain.

Douglas moved deeper into pantry darkness.

"Savory . . . that's a swell word. And Basil and Betel. Capsicum. Curry. All great. But Relish, now, Relish with a capital R. No argument, that's the best."

Trailing veils of steam, Grandma came and went and came again with covered dishes from kitchen to table while the assembled company waited in silence. No one lifted lids to peer in at the hidden victuals. At last Grandma sat down, Grandpa said grace, and immediately thereafter the silverware flew up like a plague of locusts on the air.

When everyone's mouths. were absolutely crammed full of miracles, Grandmother sat back and said, "Well, how do you like it?"

And the relatives, including Aunt Rose, and the boarders, their teeth deliciously mortared together at this moment, faced a terrible dilemma. Speak and break the spell, or continue allowing this honey-syrup food of the gods to dissolve and melt away to glory in their mouths? They looked as if they might laugh or cry at the cruel dilemma. They looked as if they might sit there forever, untouched by fire or earth-quake, a shooting in the street, a massacre of inno-cents in the yard, overwhelmed with effluviums and promises of immortality. All villains were innocent in this moment of tender herbs, sweet celeries, luscious roots. The eye sped over a snow field where lay fricassees, salmagundis, gumbos, freshly invented succotashes, chowders, ragouts. The only sound was a primeval bubbling from the kitchen and the clocklike chiming of fork-on-plate announcing the seconds instead of the hours.

And then Aunt Rose gathered her indomitable pinkness and health and strength into herself with one deep breath and, fork poised on air, looking at the mystery there impaled, spoke in much too loud a voice.

"Oh, it's beautiful food all right. But what *is* this thing we're eating?"

The lemonade stopped tinkling in the frosty glasses, the forks ceased flashing on the air and came to rest on the table.

Douglas gave Aunt Rose that look which a shot deer gives the hunter before it falls dead. Wounded surprise appeared in each face down the line. The food was self-explanatory, wasn't it? It was its own philosophy, it asked and answered its own questions. Wasn't it enough that your blood and your body asked no more than this moment of ritual and rare incense?

"I really don't believe," said Aunt Rose, "that anyone heard my question."

At last Grandma let her lips open a trifle to allow the answer out.

"I call this our Thursday Special. We have it regularly."

This was a lie.

In all the years not one single dish resembled another. Was this one from the deep green sea? Had that one been shot from blue summer air? Was it a swimming food or a flying food, had it pumped blood or chlorophyll, had it walked or leaned after the sun? No one knew. No one asked. No one cared.

The most people did was stand in the kitchen

door and peer at the baking-powder explosions, enjoy the clangs and rattles and bangs like a factory gone wild where Grandma stared half blindly about, letting her fingers find their way among canisters and bowls.

Was she conscious of her talent? Hardly. If asked about her cooking, Grandma would look down at her hands which some glorious instinct sent on journeys to be gloved in flour, or to plumb disencumbered turkeys, wrist-deep in search for their animal souls. Her gray eyes blinked from spectacles warped by forty years of oven blasts and blinded with strewings of pepper and sage, so she sometimes flung cornstarch over steaks, amazingly tender, succulent steaks! And sometimes dropped apricots into meat loaves, cross-pollinated meats, herbs, fruits, vegetables with no prejudice, no tolerance for recipe or forumla, save that at the final moment of delivery, mouths watered, blood thundered in response. Her hands then, like the hands of Great-grandma before her, were Grandma's mystery, delight, and life. She looked at them in astonishment, but let them live their life the way they must absolutely lead it.

But now for the first time in endless years, here was an upstart, a questioner, a laboratory scientist almost, speaking out where silence could have been a virtue.

"Yes, yes, but what did you put *in* this Thursday Special?"

"Why," said Grandma evasively, "what does it *taste* like to you?"

Aunt Rose sniffed the morsel on the fork.

"Beef, or is it lamb? Ginger, or is it cinnamon? Ham sauce? Bilberries? Some biscuit thrown in? Chives? Almonds?"

"That's it *exactly*," said Grandma. "Second helpings, everyone?"

A great uproar ensued, a clashing of plates, a swarming of arms, a rush of voices which hoped to drown blasphemous inquiry forever, Douglas talking louder and making more motions than the rest. But in their faces you could see their world tottering, their happiness in danger. For they were the privileged members of a household which rushed from work or play when the first dinner bell was so much as clapped once in the hall. Their arrival in the dining room had been for countless years a sort of frantic musical chairs, as they shook out napkins in a white fluttering and seized up utensils as if recently starved in solitary confinement, waiting for the summons to fall downstairs in a mass of twitching elbows and overflow themselves at table. Now they clamored nervously, made obvious jokes, darting glances at Aunt Rose as if she concealed a bomb in that ample bosom that was ticking steadily on toward their doom.

Aunt Rose, sensing that silence was indeed a blessing devoted herself to three helpings of whatever it was on the plate and went upstairs to unlace her corset.

"Grandma," said Aunt Rose, down again. "Oh, what a kitchen you keep. It's really a mess, now, you must admit. Bottles and dishes and boxes all over, the labels off most everything, so how do you tell what you're using? I'd feel guilty if you didn't let me help you set things to rights while I'm visiting here. Let me roll up my sleeves."

"No, thank you very much," said Grandma.

Douglas heard them through the library walls and his heart thumped.

"It's like a Turkish bath in here," said Aunt Rose. "Let's have some windows open, roll up those shades so we can see what we're doing."

"Light hurts my eyes," said Grandma.

"I got the broom, I'll wash the dishes and stack them away neat. I got to help, now don't say a word."

"Go sit down," said Grandma.

"Why, Grandma, think how it'd help your cooking. You're a wonderful cook, it's true, but if you're this good in all this chaos—pure chaos—why, think

228

how fine you'd be, once things were put where you could lay hands on them."

"I never thought of that. . . ." said Grandma.

"Think on it, then. Say, for instance, modern kitchen methods helped you improve your cooking just ten or fifteen per cent. Your menfolk are already pure animal at the table. This time next week they'll be dying like flies from overeating. Food so pretty and fine they won't be able to stop the knife and fork."

"You really think so?" said Grandma, beginning to be interested.

"Grandma, don't give in!" whispered Douglas to the library wall.

But to his horror he heard them sweeping and dusting, throwing out half-empty sacks, pasting new labels on cans, putting dishes and pots and pans in drawers that had stood empty for years. Even the knives, which had lain like a catch of silvery fish on the kitchen tables, were dumped into boxes.

Grandfather had been listening behind Douglas for a full five minutes. Somewhat uneasily he scratched his chin. "Now that I think of it, that kitchen's been a mess right on down the line. Things need a little arrangement, no doubt. And if what Aunt Rose claims is true, Doug boy, it'll be a rare experience at supper tomorrow night."

"Yes, sir," said Douglas. "A rare experience."

"What's that?" asked Grandma.

Aunt Rose took a wrapped gift from behind her back.

Grandma opened it.

"A cookbook!" she cried. She let it drop on the table. "I don't need one of those! A handful of this, a pinch of that, a thimbleful of something else is all I ever use——"

"I'll help you market," said Aunt Rose. "And while we're at it, I been noticing your glasses, Grandma. You mean to say you been going around all these years peering through spectacles like those, with chipped lenses, all kind of bent? How do you see your way around without falling flat in the flour bin? We're taking you right down for new glasses."

And off they marched, Grandma bewildered, on Rose's elbow, into the summer afternoon.

They returned with groceries, new glasses, and a hairdo for Grandma. Grandma looked as if she had been chased around town. She gasped as Rose helped her into the house.

"There you are, Grandma. Now you got everything where you can find it. Now you can *see!*"

"Come on, Doug," said Grandfather. "Let's take a walk around the block and work up an appetite. This is going to be a night in history. One of the best damned suppers ever served, or I'll eat my vest."

Suppertime.

Smiling people stopped smiling. Douglas chewed one bite of food for three minutes, and then, pretending to wipe his mouth, lumped it in his napkin. He saw Tom and Dad do the same. People swashed the food together, making roads and patterns, drawing pictures in the gravy, forming castles of the potatoes, secretly passing meat chunks to the dog.

Grandfather excused himself early. "I'm full," he said.

All the boarders were pale and silent.

Grandma poked her own plate nervously.

"Isn't it a *fine* meal?" Aunt Rose asked everyone. "Got it on the table half an hour early, too!"

But the others were thinking that Monday followed Sunday, and Tuesday followed Monday, and so on for an entire week of sad breakfasts, melancholy lunches, and funereal dinners. In a few minutes the dining room was empty. Upstairs the boarders brooded in their rooms.

Grandma moved slowly, stunned, into her kitchen.

"This," said Grandfather, "has gone far enough!" He went to the foot of the stairs and called up into the dusty sunlight: "Come on down, everyone!"

The boarders murmured, all of them, locked in the dim, comfortable library. Grandfather quietly passed a derby hat. "For the kitty," he said. Then he put his hand heavily on Douglas's shoulder. "Douglas, we have a great mission for you, son. Now listen . . ." And he whispered his warm, friendly breath into the boy's ear.

Douglas found Aunt Rose, alone, cutting flowers in the garden the next afternoon.

"Aunt Rose," he said gravely, "why don't we go for a walk right now? I'll show you the butterfly ravine just down *that* way."

They walked together all around town. Douglas talked swiftly, nervously, not looking at her, listening only to the courthouse clock strike the afternoon hours.

Strolling back under the warm summer elms toward the house, Aunt Rose suddenly gasped and put her hand to her throat.

There, on the bottom of the porch step, was her luggage, neatly packed. On top of one suitcase, fluttering in the summer breeze, was a pink railroad ticket.

The boarders, all ten of them, were seated on the porch stiffly. Grandfather, like a train conductor, a mayor, a good friend, came down the steps solemnly.

"Rose," he said to her, taking her hand and shaking it up and down, "I have something to say to you."

"What is it?" said Aunt Rose.

"Aunt Rose," he said. "Good-by."

They heard the train chant away into the late afternoon hours. The porch was empty, the luggage gone, Aunt Rose's room unoccupied. Grandfather in the library, groped behind E. A. Poe for a small medicine bottle, smiling.

Grandma came home from a solitary shopping expedition to town.

231

"Where's Aunt Rose?"

"We said good-by to her at the station," said Grandfather. "We all wept. She hated to go, but she sent her best love to you and said she would return again in twelve years." Grandfather took out his solid gold watch. "And now I suggest we all repair to the library for a glass of sherry while waiting for Grandma to fix one of her amazing banquets."

Grandma walked off to the back of the house.

Everyone talked and laughed and listened—the boarders, Grandfather, and Douglas, and they heard the quiet sounds in the kitchen. When Grandma rang the bell they herded to the dining room, elbowing their way.

Everyone took a huge bite.

Grandma watched the faces of her boarders. Silently they stared at their plates, their hands in their laps, the food cooling, unchewed, in their cheeks.

"I've lost it!" Grandma said. "I've lost my touch. . ."

And she began to cry.

She got up and wandered out into her neatly ordered, labeled kitchen, her hands moving futilely before her.

The boarders went to bed hungry.

Douglas heard the courthouse clock chime ten-thirty, eleven, then midnight, heard the boarders stirring in their beds, like a tide moving under the moonlit roof of the vast house. He knew they were all awake, thinking, and sad. After a long time, he sat up in bed. He began to smile at the wall and the mirror. He saw himself grinning as he opened the door and crept downstairs. The parlor was dark and smelled old and alone. He held his breath.

He fumbled into the kitchen and stood waiting a moment.

Then he began to move.

He took the baking powder out of its fine new tin and put it in an old flour sack the way it had always been. He dusted the white flour into an old cookie crock. He removed the sugar from the metal bin marked sugar and sifted it into a familiar series of smaller bins marked spices, cutlery, string. He put the cloves where they had lain for years, littering the bottom of half a dozen drawers. He brought the dishes and the knives and forks and spoons back out on top of the tables.

He found Grandma's new eyeglasses on the parlor mantel and hid them in the cellar. He kindled a great fire in the old wood-burning stove, using pages from the new cookbook. By one o'clock in the still morning a huge husking roar shot up in the black stovepipe, such a wild roar that the house, if it had ever slept at all, awoke. He heard the rustle of Grandma's slippers down the hall stairs. She stood in the kitchen, blinking at the chaos. Douglas was hidden behind the pantry door.

At one-thirty in the deep dark summer morning, the cooking odors blew up through the windy corridors of the house. Down the stairs, one by one, came women in curlers, men in bathrobes, to tiptoe and peer into the kitchen—lit only by fitful gusts of red fire from the hissing stove. And there in the black kitchen at two of a warm summer morning, Grandma floated like an apparition, amidst bangings and clatterings, half blind once more, her fingers groping instinctively in the dimness, shaking out spice clouds over bubbling pots and simmering kettles, her face in the firelight red, magical, and enchanted as she seized and stirred and poured the sublime foods.

Quiet, quiet, the boarders laid the best linens and gleaming silver and lit candles rather than switch on electric lights and snap the spell.

Grandfather, arriving home from a late evening's work at the printing office, was startled to hear grace being said in the candlelit dining room.

As for the food? The meats were deviled, the sauces curried, the greens mounded with sweet butter, the biscuits splashed with jeweled honey; everything toothsome, luscious, and so miraculously refreshing that a gentle lowing broke out as from a pasturage

233

of beasts gone wild in clover. One and all cried out their gratitude for their loose-fitting night clothes.

At three-thirty on Sunday morning, with the house warm with eaten food and friendly spirits, Grandfather pushed back his chair and gestured magnificently. From the library he fetched a copy of Shakespeare. He laid it on a platter, which he presented to his wife.

"Grandma," he said, "I ask only that tomorrow night for supper you cook us this very fine volume. I am certain we all agree that by the time it reaches the table tomorrow at twilight it will be delicate, succulent, brown and tender as the breast of the autumn pheasant."

Grandma held the book in her hands and cried happily.

They lingered on toward dawn, with brief desserts, wine from those wild flowers growing in the front yard, and then, as the first birds winked to life and the sun threatened the eastern sky, they all crept upstairs. Douglas listened to the stove cooling in the faraway kitchen. He heard Grandma go to bed.

Junkman, he thought, Mr. Jonas, wherever you are, you're thanked, you're paid back. I passed it on, I sure did, I think I passed it on. . . .

He slept and dreamed.

In the dream the bell was ringing and all of them were yelling and rushing down to breakfast.

AND then, quite suddenly, summer was over.

He knew it first when walking downtown. Tom grabbed his arm and pointed gasping, at the dimestore window. They stood there unable to move because of the things from another world displayed so neatly, so innocently, so frighteningly, there.

"Pencils, Doug, ten thousand pencils!"

"Oh, my gosh!"

"Nickel tablets, dime tablets, notebooks, erasers, water colors, rulers, compasses, a hundred thousand of them!"

"Don't look. Maybe it's just a mirage."

"No," moaned Tom in despair. "School. School straight on ahead! Why, why do dime stores show things like that in windows before summer's even over! Ruin half the vacation!"

They walked on home and found Grandfather alone on the sere, bald-spotted lawn, plucking the last few dandelions. They worked with him silently for a time and then Douglas, bent in his own shadow, said:

"Tom, if this year's gone like this, what will next year be, better or worse?"

"Don't ask me." Tom blew a tune on a dandelion stem. "I didn't make the world." He thought about it. "Though some days I *feel* like I did." He spat happily.

"I got a hunch," said Douglas.

"What?"

"Next year's going to be even bigger, days will be brighter, nights longer and darker, more people dying, more babies born, and me in the middle of it all."

"You and two zillion other people, Doug, remember."

"Day like today," murmured Douglas, "I feel it'll be . . . just me!"

"Need any help," said Tom, "just yell."

"What could a ten-year-old brother do?"

"A ten-year-old brother'll be eleven next summer. I'll unwind the world like the rubber band on a golf ball's insides every morning, put it back together every night. Show you how, if you ask."

"Crazy."

"Always was." Tom crossed his eyes, stuck out his tongue. "Always will be."

Douglas laughed. They went down in the cellar with Grandpa and while he decapitated the flowers they looked at all the summer shelved and glimmering there in the motionless streams, the bottles of dandelion wine. Numbered from one to ninety-odd, there the ketchup bottles, most of them full now, stood burning in the cellar twilight, one for every living summer day.

"Boy," said Tom, "what a swell way to save June, July, and August. Real practical."

Grandfather looked up, considered this, and smiled.

"Better than putting things in the attic you never use again. This way, you get to live the summer over for a minute or two here or there along the way through the winter, and when the bottles are empty the summer's gone for good and no regrets and no sentimental trash lying about for you to stumble over forty years from now. Clean, smokeless, efficient, that's dandelion wine."

The two boys pointed along the rows of bottles.

"There's the first day of summer."

"There's the new tennis shoes day."

"Sure! And there's the Green Machine!"

"Buffalo dust and Ching Ling Soo!"

"The Tarot Witch! The Lonely One!"

"It's not really over," said Tom. "It'll never be over. I'll remember what happened on every day of this year, forever."

"It was over before it began," said Grandpa, unwinding the wine press. "I don't remember a thing that happened except some new type of grass that wouldn't need cutting."

"You're joking!"

"No, sir, Doug, Tom, you'll find as you get older the days kind of blur . . . can't tell one from the other. . . ."

"But, heck," said Tom. "On Monday this week I rollerskated at Electric Park, Tuesday I ate chocolate cake, Wednesday I fell in the crick, Thursday fell off a swinging vine, the week's been *full* of things! And today, I'll remember today because the leaves outside are beginning to get all red and yellow. Won't be long they'll be all over the lawn and we'll jump in piles of them and burn them. I'll never forget today! I'll always remember, I know!"

Grandfather looked up through the cellar window at the late-summer trees stirring in a colder wind. "Of course you will, Tom," he said. "Of course you will."

And they left the mellow light of the dandelion wine and went upstairs to carry out the last few rituals of summer, for they felt that now the final day, the final night had come. As the day grew late they realized that for two or three nights now, porches had emptied early of their inhabitants. The air had a different, drier smell and Grandma was talking of hot coffee instead of iced tea; the open, white-flutter-curtained windows were closing in the great bays; cold cuts were giving way to steamed beef. The mosquitos were gone from the porch, and surely when they abandoned the conflict the war with Time was really done, there was nothing for it but that humans also forsake the battleground.

Now Tom and Douglas and Grandfather stood, as they had stood three months, or was it three long centuries ago, on this front porch which creaked like a ship slumbering at night in growing swells, and they sniffed the air. Inside, the boys' bones felt like chalk and ivory instead of green mint sticks and licorice whips as earlier in the year. But the new cold touched Grandfather's skeleton first, like a raw hand chording the yellow bass piano keys in the dining room.

As the compass turns, so turned Grandfather, north.

"I guess," he said, deliberating, "we won't be coming out here any more."

And the three of them clanked the chains shaken down from the porch-ceiling eyelets and carried the swing like a weathered bier around to the garage, followed by a blowing of the first dried leaves. Inside, they heard Grandma poking up a fire in the library. The windows shook with a sudden gust of wind.

Douglas, spending a last night in the cupola tower above Grandma and Grandpa, wrote in his tablet:

"Everything runs backward now. Like matinee films sometimes, where people jump out of water onto diving boards. Come September you push down the windows you pushed up, take off the sneakers you put on, pull on the hard shoes you threw away last June. People run in the house now like birds jumping back inside clocks. One minute, porches loaded, everyone gabbing thirty to a dozen. Next minute, doors slam, talk stops, and leaves fall off trees like crazy."

He looked from the high window at the land where the crickets were strewn like dried figs in the creek beds, at a sky where birds would wheel south now through the cry of autumn loons and where trees would go up in a great fine burning of color on the steely clouds. Way out in the country tonight he could smell the pumpkins ripening toward the knife and the triangle eye and the singeing candle. Here in town the first few scarves of smoke unwound from chimneys and the faint faraway quaking of iron was the rush of black hard rivers of coal down chutes, building high dark mounds in cellar bins.

But it was late and getting later.

Douglas in the high cupola above the town, moved his hand.

"Everyone, clothes off!"

He waited. The wind blew, icing the window-pane.

"Brush teeth."

He waited again.

"Now," he said at last, "out with the lights!"

He blinked. And the town winked out its lights, sleepily, here, there, as the courthouse clock struck ten, ten-thirty, eleven, and drowsy midnight.

"The last ones now . . . there . . . there . . ."

He lay in his bed and the town slept around him and the ravine was dark and the lake was moving quietly on its shore and everyone, his family, his friends, the old people and the young, slept on one street or another, in one house or another, or slept in the far country churchyards.

He shut his eyes.

June dawns, July noons, August evenings over, finished, done, and gone forever with only the sense of it all left here in his head. Now, a whole autumn, a white winter, a cool and greening spring to figure sums and totals of summer past. And if he should forget, the dandelion wine stood in the cellar, numbered huge for each and every day. He would go there often, stare straight into the sun until he could stare no more, then close his eyes and consider the burned spots, the fleeting scars left dancing on his warm eyelids; arranging, rearranging each fire and reflection until the pattern was clear. . . .

So thinking, he slept.

And, sleeping, put an end to Summer, 1928.

# ABOUT THE AUTHOR

RAY DOUGLAS BRADBURY was born in Waukegan, Illinois, in 1920. He graduated from a Los Angeles high school in 1938. His formal education ended there, but he furthered it by himself at night in the library and by day at his typewriter. He sold newspapers on Los Angeles street corners from 1938 to 1942—a modest beginning for a man whose name would one day be synonymous with the best in science fiction! Ray Bradbury sold his first science fiction short story in 1941, and his early reputation is based on stories published in the budding science fiction magazines of that time. His work was chosen for best American short story collections in 1946, 1948 and 1952. His awards include: The O'Henry Memorial Award, The Benjamin Franklin Award in 1954 and The Aviation-Space Writer's Association Award for best space article in an American magazine in 1967. Mr. Bradbury has written for television, radio, the theater and film, and he has been published in every major American magazine. Editions of his novels and shorter fiction span several continents and languages, and he has gained worldwide acceptance for his work. His titles include: *The Martian Chronicles, Dandelion Wine, I Sing the Body Electric, The Golden Apples of the Sun, A Medicine for Melancholy* and *The Illustrated Man.*

# RAY BRADBURY

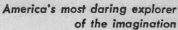

*America's most daring explorer
of the imagination*

| | | | |
|---|---|---|---|
| ☐ | 01484 | **RAY BRADBURY'S DINOSAUR TALES w/B. Preiss (A Large Format Book)** | $6.95 |
| ☐ | 23120 | **THE MACHINERIES OF JOY** | $2.75 |
| ☐ | 23248 | **S IS FOR SPACE** | $2.75 |
| ☐ | 22555 | **SOMETHING WICKED THIS WAY COMES** | $3.95 |
| ☐ | 20064 | **THE HALLOWEEN TREE** | $2.25 |
| ☐ | 24223 | **THE ILLUSTRATED MAN** | $2.75 |
| ☐ | 24219 | **DANDELION WINE** | $2.75 |
| ☐ | 23410 | **R IS FOR ROCKET** | $2.75 |
| ☐ | 23672 | **I SING THE BODY ELECTRIC** | $2.95 |
| ☐ | 22968 | **THE MARTIAN CHRONICLES** | $2.75 |
| ☐ | 23675 | **GOLDEN APPLES OF THE SUN** | $2.95 |
| ☐ | 22867 | **LONG AFTER MIDNIGHT** | $2.75 |
| ☐ | 20426 | **MEDICINE FOR MELANCHOLY** | $2.25 |

**Buy them at your local bookstore or use this handy coupon for ordering:**

# OUT OF THIS WORLD!

That's the only way to describe Bantam's great series of science fiction classics. These space-age thrillers are filled with terror, fancy and adventure and written by America's most renowned writers of science fiction. Welcome to outer space and have a good trip!